The Roads of My Relations

VOLUME 44

SUN TRACKS

An American Indian Literary Series

The Roads of My Relations

STORIES BY DEVON A. MIHESUAH

The University of Arizona Press

Tucson

The University of Arizona Press

This book is printed on acid-free, archival-quality paper
Manufactured in the United States of America
First printing

Library of Congress Cataloging-in-Publication Data
Mihesuah, Devon A. (Devon Abbott), 1957–
The roads of my relations : stories / by Devon A. Mihesuah.
p. cm. — (Sun tracks ; v. 44)
ISBN 0-8165-2040-2 (alk. paper) —
ISBN 0-8165-2041-0 (pbk. : alk. paper)
1. Choctaw Indians—Fiction. 2. Indians of North America—Mississippi—Fiction. 3. Indians of North America—Oklahoma—Fiction. 4. Family—Mississippi—Fiction. 5. Family—Oklahoma—Fiction. 6. Historical fiction, American. 7. Domestic fiction, American. I. Title. II. Series.
PS501 .S85 vol.44
[PS3563.I371535]
810.8′0054 s—dc21
[813/ 99-050808

British Cataloguing-in-Publication Data

A catalogue record for this book is available from the British Library.

Publication of this book was made possible in part by a grant from the National Endowment for the Arts.

FOR MY CHILDREN,

TANNER MATTHIAS AND ARIANA TARYN

Contents

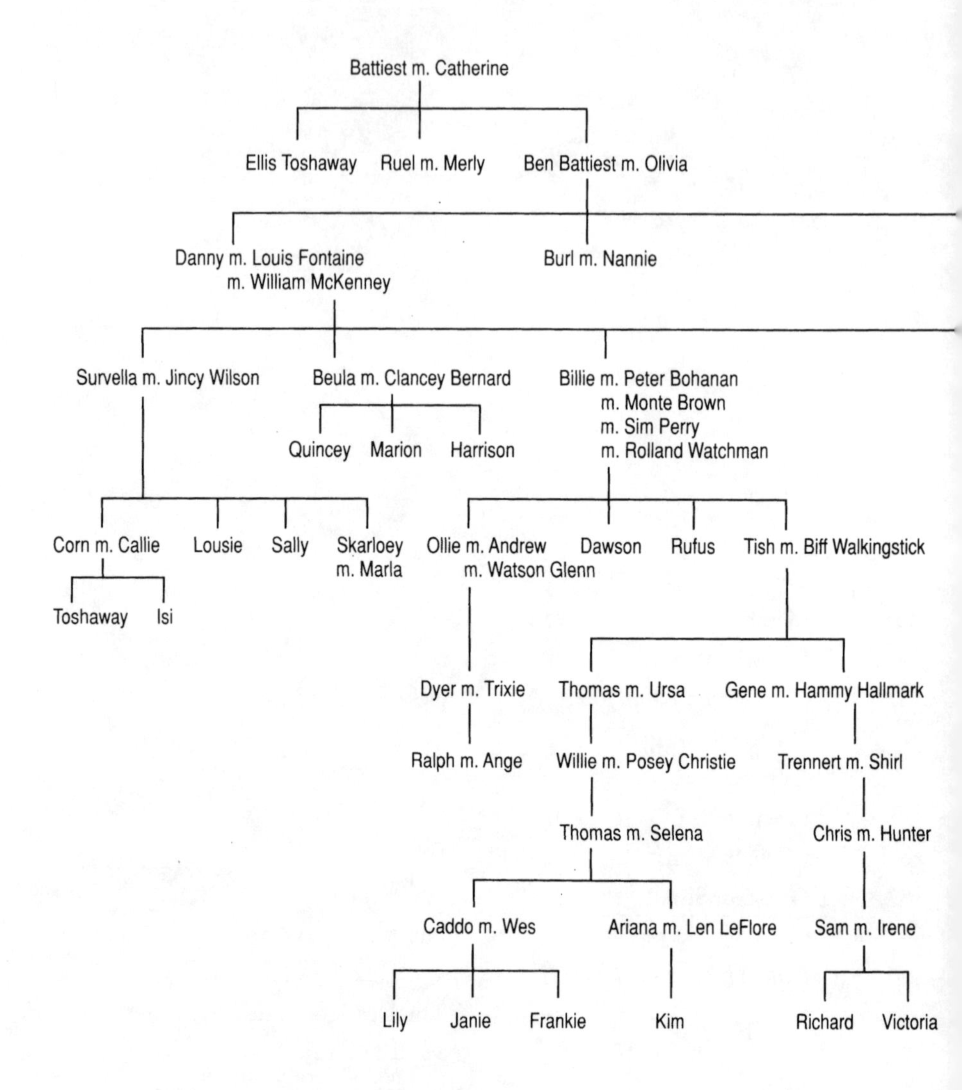
Battiest m. Catherine
Ellis Toshaway
Ruel m. Merly
Ben Battiest m. Olivia
Danny m. Louis Fontaine
m. William McKenney
Burl m. Nannie
Survella m. Jincy Wilson
Beula m. Clancey Bernard
Billie m. Peter Bohanan
m. Monte Brown
m. Sim Perry
m. Rolland Watchman
Quincey
Marion
Harrison
Corn m. Callie
Lousie
Sally
Skarloey
m. Marla
Ollie m. Andrew
m. Watson Glenn
Dawson
Rufus
Tish m. Biff Walkingstick
Toshaway
Isi
Dyer m. Trixie
Thomas m. Ursa
Gene m. Hammy Hallmark
Ralph m. Ange
Willie m. Posey Christie
Trennert m. Shirl
Thomas m. Selena
Chris m. Hunter
Caddo m. Wes
Ariana m. Len LeFlore
Sam m. Irene
Lily
Janie
Frankie
Kim
Richard
Victoria

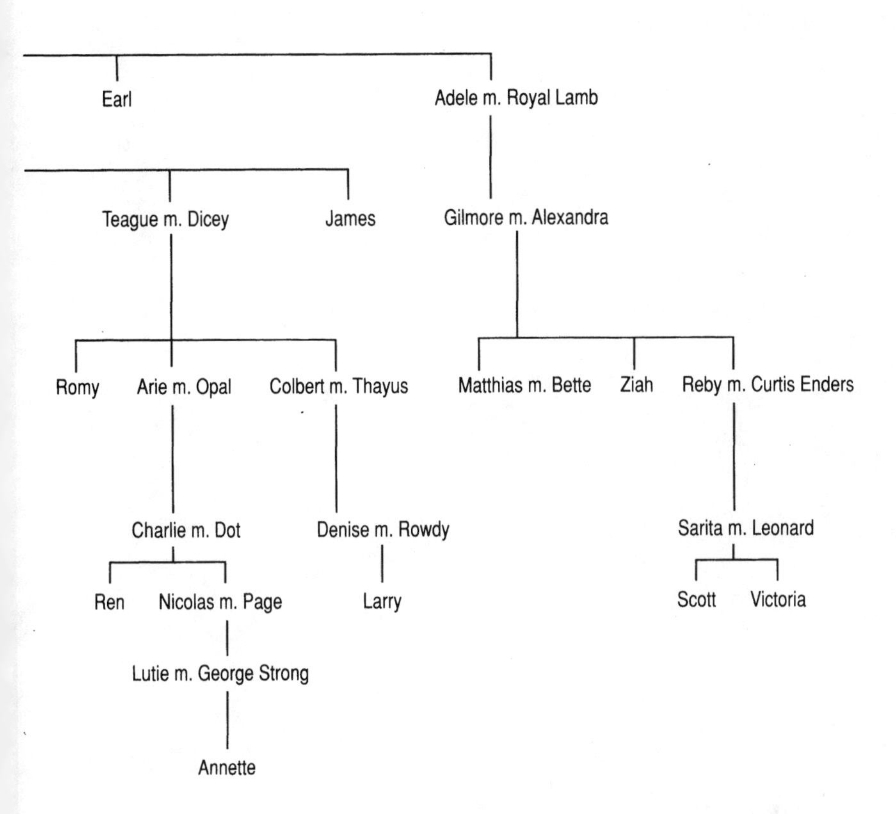

Earl
Adele m. Royal Lamb
Teague m. Dicey
James
Gilmore m. Alexandra
Romy
Arie m. Opal
Colbert m. Thayus
Matthias m. Bette
Ziah
Reby m. Curtis Enders
Charlie m. Dot
Denise m. Rowdy
Sarita m. Leonard
Ren
Nicolas m. Page
Larry
Scott
Victoria
Lutie m. George Strong
Annette

The Roads of My Relations

My House

BILLIE

Red Oak, Southeastern Oklahoma. 1922.

Eastern Oklahoma is a land of forests and streams. Blue and yellow wildflowers cover hillsides and meadows and dense thickets of oaks grow among taller pecan or cottonwood trees. Fat hawks perch on dead trees and telephone poles, watching for prey in the fields and woods below. The summer air is thick and hot and if I breathe deep, the smell of damp, green foliage rushes into my lungs, making me sneeze.

The trail to my creek is hard to see because of the vines. Every morning I walk my trail to get water for my garden, just as I hauled heavy buckets of river water to our farm in Mississippi. The bank is high enough to keep the creek from flooding. In a hundred years, it only reached the edge twice.

Fish big enough to eat lived in this water when my family first moved here. I liked to catch them and Papa'd clean them. He'd throw the guts to the cats and I put the fish heads on the fence posts, their noses pointing upwards. Since then, people living upstream made the water flow in different directions. The water level dropped and the fish are so small they aren't worth catching anymore.

The stream barely moves and is clear enough to see its copper bottom. Small frogs with strong legs push through the water. Black dirt daubers move inside dime-sized holes that dot the opposite bank. Others buzz around my house looking for places to make their mud homes. Every summer I knock down their nests with a broom.

I sit on the bank and listen to locusts. They make the same up-and-down song in Mississippi. If locusts live long enough they climb out the split in their backs and leave their old, dry skins attached to trees and fence posts. Otherwise, I find their body parts on the ground where birds drop them.

When the water is warm enough, I like to feel the creek mud between my toes. At the same time I have to watch for water moccasins that grow to five feet and sometimes crawl into the trees and curl in the branches. One year a mama moccasin had babies that were thin as twigs. They swam fast and chased me out of the water.

Blue jays, robins, and purple martins feed from feeders nailed to my trees or hung from branches out of reach of cats. Scissortail flycatchers chase flying bugs across the yard. Mourning doves hide among the leaves, their sad voices welcoming guests and saying good-bye. At night bats fly from their secret places to hunt biting insects. I see their tiny outlines and hear their squeaks.

Spiders stretch their webs between the redbud trees along the path to my creek. One summer twenty years ago, a big spider spun her web across the path every night, so early each morning I saw sparkly dewdrops on the strands. I left the path so I wouldn't disturb her.

One morning she was gone. The top part of her web had come loose that night and by the next day, only a few strands moved gently on the breeze. I looked on the ground thinking that I might find her body, but she wasn't there. Ravens liked to gather in the same trees and maybe one took her.

My last husband, Rolland, never liked spiders. Spiders are good luck, you know, and I hurried to catch them in a cup and throw them outside before Rolland swatted them. Spiders still live here, for the most part giving off good luck.

A lot of life has passed through this house. I've lived almost a hundred years and things haven't always gone the way I wanted. Still, a lot has. Maybe good luck and bad luck balance out.

My garden is half an acre of straight rows of potatoes, tomatoes, green beans, squash, peppers, cucumbers, cabbage, okree, and corn. It looks the same as our garden in Mississippi. Three fences are covered with blackberries and raspberries, their old stems thick and tough. Mama arranged our Mississippi garden the same way her papa planted his. Now my grandchildren have gardens like mine.

Papa made a scarecrow to keep ravens and jays away even though they're smart enough to figure out the difference between a real man and a straw one. Papa nailed wooden slats along the bottom so rabbits couldn't push through. I remember the first time I dug for potatoes with Papa. I was surprised to see them underground and not on trees like peaches.

My sturdy fence is made of vertical rolls of hog wire formed into tubes and filled with rocks. I feel comforted seeing my rocks. Someday the wood posts will splinter and fall, but the rocks never will. I planted sunflowers with heads big as plates along the fence line and their faces follow the warmth of the sun.

We built this house in 1836 after our removal from Mississippi. This wasn't called Red Oak then. Papa hurried to build a one-room house so we'd have a safe place to sleep. A lot of what we owned was left in Mississippi and we lost almost everything else on the trail.

Some parts of my house are just about ninety years old. It almost burned three times, twice in one year. Now it has three bedrooms, the kitchen, parlor, and bathing room. I put up wallpaper about twenty years ago and a new layer last summer. The original chimney stands as straight as the day Papa finished it.

Papa was Irish Catholic and believed that we should be surrounded by symbols of God, so he inlaid little crosses made of red pebbles throughout the chimney. It looks odd, but makes for conversation. Once I sat too close with my back to the fire and singed my hair. I'm pretty sure God made that happen on purpose.

Once there were seven people in this house. Now there's only me and the animals and my great-grandchildren who visit in the summers. Every day I water the flowers and throw feed to the chickens, and sometimes I go into town with my grandson Tom. My hound Tecumseh has given up on catching squirrels and sits on the porch with me while I sketch. I've drawn hundreds of pictures of my family, animals, and trees. My favorites are on the walls and the rest stay under my bed, waiting for the day I pass away and my relatives decide which ones they want to keep.

I have a lot of time to think. I've not been back to Mississippi, but I can still see my house, the trees, the sky. I most recall the smell of wild onions on my hands and the warm nights. In summer we cooked outdoors and slept with netting over the beds to keep out insects. As the sky darkened, I saw stars low on the horizon where the tree branches grew apart. My brother

Teague threw pebbles in the air and watched bats try to catch them. Locusts and crickets sang until the sun came up. We heard the night varmints' nails scratching on the porch or digging around the baseboards.

Those days went on forever, crowded with people and work, with my family and neighbors trying to keep our lives as happy and full as the times allowed. I've lived in a hurry, the same as other Indians did, like we expected to have only a few years to fit a lifetime into. That is how Indians have to live.

Mama and Papa

BILLIE

Mama was half Choctaw and she looked all Indian. The man I call Papa wasn't my real father, but I called him Papa anyways. He was white and didn't like us to talk Choctaw. He was like the missionaries who refused to speak Indian in hopes that the Indians would learn English.

Papa was handsome, smart, and determined but much too self-righteous. He believed his was the only way to farm, to pray, to dress, to raise us kids. Choctaws looked and acted different from him and it seems he'd want to change to fit in, but not Papa. He was like all the others who came here.

Papa pulled back his dark blond hair with a ribbon and some strands always fell in his face. His deep-set eyes looked like a hawk's and we paid attention to him. When he was a child, Papa got a deep tear across his cheek when his horse ran him through tree branches. That scar turned red whenever he was mad, which was often. Papa was serious about everything and never stopped finding work to do around the farm. Papa thought that if he didn't do everything his way, he'd somehow become like the fulls. The last thing he wanted was for people to think he was trying to be an Indian.

He got angry when Mama told him about the old traditions, like when Choctaw women owned property and children belonged to their mamas' clans.

"All that changed when white men married into the tribe, William," Mama'd lecture to him as she rolled out biscuits or scrubbed the table. "White men and their half-blood sons worked things around so now they control everything and women don't have choices." When Mama talked like that, Papa'd ignore her.

Papa was hard to live with. He started each day by lecturing to my mother and then to us about what we needed to do that day. Papa wasn't always direct, but we always knew what he meant.

"Barn needs a cleaning," he'd say, then look at my brother Teague. Or, "Dead vines need to be taken down," then he'd look to my sister Survella.

Visitors came by often, many of them family. We had enough food for everybody and we enjoyed talking with them, but Papa was afraid that every relative of Mama's wanted to move in with us.

"If they were smart, Danny, they would learn to raise cattle and make money like the LeFlores," Papa would say.

Then Mama'd needle him back. "The LeFlores have more money than anyone else in the tribe and more than most whites. More than we'll ever have. So what is it you're doing wrong?"

Papa's thoughts weren't right. Some of Mama's relatives were fulls who could read and write and worked farms and herds bigger than ours. Papa talked like all fulls were lacking something in their heads. Most Choctaws I knew were half-bloods. They didn't seem any smarter than the fulls.

Papa and his brother, Roger, inherited their farm after their daddy, Angus, died a few years before Papa came to Mississippi in 1812. He and his brother sold a portion of the farm so Papa had money to take a boat here. It was a long trip, taking almost three months. Papa said many people died from sickness and he got a bad cough that stayed with him for a long time after he arrived. Roger stayed to help their mama for two years until she died.

Roger came over in 1814 and married a Choctaw woman. He was different from Papa. Roger learned to speak Choctaw and to farm the way his wife taught him. He also stopped going to the mission because he wanted to completely change his life. Papa didn't talk to Roger much after his marriage because he was disappointed with him.

Our house had to fit Papa's standards and he tinkered on it every day. It was small but sturdy with two rooms, one for us children and the big room for him and Mama, along with the woodstove, table, and two benches. Unlike most other Choctaw houses, it had lots of windows. It took several months to finish, but Papa laid a puncheon floor. He built our beds two feet off the ground, insisting that fleas couldn't reach us at that height. The straw stuffing poked through the material and made us scratch—along with the flea bites.

Papa read from the Bible every night. Some of the book was interesting while other parts sounded like threats. From what Papa told us about God, I got the feeling He was usually in a bad mood and hard to please. Even though we didn't go to church Mama had us baptized Presbyterian just to spite Papa. I guess Mama married him because she thought our family had a chance to make a living if she married a white man. I can't say I liked him, but my papa was one of the most important people in my life. Without him I wouldn't be educated and I'd only know one way of living.

My real papa was Louis Fontaine. He was half white and half Choctaw. His mama was Choctaw who spoke Indian. His daddy came from France in 1789 and made money selling deer hides. Before I turned two, something happened inside my papa's head one day while he plowed the garden and afterwards he couldn't move one side of his body. He couldn't talk or swallow, either, and starved to death after a month. I don't recall him, but my older sister Survella remembered that he smiled a lot.

Fontaine's daddy was tall and so was Mama's, while both their mothers were short. Mama was just over five feet and her brother Burl was six feet. I recall Burl's ears because they were large and didn't match. His voice was big and people listened to him. He sat on the tribal council, but never drank before meetings. No one wanted to stay around him after he had his whiskey. Burl's twin brother Earl looked just like him except his ears were bigger. Earl didn't care for anybody. Earl was a hermit and I only saw him once before he drowned after an alligator snapping turtle got ahold of his foot while he was fishing and pulled him into deep water.

The 200 acres of land Mama worked with Fontaine was around today's LeFlore County, on the west side of the Yazoo River. Since Mama and Fontaine used it all either by farming or grazing, they called it theirs even though it wasn't. All that was tribal land, but families or individuals could work it.

Six months after Louis died, Mama married the man I called Papa, William McKenney. They only had two children together, but we all took his name. My younger twin brothers James and Teague always gave Mama a hard time, even before they were born. Mama had to lie down the entire pregnancy and relatives that Papa didn't like tended to her. Mama loved it.

Mama and William bought forty head of cattle and Spanish mustangs from a trader in Mobile for cheap, then we bred them and sold the young ones for more. My stallion and two of the mares come from Papa's herd. I wonder how they can see with their manes in their eyes.

Poor Choctaws shot our cattle for food. They didn't know some cattle belonged to certain people and not to the whole tribe. Some knew better, though, and acted like what they killed were just slow deer.

Us children we were colored all shades of brown and my sister Beula was the darkest. More than anything she wanted blond hair and blue eyes and she carried a parasol so her skin wouldn't get darker. My other sister, Survella, could've passed for white but she refused to pretend she was anything besides herself.

People could tell I was Indian. Even if I looked white I'd choose to be Indian. Else I'd be cheating. Like I could get something the rest of my family and tribe couldn't.

Survella was my favorite sister and the handsomest of us. Her easy nature made everyone want to be around her. Her thick dark hair was hard to comb so she wore it in one braid that fell across her shoulder to her waist. Her black eyebrows made her eyes look even darker. That left eyebrow came up when she thought hard.

Survella had the talent for growing flowers. She had the sense of how to cut the stem at the right place, to sacrifice one portion to allow the rest to blossom. She'd make the roses and wildflowers grow around the base of the house so thick the colors and smells made me dizzy. I'd cut flowers for arrangements and the mix never looked right, while Survella'd cut a handful and her vases looked like perfect pictures.

Survella wasn't very talkative. Unlike me, she gave thought to everything before speaking and sounded smart. As soon as we learned to write, she put her thoughts in writing. Mama and Aunt Adele liked to tell their stories while Survella recorded them. I still have my sister's journals.

My little brother James didn't say a lot, either. He knew he was different because he was sickly. James had a hard time helping with the chores and even as a child his weakness shamed him. He was small and had difficulty breathing when he moved too fast. Horsehair made his eyes burn so he never rode, and he scared us sometimes when he tried so hard to breathe that he grabbed the sides of the bed and his hands turned white. We almost lost him one spring when his face swelled after a bee stung him. After that Mama made him wear long sleeves and a hat. During the hot Mississippi summers we sweated all day and jumped in the creek to cool off. Poor James never had any fun. He bathed in the water barrel so Mama could watch him.

Papa brought back a harmonica from Mobile one spring and nobody was interested in it except James. Mama sent him to the creek so we couldn't hear him practice. Uncle Burl also taught him to make whistles, what we call *uskula*, from canes in the river. Neither one was pleasing to our ears.

My skinny brother Teague had bucked teeth and wore his hair long all his life. Papa and missionaries tried to cut it and he'd hide at the talk of scissors. I remember him as a little wart, as our Aunt Adele called him. When he was a child Teague didn't fall asleep until midnight. Mama and Papa tried warm baths and let him run in the pasture until he wore out. They shut off the lantern early but he chattered and wandered around the house in the dark.

When he was just a baby, he'd stand on Mama's trunk and climb out the window onto the porch chair. He walked around at night and returned before Mama and Papa woke up. One night he got tired and fell asleep in the strawberries and Mama was frantic when she didn't find him in bed. From then on, she locked the window so he couldn't get out. That was just the start of his life. He called me "Cat Eyes" and "Canoe Feet," which I guess were right descriptions of me, but I loved him dearly.

Teague was like Survella in that he always asked Mama about the old Choctaws. And he liked to irritate Papa.

"The old ones plant squash like this," Teague'd say in the garden.

Then Papa'd say, "Not around here, they don't."

Or Teague would ask what we planned to take to the summer corn dances, knowing that Papa wouldn't allow us to attend.

"The old ones will let you dance if you ask them, Papa," Teague said one evening at dinner. Mama didn't stop him from teasing his papa because she liked to hear him do it.

"I don't dance and I never will so button your lip, son." Papa's scar would turn red and we'd try not to giggle.

After we ate we always moved outside to watch the bats. Teague'd look at me and wink, then ask Mama if it was going to rain—"*Himmaḳ nitaḳ omba chi ho?*"

Mama'd look up and answer, "*Oḳblaḳa*."

"Talk English!" Papa yelled before he stormed off to the barn. Mama just stood there with her hands on her hips and a smirk on her face, watching him get mad.

Teague rode all the just-broke horses Papa brought home and he played stickball alone out in the yard, bouncing the ball off the barn while our cats sat on the fence rails and watched him. Teague always wanted to pet one, but could never get close enough. Mama told us to stay away from the kittens that were born one spring, but Teague cornered them under the porch and they clawed his hand so bad he got a fever. They gave him scars and he never liked cats after that.

Teague started roaming when he was two. Papa put a rope around his middle so he couldn't go too far. When he was three, the rope came off and he walked down our road, first a quarter mile, then farther. If we had a place to go, Papa let him walk ahead then picked him up in the wagon on their way to town. Sometimes he ran just to see how far he could go. When he was a child he ran along the Yazoo River, sometimes barefoot, sometimes in thin-soled moccasins or in shoes too large for him. He liked to run barefoot best, but he stepped on stickers. He made leather sandals with a strap that wrapped around his heel and a thong between his toes. After the leather rubbed his skin tough he wore them for eighty miles before making another pair.

One day Teague told us he wanted to run as fast as our horses, as fast as the river water. Mama didn't mind his running because her brothers ran, but Papa thought Teague might have a problem.

"Waste of time, son," Papa'd yell when Teague ran down the path to meet the main road.

Teague would just wave without looking back.

"He gets tired doing that when he should be working here," Papa grumbled. "He's going no place."

"He is in his mind, William. Like you do when you read," said Mama. "Let him run." Then she'd wipe her hands on her apron and go back inside to let Papa talk to himself.

There was, however, something very wrong with my sister Beula. She was four years older than me. Her skin and hair were dark, and unlike Teague and James who also were dark, she was troubled by her Indian appearance. She preferred Papa to Mama and sounded strange talking with his Irish accent. Beula stayed away from us kids unless she didn't have a choice, like at mealtimes. I always felt uncomfortable around her. We lived together for sixteen years, but didn't hardly know each other. She didn't make life easy for us.

All of us except Beula learned to speak Indian from Adele and Mama. Like Papa, Beula wasn't interested in learning about Choctaws. She believed that we couldn't live like both whites and Indians and that white ways were best. As we watched whites move into the Choctaw Nation, we realized we should learn about them, but Beula actually wanted to *be* white.

Mama's sister Adele, her husband Royal, and their son Gilmore lived a mile away. Adele didn't eat meat or drink coffee because she said both were bad for digestion. She smoked a cob pipe and believed that a sip of whiskey every now and then was good for concentration. Adele usually smelled like liquor, but she wasn't ever corned except one time when she came over at suppertime and didn't stop drooling and laughing to herself until it was time for dinner. She talked in Choctaw and later Mama said she couldn't understand a word her sister said. Papa got mad at her and took his plate outside to eat and didn't come back in until she went home.

When I was nine, Adele was thirty. She cut her hair to her shoulders and at night she twirled it into a bun so the next morning there'd be some curl. She always wore a brown straight-lined skirt with pleats, a man's button-down shirt, and a gray long-sleeved jacket. She stuck feathers in her wide-brimmed hat and had more on her head than in her pockets.

Adele tamed her farm cats and talked to her horses and cows. She was sentimental about her animals and didn't like it when Uncle Royal butchered a chicken or hog. If one of her cats died, or if she found a dead possum or raccoon, she got melancholy. Papa said Adele was light in her head and avoided her. She was peculiar to a lot of people, but she made sense to me.

My Uncle Royal wasn't easy to know. He never hugged or played with us kids much, probably because his son was deaf. He had no front teeth and talked to Mama and Papa at meals with his mouth full. I tried not to look at him. Royal ate so many sweets his belly stuck out past his chest. Worse, he didn't use a handkerchief. He'd just put his finger up to one side of his nose and blow real hard into the air. Teague liked that way of nose-clearing and Papa was always after him to use his hankie.

My cousin Gilmore was the same age as me. He got a fever when he was five and lost his hearing so he talked real loud trying to hear himself. Adele didn't allow Royal to take him hunting and she didn't let him go to regular school. She wanted to keep Gilmore in sight for fear that someone would kidnap him and put him in the Deaf, Dumb, Blind, and Insane Asylum over in Arkansas. So instead of hunting, Gilmore stayed at home and learned to read from Papa. He read everything he could find and pestered Papa to lend him his Bible. Papa let Gilmore read it, but he had to sit on our porch and not take it home.

Gilmore also made fine blowguns. When Burl came to visit, Gilmore sat on the porch and watched our uncle take an eight-foot cane and hollow it out with a metal rod, then rub the cane smooth with the same file he used to shave down horses' hooves. Burl made little arrows from hickory wood or small strips of cane. He sharpened one end and balanced the other with cotton bits. Burl also taught Gilmore to make rabbit sticks.

My cousin always carried a homemade blowgun and was a sure shot. Most Choctaws killed rabbits with a special-made rabbit stick while Gilmore killed with his blowgun. My aim with a stick and gun was never good, probably because I didn't really want to kill a rabbit.

Gilmore eventually learned to sign with his hands and to read lips. Because he didn't talk much people believed him stupid, but he was smarter than all of us.

Adele and Royal lived in a two-room house with peach and pecan trees around it. Adele raised chickens and I'd watch her mix up eggs and milk in a bowl, then cook it on her iron griddle until almost done. Then she'd put onions and fried potatoes in the middle and fold one side over.

Evenings she took Gilmore and me to look for pretty stones and acorns to string on necklaces. We picked ripe peaches and she taught us to find onions and how to tell when pigweed was ready. Deer and black bears looked for food on our trail at dusk. We hid in the oaks and watched them while eating salty roasted pumpkin seeds. Then I'd come home and sit by the wax-and-tallow candles and sketch pictures of what I'd seen that day. Mama hung my drawings all over the house, even the ones that weren't so good. Her doing that made me feel like I had a talent for something and wasn't wasting my time.

The next closest neighbors to us were the Hackers, and we didn't care for Mr. Hacker. He thought all Indians were heathens and doomed to hell, although that didn't stop him from marrying one. He came from England with nothing, and after looking for a woman with some land or money he found a full-blood named Hettie Baker who had lost her husband to consumption. She and her first husband, along with two of his cousins, had started a nice farm with a cornfield and peach orchard. They marketed their crops to travelers.

Hettie didn't have children and must've been lonely to marry the likes of Hacker. Sometimes Mama saw her with bruises on her face and once with her arm wrapped up tight like it was broken. Hacker was too lazy to work the fields so some of her relatives moved closer so they could work the land—under his direction. At the first talk of removal Hacker took all ten of their horses and left.

My parents argued about Hacker, Mama saying that Hettie should've known better. "White men come here to make a living," Mama said, "and they marry Indian women to get what they want."

Papa was insulted, believing that white men made life better for Choctaws. We were *anumpuli*—dense—and needed someone to tell us what to do. That was one of the few Choctaw words Papa bothered to learn and he used it a lot.

"If Choctaws are so stupid, then why did you marry one?" Mama asked calmly, stirring corn batter. She stood still, waiting for his answer. Papa couldn't think of what to say so Mama threw the bowl at him and bruised his head. They never finished their discussion.

Crow Witches

East Mississippi. 1829.

Kneeling over his work, Jackson Crow pivoted his head. His owl eyes didn't blink. "That's enough, boys."

Jackson's son Dew turned to his father in the same manner that his father looked at him, pivoting his head without moving his body. The other men, Sweeney and Jeffrey, looked up from their kills and turned their heads, too. All the men were of slightly different heights and builds but their faces were the same. Even Dew had the adult face of his father, uncle, and cousin.

A Negro woman wailed from where she crouched under a redbud tree. "Jackson, don't do me no more," she cried. Jackson felt his face, which was torn by her knife. After considering his bloody hand a moment, he shot her through the left eye.

The men rose from their crouched positions and started toward the boy, who stood by the horses. Woven into their manes were human ears and hairs—blond, black, and red. The three men walked shoulder to shoulder, their heads bobbing from side to side. The boy thought they looked like a family of owls he once saw perched together on a branch, staring, identical.

Young Mel Mills could not run for he was held fast to the ground by snakes. He covered his face and felt the Crows' breath on the back of his hands. He felt a sharp pain across his neck and then, nothing.

"Dew, go see what's out there," Jackson said to his son without looking at him.

The son, who only looked young, squatted to the ground, smiling. He lowered his chin and stared at the ground as if in a trance.

Sweeney watched as Dew's hands disappeared into his coat sleeves and his head shrank until his hat fell off. The older Crow cocked his head and looked while Dew's clothes crumpled into a pile and an owl emerged from the neck collar. The four-pound brown bird then circled the camp once and flew to the south.

"I'm hungry," said Jackson. "Let's eat and git."

"Want me to take Dew's clothes?" asked Sweeney.

"Nah," said Jackson as he took up the reins to his wild-eyed bay. "He'll find some more."

Hattak Fullih Nipi Foni: The Bonepicker

BILLIE

1834.

The summer I turned ten we visited Mama's cousins, the Colberts, who lived forty miles downstream on the Yazoo River. James didn't feel well so he stayed home with Uncle Royal.

My cousins Jo and Lizzie spoke English to be nice since their Choctaw was too fast for us. Their mother, Susan Catherine, was a fat friendly woman whose hands stayed dirty from gardening. Her husband, David—that's the name missionaries gave him—had rheumatism and put bear grease on his joints. He never washed off the old grease and I smelled him across the yard. I'm not sure how his family tolerated him.

David didn't think much of Papa, or of any other white man. Beula took as much offense to David's attitude as Papa did, so they sat outside all day, even to eat. At night they slept under the wagon. Mama seemed to enjoy them staying out of the house.

Susan Catherine's mother had arthritis and lay on a cot in the dark part of the kitchen with her hands balled into fists. Every morning David moved her to the porch where the sun warmed her, like a lizard.

Raspberry vines draped the sagging wood fences and their peach tree about split from the weight of fruit. David killed a hog the day we arrived and all our meals for those four days included pork and fruit pies. Susan Catherine's hogs were so big Papa could've ridden one. She grew pumpkins just for them, although they ate anything they got their mouths on.

One morning Gilmore, Teague, Survella, and I packed a basket of biscuits and apples to take on our adventure to see the waterfall that flowed near the farm. Beula stayed with Papa so they could pout together, which was fine with me as I didn't enjoy my sister's company. Adele said the ways of others rub off on us the more we're around them, and I sure didn't want to be like Beula.

"You comin'?" Lizzie asked Beula, who was sitting on the porch making a show of fanning herself with a turkey wing.

"No. My stomach hurts," Beula answered in her little voice. Her insides hurt whenever she was upset or had to visit relatives.

"Walk'll do you good," Lizzie persisted. "Might see some fulls." Lizzie didn't like Beula either, and liked to tease her.

Papa sat on the edge of the porch looking out into the cow pasture. Beula looked to him with her most desperate expression. "Papa," she whined. "Do I have to go?"

"Your sister will stay here, Billie. Go on now."

Nobody argued with that. "I'll go," Jo said, tying back her hair.

We enjoyed our slow walk under the shade of gray summer clouds for about a mile. A mama quail and her babies ran across the road in front of us when we heard crying coming from behind a small house built to the east of the road. The mud home had a roof made of sod, no windows, and a front door shorter than most grown people. No barn, just mesquite-pole corrals under the trees.

"Old man Tushkochaubbee died a half year ago," Lizzie explained after we stopped to listen to the wailing. "His family put him out in the trees so his flesh could rot. Now the *hattaķ fullih nipi foni* gets to finish him while the women cry."

"What? The what?" Teague was excited.

"The bonepicker. When a person dies, a picker comes to take the flesh with his fingernails. Then the stripped bones get put in a bone house."

"When who dies? Our family doesn't use bonepickers," Survella said. Then she looked at me with big eyes. "Do we?"

"Usually just the fulls call them out," answered Lizzie. "Most Choctaws won't even allow talk of pickers, especially the Christians."

Well, Teague, Gilmore, and I decided to sneak into the trees to see the picker for ourselves. Everyone else was scared and waited by the road.

We saw women wrapped in shawls, but the scaffold was half hidden by trees. We held our breath when dry branches on the ground crunched under our feet. The mourners didn't take notice and stayed occupied with their crying. Then we saw the bonepicker and my heart almost stopped.

His long hair stuck out like a back-combed chicken. His dirty brown clothes were stained and his long fingernails worked quickly, pulling off strips of old Tushkochaubbee.

I thought I'd be sick so I grabbed Gilmore's arm and stepped back slowly over the branches, then all three of us ran back to the others. We didn't see enough to give us clear answers, but we thought hard. Where does he live? Is he a witch?

Teague was breathing fast. "Let's go back," he said. "Maybe he'll talk to us."

I looked at him like he was mad. "Talk to us?" I squealed.

"He?" asked Lizzie. "I heard bonepickers were women."

"Was it a woman?" I asked Teague. Perhaps it was. "Looked like a wild man to me."

"Me too," said Gilmore.

"Well . . . maybe." Teague slowed his steps like he was about to turn around and go find out.

"No, Teague," said Survella. "We better not until we ask Mama or Adele."

"Later, then." Teague kept walking and said nothing else, but I knew he was planning another way to see the picker.

After we left the Tushkochaubbee farm we branched off the main road and followed a game trail that led to a stream. It was the same stream that ran past our house except this part was wider and faster.

"So how many people use bonepickers? Has your family used one?" I asked Jo.

"Hmmm, not too many, I don't think. Most use cemeteries. The older Choctaws say we're not supposed to speak the names of the dead."

"How do the dead person's grandchildren ever learn about them?" asked Survella.

"Yeah," said Teague. "If no one mentions the dead are they lost forever to the family that comes later? Can you write about them?"

"I'm not sure what those older people do." Jo walked faster, a sign that she didn't want to talk about it. I always figured that she did know, but got tired of lecturing to us ignorant Choctaws who should already know about such things.

About 300 yards after we met the stream, the trees got thicker and so did the plants along the bank. We started up the hill and heard loud water. At the crest of the small hill we walked into an open area.

It was a strange place. The half-circle waterfall dropped thirty feet to the pool below and stretched eighty feet across. Big snail shells were pressed into the brown rock around the frothy pool. The clear runoff turned into a thin stream that disappeared into the thick woods behind us.

"Snails," said Jo, examining the hardened impressions.

"They'd sure eat Papa's tomatoes quick," said Survella. "I'd like to see his face if these things found his garden." We all laughed, secretly wishing it could happen.

"You sure they're snails?" asked Teague. "They look like something that lived in the water."

"Who knows?" I said, straightening up from putting a little broken shell in my dress pocket. Right then I saw movement at the top of the falls.

I stared for a minute and nothing was there. I looked away, then back, and saw the bonepicker with all his wild hair standing with one arm to his side, the other pointing to the sky. He watched us.

"Look, look there," I yelled to the others, but when they turned their heads the sun had risen behind the falls making it too bright to see.

"Teague, the bonepicker! I saw him. Right there."

Teague spidered up the side of the falls where the rocks were big and stable. He disappeared over the top for about fifteen minutes. Just when I thought the picker had caught my brother and pulled off his skin, Teague reappeared and started climbing down.

After watching my panicked face, Jo reassured me. "Pickers don't kill, Billie."

"So what's he doing here?" asked Survella.

Teague jogged back to us, shaking his head. "Nothing. Didn't see tracks, either. Let's go back and see if he's at the house."

We reluctantly followed my brave brother.

When we reached the Tushkochaubbee house, Gilmore, Teague, and I sneaked back to the same spot and saw him, still there, picking bones. He looked up to where we hid, his face unseen under tangled hair, then he looked back down at Tushkochaubbee.

"He knows we're here," I whispered to Teague.

"Yeah, but I want to see him closer."

Teague moved forward, but Gilmore grabbed his arm and shook his head "no."

Then the picker stood and faced us. He folded his arms so that his hands cupped under his armpits, then he started making a motion like a bird flying. Then he pointed at the sky, flapped his arms a few more times, and settled back into his picking.

"Come on." I had to pull my brother after me.

We returned to the others, told them what we saw, and decided to go home. Mama and Adele were pleased we got to see a picker since they never had, but they seemed troubled that he communicated with us. Papa and Beula didn't want to hear anything about it.

The next day Mama and Adele went with us to Tushkochaubbee's house thinking that we might see the bonepicker or hear some crying. It was quiet. Nobody was there, just a warm, quiet wind and some hens scratching in the yard. We went around back and saw an empty scaffold. The picker had completed his task and went back to where he came from.

For years afterwards I looked for bonepickers with long fingernails and tangled hair. I have seen only one, and have drawn hundreds of sketches of him.

It was within a day, however, that I knew what he was trying to tell us.

Five miles away along the Yazoo. The next morning.

"William, I want to stop now," said Mama.

"Dammit, Danny, this is the second time this morning."

"I got the runs and I wanta git in the river. Now stop."

We had listened to our parents argue ever since we left David and Susan Catherine's house. Papa had tolerated his heathen in-laws for several days. Now he wanted to get home and Mama wouldn't let him.

"Come on, Survella and Adele," Mama said. "You come with me."

My mother, aunt, and sister walked off through the shallow water and around a bend, leaving me, Gilmore, Teague, Beula, and Papa to skip stones. Ten minutes later we heard Mama scream.

Papa pulled his musket from under the wagon seat and ran through the shallow, sparkly water toward the bend in the river.

"William!" Mama yelled. All three ran toward us, Adele in front. Mama held her dress in one hand and her shoes in the other. All she had on was her yellowed slip. My naked sister ran after Mama, her dress over her shoulder.

Two men and a tall boy ran through the water behind them. They stopped when they saw Papa's musket. It was plain that all three were Choctaws, but the boy was very dark, like he was part Negro. One man had a fresh scar across his left cheek, and the other had dry white patches all over his head, each with a bloody center. He didn't wear a hat to cover the bald spots where the crud had spread.

"What you boys want?" Papa yelled.

They didn't answer. Their eyes were round and a strange copper color. They looked like owls.

Then they turned and disappeared around the bend. "I forgot my brush, Mama," said Survella.

"I'll buy you a new one," Papa said as he roughly picked her up by the waist and tossed her in the wagon. "Teague. Gilmore. Get in," he yelled. My brother stood at the bank like he was waiting for the men to come back. Then Teague swatted Gilmore on the rump and both ran to the wagon, climbed the wheel spokes, and jumped in. Then we ran home as fast as the horses could pull us.

That night, Mama and Papa sat looking out the windows, muskets loaded. Us kids huddled beneath our window, looking outside and listening to our parents' talk. It was a clear, moonless night. Around eleven or twelve o'clock stars ran across the sky.

"Witches are out," said Mama.

"Don't start that," said Papa.

Mama kept talking. "When stars run like that, it means witches are moving. When a witch dies, the star falls. None are falling so they aren't dead. Those men we saw. They're part of it. I know it. Tomorrow I want Ellis over here. He'll take care of them."

They were quiet for a few moments.

"Go on to bed," Papa said quietly to us. "We'll watch."

From our beds, we watched the outlines of our parents until we fell asleep.

Uncle Ellis

BILLIE

That next morning Teague took Papa's horse Percy over to Adele's. Then she and my brother rode the twenty miles to Adele and Mama's Uncle Ellis Toshaway Battiest. Ellis made Papa uncomfortable just like other full-bloods did. Ellis was an Indian doctor like his brother Ruel, what we call an *alikchi*. After hearing that, I knew I must keep an eye on him in case he did something special.

Papa said that Choctaw doctors weren't real doctors, they were heathens, and he didn't want one touching us. Mama got so mad at Papa that she refused to talk to him for a week. They acted like children around each other.

The next morning, Ellis rode into the yard followed by three men, Lewis Wilson, Wood Nall, and Jest Wesley. Behind them ran a long-legged white dog. They dismounted and tied their horses to the pole fence by the porch. After Mama called them in to dinner they went to the water barrel to wash.

Ellis was thin as a skeleton and his dark skin stretched tight across his bony face and across his hands; the veins showed through like blue worms. He tied back his thin hair with a bright red ribbon. A string of blue and brown beads hung around his neck and he wore earrings through both earlobes and a tattoo on his arm. Ellis's clothes were as tattered and gray as he was.

The other men were what we called real Choctaws. They were dark with their hair cut above their ears. Each wore boots with high heels, shirts with no collars, and vests. Their hair and pants were wet where they had wiped their hands.

All three were Lighthorsemen, a group formed a few years earlier by

Greenwood LeFlore and David Folsom to enforce the laws. Lighthorsemen had big responsibility. They decided if a person was guilty of a crime and, if so, they served punishment.

"So, you all right?" the tall man named Lewis asked Mama. It was plain they knew each other.

Mama looked at him the same way he looked at her. Papa got mad and answered for her. "We are fine. What do you plan to do?"

"William, wait a minute. Everyone eat. There's plenty." She greeted the other men. "*Halito*, Wood. Jest."

Wood nodded his head and said "Danny," while Jest nodded and kept his eyes down.

I followed Ellis while he tended to the horses. "Billie Louise," he said. "Little one." He had a rough laughing voice and no teeth.

I stood next to him in my blue dress, with one hand on the wagon wheel and the other holding my white apron stained pink from cooking raspberry pies. Right there in front of me was a man who knew everything I wanted to know. He was all the old Choctaws rolled into one.

I couldn't think of what to say, so I watched Ellis rub his lathered horse with handfuls of straw. Then we went to the house without saying a word. Once inside, I felt foolish again because I had made the *tanfula* for dinner and I didn't make it the way most Choctaws like it. *Tanfula* is made with pounded and boiled corn mixed with strained wood ash lye, but I add a special ingredient.

When I was three, I ate a green pepper off a bush at Adele's. There were green ones mixed in with yellow and red ones. Adele liked the bushes for decoration and told me never to eat one of the peppers or else I'd be sorry. She was part right. My mouth felt like it was on fire and I drank four or five dippers of water from the barrel. Water only made the pain worse. Adele gave me a glass of cream and the fire went out. Even though my mouth blistered, I had liked the taste of those little peppers. Adele laughed then picked a few, dried them out, and a week later I planted the seeds in Papa's garden. Every summer those red, yellow, and green peppers grew like wildflowers and I ate every one. They're best when pickled. I'm also partial to onions and jalapeño peppers.

Not everybody likes peppers in their food. I was the cook in the family and I made several batches of everything, one with spice and the others plain. Papa said I could use the extra corn as long as I ate it all. And I always did since the time Mama made a strawberry pie and the ball I tossed around the kitchen landed in the middle of it. Papa made me eat the whole thing by myself, so I knew he was serious about me eating anything I made that nobody else wanted. I always had my shaker bottle of peppers and vinegar when we went visiting, and I still have my bottles marinating on the kitchen windowsill. They make nice gifts, although I don't know of anybody who eats them.

When family and friends came to visit, they'd ask who made the bread or *tanfula*. If I made it, they'd take only a little. Nobody liked the way I cooked meat for myself either. I couldn't tolerate deer unless it was almost burnt while the rest of my family liked it bloody.

Well, Ellis sat down and took some *tanfula* from the red wooden bowl and Mama said, "You won't like that, Ellis," but he took some anyway. Survella looked at me, wondering what he'd say after tasting it.

He grinned real big and said, "This is tasty, little one." Still, he put his plate down, got another, and took food from the other bowls. The other men didn't even try my spicy dish. I wanted to run and hide.

Everyone filled their plates with strawberries, biscuits, fried onions, and eggs with mushrooms. Wood Nall took tiny bites. He had big hands and his daintiness looked funny. Afterwards the adults moved to the front porch and drank three pots of coffee and ate two raspberry pies. All us kids except Beula found them interesting so we sat inside the kitchen door and listened to them. They all spoke English as well as we did. They had thick Choctaw accents, but they knew the big English words.

"About these men," said Lewis. "A month ago two men and a boy stole some cows from a mission school and killed a family the next afternoon. Took their hair and ears. One man has a *yanfa*." He made a motion across his face. "That's Jackson Crow. The boy's his son Dew. Mother was a Negra. The man with the nasty skin's Jackson's cousin. We've been looking for weeks but we haven't found anyone who's seen them. Till you."

Lewis had a funny way of saying "Negro." It came out "Negra."

Survella sat up straighter, and I moved closer to the door. Mama started talking real fast, asking questions.

"Jackson killed his boy's mother after an argument," he continued. "She cut his face before she died."

"You're going after them?" Mama asked Lewis.

"Soon as Jest gets outta your outhouse."

Ten minutes later we watched the three Lighthorsemen ride away. Ellis stayed to visit with Mama and Adele. Wood tried to get his dog to follow, but Gomer was happy to sit in the porch shade, petted by us kids who had always wanted a dog.

Ellis talked to Mama and Adele for the rest of the day. I've thought about Ellis a thousand times since then and of what I could have asked him. All gone now. For a long time I wondered if he was mad because of the way I cooked, but now I know it was the least of his thoughts.

My grandson Tom says that medicine people keep secrets and don't let them go. Like crotchety old Pel Postoak, who lives about forty miles from here. He only talks to fulls and a few half-bloods that need him. Pel's family worked a pecan orchard until they lost it in the allotment. Now white folks live on Pel's farm and make their business selling nuts from the same trees. Pel's been bitter ever since and has nothing to do with white people or Choctaws who act like them. From what I could tell, Ellis wasn't angry toward whites but he ignored Papa. Come to think of it, everyone did except Mama and us kids.

Before Ellis left the next day, he gave each of us children a leather bundle. He put his hands on my shoulders and in his old creaky voice said, "Billie Lou, you will have this a long time. You will travel many roads but never alone."

Then he looked at us standing there on the porch watching him, and he stopped smiling. "Careful," he said. "Witches about."

After Ellis rode away, Aunt Adele and Mama talked quietly for a while and they both kept looking at the sky. They came in while my sisters and I washed dishes and Adele said she'd spend the night, something she never did.

That night, while we sat in the front room lit by firelight, Adele told us never to forget the old Choctaws. "They're part of us, children." She looked to where Beula was sitting by the window, gazing out. I remember thinking that my sister probably was dreaming of marrying a white man and moving far away from us. "Even you, Beula," Adele said softly.

"I already forgot."

"Don't be so hateful, sister," said Teague. "You are who you are. You can't forget if you try."

Beula ignored him. I was surprised that Papa stayed out of the conversation.

I never have forgotten. My sketches of Ellis are my best, probably because I paid such close attention to him. Even though I don't understand the old ones, they've pulled me towards them all my life. I feel comfortable with yet distant from them, like they're from a different tribe. It's interesting that Ellis was more Indian than me, but to white people there wasn't any difference between us. But Indians are very different from each other. I had never thought much about it until we visited Mobile.

Papa always missed what he called civilization and he longed to visit white people. He needed conversation and since no Irishmen lived in our area, he tried to lose himself in books. He read the same books over and over, especially the Bible. I didn't mind when he read aloud from it because I like adventure stories.

Once a year Papa went to Mobile to buy supplies we couldn't find in Mississippi, like kitchen pots or knives for Mama, and dresses, pants, and hard stick candy for us kids. He stuffed the saddlebags with books for him.

Survella and I traveled with him the year before we moved to Indian Territory. We'd never seen big water and in Mobile the smell of the sea stuck to us. Boats came and went, and seagulls glided head-high scouting for food.

The fish markets smelled worse than anything I'd ever been around and at the same time were interesting. Fish of all kinds were stretched out on wooden shelves, including a catfish five feet long, giant crawdaddies, sea animals living in shells, and others with claws and eyes on stalks that looked like cousins to armadillos.

There were lots of different kinds of people, too. Black folks with skins all shades of dark and toting heavy loads trailed behind their white masters. Fancy-dressed men rode shiny trotting horses. The only white women were missionaries in dreary dresses. Chickasaws came to trade dressed in regular pants and bright shirts. They were taller than Choctaws and looked to be lighter in color. Papa said they were a mean bunch and fought a lot.

Those Indians looked serious and didn't seem the type to deal with white people unless they had to. I saw Chickasaws and Osages in Oklahoma City after the Civil War. Those Cherokee women looked white, and the Osages still wore their hair plucked except for a strip down the middle of their heads. Why did they do that, I wondered. Did their women think it made them look handsome? Where did that idea start? 'Course, lots of full Choctaws never cut their hair and I couldn't figure how that style made their life easier, what with all that hair either dragging on the ground or piled heavy on top of their heads.

I figured other Indians were as varied as us Choctaws. All Cherokees didn't look like the ones we saw, and neither did Osages. White people saw us Indians as all alike. I still wonder what Indians think of each other.

A week after the Lighthorsemen left our home, the bodies of Lewis Wilson and Jest Wesley were found together floating in a mossy creek pool, their hair and ears missing. Wood Nall wandered the road above the creek dressed only in his long johns. He tried, but he couldn't talk. His mouth moved, but no sound came out. When other Lighthorsemen took Wood home, he set his house on fire then poked on his leg with a knife until he cut the big muscles in his thigh. Then he drank two full bottles of whiskey from his collection in his barn, crawled to his wife's grave, which lay under a sunflower patch outside the corral, and died. Wood never said what happened to him and his friends and no tracks were found other than the Lighthorsemen's, but everyone knew who killed them.

Ishtaboli

BILLIE

1834

Mama and Adele were sad at the loss of their friends and Mama was especially aggrieved at Lewis's death. It wasn't until a year later that Adele told Survella about Mama and Lewis. They would have married except that when they met, he already was married and had six kids. I thought about that a lot as I grew older and figured that Mama was able to deal with Papa because she thought of Lewis. She believed in the possibility of him. Papa knew it, too, but still treated Mama like she was stupid. What mattered was that she was *his* wife, and as far as Papa was concerned, nothing was going to change. Mama was as unhappy as Beula afterwards, but life had to go on.

Shortly after the Lighthorsemen were buried, Papa finally gave in to our pestering to let us see an *ishtaboli*—a ball game. Adele said it was played on a field with sometimes a hundred players to a team. She saw several games when she was younger, and in those days a thousand people came to watch. She said that players hit each other with their sticks so hard they'd break an arm, leg, or face. Papa didn't like the sound of that, but the rest of us did so we made plans to travel the twenty miles to see the game.

We loaded our wagon and left plenty of food scattered about for the chickens. Papa didn't like to leave the farm alone, but the Crows scared Mama and Survella so much that they made sure we all stayed together.

Adele said Choctaws blew whistles at the games so we took ours that James had made. Papa rode Percy and Mama drove the wagon. Adele, Royal, and Gilmore followed us in their wagon.

By the time we were fifteen miles south, the roads were crowded with more people than I'd ever seen. People on wagons, on horses, and on foot all headed in the same direction. Wagons and horses were loaded and those walking carried wrapped bundles. Most of them were fulls and only a few said hello.

"What's everyone carrying?" James yelled to Adele.

"Watchers bet on the game," she yelled back. "Sometimes all their belongings and sometimes their wives."

"Not God's way," Papa said very loudly from twenty feet away.

"William, hush." Mama was afraid the people around would hear him.

Papa dropped back behind Adele's wagon and stayed quiet.

That night we ate supper at friends of Adele and Royal's, the Durants. Because they lived on the main road to the southern district, they made a healthy living selling meals to travelers. They kept people from coming onto their property during the game by blocking the road with a dead cottonwood tree. We had to cross a field to get to the back part of their house.

After we cared for the horses and washed, we sat at the big table to eat. Beula looked at the piles of food in the center of the table and asked, "What's that?" She had no intention of eating it.

"*Banaha*," Adele said. "Boiled cornmeal, potatoes, onions, and beans inside cornshucks. Same as you get at home except it looks different. Eat some."

"No, thank you." Then she crossed her arms and sat still.

The Durants talked Choctaw to Mama, Adele, and Royal. They never looked at Papa so he took his plate outside. Beula went with him. They spent lots of time outside our relatives' homes.

We mostly lived around half-bloods in the *Okla falaya* district and didn't see a lot of fulls. Aunt Adele and Uncle Royal always went off to visit some and I was jealous that Gilmore got to go with them. It was frustrating, too, because it was hard to understand my cousin when he tried to tell me about his trips.

After noontime supper, Teague, Gilmore, Survella, and I walked to the ball field. We stayed on top of the rise that overlooked the field and watched people set up camp. Some men dug a tree stump out from the center of the pasture. Other men, players it looked like, sat together in tight circles, maybe talking strategy.

Two men stood near us, one holding his playing sticks that were half wrapped with a red blanket. The sticks are about three feet long with little pockets at one end. The pieces are sewn together with sinew and they stay tight even if they hit something solid, like a person. The idea is for the teams to hit or catch and then throw the leather ball with their sticks until the ball touches the other team's pole at the end of the field. The men were young, maybe around eighteen, and both were dark, one with hair to his shoulders and the other with his cut short. They studied the field, thinking about the next day.

We walked back toward the house along with several dozen other people who headed in that direction.

"I feel funny," said Survella.

"What do you mean?" asked Teague. "You gonna throw up?"

"No, I feel scared, like there's something around us."

"You're right. There's a lot of trees around us," Teague answered. The other people had walked ahead of us and around a bend, out of sight.

Survella was breathing fast. "That's not what I mean."

Gilmore looked all around, then touched my arm and nodded. He mouthed, "Something's here."

Then I saw the outline of a horse and rider under the shade of cottonwood trees about twenty feet from the road. I don't know why I looked in that direction because my attention was the other way. I kept watching the rider and bumped into Teague.

"Watch it, sister," he said. Then he saw me staring and turned to where I pointed. "I don't see anything," he said. As we got a few feet closer, I saw that the rider was Jackson Crow sitting on his black horse. He was facing away from us, but I was certain he knew we saw him.

Gilmore squinted hard and tried to say, "I see nothing, but there is something there. I feel it."

I touched Survella's arm. "I know," she said without looking. "It's him." Then she began crying and started running to the Durants'.

"Survella, slow down," I yelled. She was crying and I thought she'd trip. Teague and Gilmore kept up with her, but had to run fast.

"What are you running for?" Teague said behind her. "I didn't see anyone."

"It was him. It was him," Survella said between gasps.

"How could you not see him, Teague?" I panted.

Something blew past my head, mussing my hair. Looking up, I saw brown bird wings. The owl flew about twenty feet out in front of us, then turned sharply in a way I'd never seen birds fly and started back. It seemed to soar in slow motion, its wings folded. *Birds can't do that*, I thought. Mama said that when an *opa* comes around it means something bad will happen. I didn't understand how an owl could be bad, but I believed her. Papa, being a Catholic, didn't. He said white owls were good luck to Christians, but we didn't have any of those big ones around Mississippi.

Survella stopped and fell to the ground, her hands over her head. "Get it away," she screamed.

"Now what are you doing?" Teague asked loudly. "Are you all right? Gilmore?" Our cousin shrugged, meaning he didn't know.

Then the owl flew directly at me, the copper bird eyes round, but I knew they were human, too. As the owl streamed past us, it turned its head to look at me. I watched the large, brown, feathery bullet disappear into the trees. Teague jerked my arm hard. "What's wrong with you two?"

"Survella's going," I answered, and we ran after her to the house. Then I noticed the sky was very dark. And there were no clouds. "Teague, it's dark," I said. "It shouldn't even be dinnertime. How long were we out there?"

"Well," he looked around, "I don't know." Clearly, Teague knew something was amiss but he didn't know what.

"What's wrong here?" Papa asked after he saw us catching our breath on the porch. Survella was still crying. I told him what we saw while Teague stood there listening to me with his mouth open. Then Papa, Royal, and Mr. Durant rode off to see if they could find Jackson. That made me feel better, but Survella felt dizzy. She went to the back room with Mama and stayed there.

"What do you mean you didn't see anything," I asked my brother. "You were there."

"Billie, all I saw was you two acting crazy."

Gilmore kept his hands in his pockets and watched us talk. How awful not to hear, I thought, but even worse not to be able to talk clearly. "What about you?" I asked, but Gilmore shook his head "no."

The men came back an hour later and said they didn't see any tracks in the grove where we had run from Jackson.

"How could Survella know Jackson was in the trees without seeing him?" I asked Adele while we washed our hands in the barrel outside. "And why didn't Teague and Gilmore see him at all? Gilmore sensed him, but couldn't see."

"Crows are witches, you know. And they can turn into *opas*," Adele said. "They can make you think bad things. Make you sick anytime they want. And to forget. My son knows things. A trade for being deaf and dumb."

Mrs. Durant made a dinner of biscuits, fried pig, wild onions, and green beans, but Survella didn't want any and neither did I. Something strange had happened and I felt dirty, although nothing had touched me. Teague was bothered only because the time passed and he didn't know why.

Everyone else was hungry and found a place at the table. As usual, I tried not to sit opposite Royal. Us kids stayed quiet while the adults talked.

"We did not see a thing, Danny," Papa argued with Mama. "No tracks, no owl hoots."

"But Survella and Billie saw. . . ."

"There were shadows by that time," Papa reasoned. "Could have been someone else. Another big bird, maybe."

"Witches hide in shadows," Mrs. Durant said.

Adele nodded. "They only let you see them if they want you to see them."

Papa shook his head. "How could the girls see the owl and Teague say he didn't? He was right there with them. Were you not, son?"

We all looked at my brother, who had started to pale. "Yeah, but. . . ." He looked confused. "I can't remember." He looked down at his hands. Gilmore gnawed half-heartedly on his pork bone and didn't try to explain.

"Witches were there," said Mrs. Durant. "They wanted the girls to see them, not Teague or Gilmore. To make you confused and to set us against each other." My brother had not eaten a bite and looked pained. "Teague, I'll get something to help you sleep." Mrs. Durant went to the shelves next to her pantry that were filled with dried plants and picked a bunch for tea.

Gilmore looked to Adele. "Witches were there," he mouthed. "And they're still around. Here."

"Not tonight they won't be," said Papa. He had taken his muzzle-loader down from above the door where the Durants kept theirs.

The conversation died since nobody had anything else to say. Adele and I cleared the plates, Mrs. Durant boiled water, and her husband took three sticks from the windowsill. He took one out, broke it, and put the pieces in the bucket by the back door as he went outside to check the horses.

"What're those?" asked Teague.

"Well, *iso*"—Adele liked to call Teague "son" even though he really wasn't—"when it's decided when the *ishtaboli* will be played, a certain number of *fuli*—that means sticks—are bundled together and the bunches given out to the players and those who want to watch. Each day a stick is taken out of the bundle until one is left. That means the game will be played that day."

"So, when he takes the next one out in the morning, he'll know to go to the ball field. Seems he'd know that a few sticks ago," Teague said. He was unimpressed.

"That's not the point. Now, time to sleep," Adele said as she took the empty teacup from Teague.

Mrs. Durant told us we must sleep since we'd be up early, but from us worrying about the Crows and having to listen to the players sing all night, we only managed to sleep a few hours total and were wobbly in the morning, as if we'd been sick.

While we washed our faces to try and wake up, Papa told us that Mama and Survella had to stay in the house with him. The rest of us could go if we promised to stay together. "None of you wander off alone, do you hear me? Hold hands and stay in the crowd."

"Yes, Papa," Teague said while cleaning his ears with his shirttail.

Nobody cooked breakfast and Adele said we'd eat biscuits and apples during the game.

"Come on and go this time, Beula," I said to my sister, who was sitting on a footstool with a wet cloth, washing her face.

"No, I. . . ."

Mama was folding our sleeping clothes and spoke from the other room. "Yes, Beula. You need to get out for once."

"Yes, girl," Papa agreed. "You need to walk."

Beula let out a sigh and threw down her cloth. I knew she'd go but would act hateful.

After we dressed and pinned up our hair, we started down the road and arrived at the field as the sun came up. We agreed to hold hands, but us kids walked faster and got ahead of the adults and soon Beula and I lost everyone else. We decided that as long as we had apples and biscuits and knew where the Durants' house was we could wander by ourselves.

There were more people that morning than I ever thought could crowd together, and we had to wind our way through them to see the field. The day was clear with only a few wispy white clouds floating around the blue sky. Beula was surely worried that without her parasol she'd turn a few shades darker.

We stood at the end of the south side of the field in two-foot-high grass, almost twenty feet from the posts where the other team had to hit to score. The field was about 400 yards long and at the ends were two tall posts set in the ground one foot apart. The stump hole was filled in and pressed flat. We could see the entire field and since there were only a few other people around, we figured it was a good spot.

Hundreds of people surrounded the field, from small children to old ones who looked like they could barely keep from toppling over. There were as many women in the crowd as there were men. Most were full-bloods, but some were half-bloods like our family, with dark brown or reddish hair and lighter skin. Some of the half-bloods were wealthy ones judging from their clothes and the way they stood away from the fulls. I saw some white men, but every one stood next to a Choctaw woman. I didn't see any white women and wondered why none married Choctaw men.

That ball game was the first time I ever saw someone with a pressed head. She was an old woman, which made sense because Adele had told us that Choctaws didn't press heads anymore. Adele said that when they were babies their mothers wrapped them tight onto their cradleboards so their heads would be flat and long. I wondered how she could think straight with her brain moved around like that.

"Good heavens," Beula said when she saw her. "Why would her family do something like that?"

"Maybe it's religious," I answered.

"No, it couldn't be. Unless it's the work of the Devil."

I ignored her. Beula believed that everything strange to her was the Devil's doing. Her comments were tiresome and I tried not to have discussions with her.

It was hot and many people tried to stay cool with turkey-wing fans. Some people dressed in their best clothes, all clean and colorful, while others were drunk and smelled bad, but every person was excited and blew their whistles. I brought my whistle but knew that Beula had left hers home on purpose.

I had not blown it twice when a noise like humming started in the oak groves around the field. Then the noise grew to yelling and the crowd on the east side parted to allow hundreds of men dressed in breechclouts to run to the field. Then they turned south to gather at their end. I didn't look at Beula, but she probably had the same expression on her face as I surely had. I felt flushed, as if I had been running. Beula had a grip on my arm that I thought would bruise me.

The players were like a dream. They painted themselves in colors and wore a wrap between their legs and around their waists. They had tails made from horsehair attached to their waists and they stuck out like a horse's. We didn't know anyone playing so I yelled for the group that came out first.

When the game started, both teams went after the little deerskin ball as fast as they could run. They jumped over each other, knocked each other down, and swung at everyone with their sticks, even their teammates. It was such a fury I was surprised they all didn't run into one another. Every time the teams ran to one side of the field a few men were left lying on the ground, holding a leg or their heads. One man lay on the field for a long time with both hands over his nose and the players ran over him. He finally crawled over to the side. I loved it and I forgot all about the Crows.

So did a lot of other people. An old woman standing near us wore a dirty white skirt with a red and brown shirt and a hat with a sloping brim. She didn't look like she had the strength, but she started jumping up and down and yelling like the Crows were after her. She wasn't the only one. By the time the game started everyone jumped and screamed. Spit flew on my neck all day.

After just an hour, people who had looked normal before the game looked like they had run ten miles. Their hair came undone, their shirttails were out, and they sweated as much as the players. After so much noise I thought I would never hear quiet again. My throat hurt, too. Beula was embarrassed to be around me, but it was so much fun I didn't care what she thought.

One time the teams crossed the line where Beula and I watched. We stood in front of the crowd on our end of the field and had to scatter with everyone else so we wouldn't be trampled. Those players came at us so fast we froze for a minute. Beula fell backwards over her feet and got up just before the sticks came swinging. As soon as the players were on us they were already back to the other end. It was just the most amazing thing.

The game lasted into the evening, and the team I cheered for won. After the game ended, about a hundred women ran onto the field to play. I couldn't believe my eyes. Some were my age and some looked like Mama. They pulled the backs of their skirts up between their legs, tucking the fabric into their belts so as not to trip. They tied their long hair back and looked ready to work their farms, but they were ready to *play*. Sticks clanked together and the women ran up and down the field as fast as the men. One woman got hit across the face and fell. When she stood we saw blood all over her. Beula could hardly stand it.

After the players left the field we went back to the house. I replayed both games in my mind and decided that if I ever got the chance I'd play, too. When I was older I got to knock the ball around with the stick Gilmore traded a blowgun for and was pretty good at catching the ball when he threw it to me, but I never found a real game to play in.

Papa, Mama, and Survella stood watch at the Durants' all day and were tired. Survella's eyes were red from crying and all wanted to go home, especially after Adele told them she heard that some men and women were found dead a little ways from the field, their hair and ears missing.

The next morning Papa and Royal threw all our belongings into the wagons and we went home, looking over our shoulders the whole way so that by the time we got home we all fell asleep. Those Crows were like the wind, either all around us without us seeing them, or they'd be so fast and vicious we'd break like oaks in a tornado.

It wasn't long after our trip that we heard our parents talk about moving to Arkansas or a place called Indian Territory. Where could that be? I wondered. If Indians were there, it couldn't be too bad.

Mama smiled around us children, but didn't look happy when she and Uncle Burl discussed the Choctaws' business with the federal government. Adele told us about the treaties and how our tribal land was shrinking. We'd been losing it for a long time, but that was the first I'd heard of it.

All the talk about treaties and government meant nothing to me. I thought all that was grown-up business. I was wrong. I was only ten and my childhood was over.

Moving

BILLIE

1834–1836.

In the fall of 1834, the oak and silver maple leaves changed from red to yellow, just like they did the years before. The end of summer in Mississippi was peaceful. Sometimes when a hot breeze blew, a sudden swirl of cool air ran past. I wondered if the coolness was sent ahead to warn the hot air it had to soon move away.

Our cold air was a removal treaty that had been signed several years before called Dancing Rabbit Creek, and it gave Choctaws the choice of either moving to Indian Territory or becoming citizens of Mississippi.

"I don't believe a word of it," said Aunt Adele. "We got to move no matter what the government promises." As usual, she was right.

At night us kids listened to the adults in the front room argue about what to take. We didn't have many clothes or other belongings but we did have a house, farm, and land. The sun looked down on us in Mississippi and I couldn't think of looking up at the sky from another place. The creek, the hills, Nanih Waiya—the place where the first Choctaws came out of the ground into the world—all of it was my home.

Mama started to wear a stern look I hadn't seen before. And she began to act strange. She had hair to her hips and rolled it around socks to make a bun then fastened it with pins. She only took it down at night and I normally brushed it every evening while she sat at the kitchen table.

"Don't brush my hair," Mama would say after she sat down and handed me her brush. She stopped putting her hair up and tied it back with a strip of cloth instead, and the front part fell in her face. Tangled hair and dark circles under her eyes caused her to look sick.

"I don't feel good," said my brothers Teague and James.

I knew we were in for pain.

Like Adele said they would, white people showed up early and told Choctaws to leave even before they packed. Some whites moved right on in, and Choctaws south of us had to find relatives to stay with. The Durants lost their cattle and horses to white thieves, and Hettie Hacker died one night when her house mysteriously caught fire. The next week white men with long beards started building their new house on her property.

By October of 1835 we sold our plow, the cattle, and all but seven horses. The government said to leave our livestock behind because we'd receive other animals in the West, but Papa wouldn't even think about leaving the mustangs and Mama didn't consider selling her milk cow, Rebecca.

"How're we gonna get those horses to the Territory, William?" Mama asked. With a wagon full of basic goods like clothes, tools, bedding, and food for us, there'd be little room for hay besides what the wagon team and Rebecca needed. Mama thought we should concentrate on ourselves, not a bunch of horses.

"Are you trying to start something?" Every time Mama asked Papa a question pertaining to a topic he was sensitive about, Papa answered her like that. It was his way of letting her know she was out of line for bringing it to his attention. Usually, Mama'd keep at it, but she was no longer in the mood to fight so she turned around and left the room.

Government men also said that if we walked we'd get food, a new rifle, gold, and a guide. Several hundred Choctaws agreed to walk, but Mama said us kids were too young. "Our wagon will carry us all. We can ride your horses, William," she said. That was Papa's out, and he said nothing.

There wasn't enough room for our furniture, and only for a few tools. Mama insisted on taking her china set that Papa brought her from Mobile. Papa thought it was unwise to try and take dishes across country, but he kept quiet and packed the delicate dishes in a crate lined with rags and blankets.

Cousin Gilmore had only a small bundle of clothes, a bag of books, and four blowguns that he strapped under Royal and Adele's wagon. Adele took her baskets filled with medicine plants. I had no treasures except the bundle Ellis gave me and a basket. It was lopsided and ugly and I wanted it because it was my first try.

Adele wove beautiful baskets. She showed me how to pick cane, then split and dry it. She used barks and roots for dye, black from walnuts and red from oak bark. Survella's baskets were good enough to sell, but mine came out uneven or loose. I made one good basket with diamond designs and a strong handle that I accidentally stepped on.

That first morning we waited an hour by the wagon for Mama. "What's she doing in there?" asked Teague.

"You in a hurry to get somewhere?" Survella asked him. Teague shook his head. "Didn't think so."

Finally, Mama came out with a blanket over her head, then stepped up to the wagon bench without a word. Beula sat with her knees drawn up at the back of the wagon, biting her nails. She made sure she got that spot, which was as far from us as she could get. Beula didn't like horses, otherwise she'd be on one, trailing a mile behind. My little brother James looked sickly and lay down with his head propped on the china box. Papa and Teague rode a horse while Mama and us girls took turns driving the wagon.

As we drove away, I turned and watched our quiet, deserted house. Our chickens pecked in the yard, their little bird brains unconcerned about anything except food. I mentally said good-bye to Red the rooster and Chickchicki, the big gray, freckled hen that came to me when I called her. The garden was as peaceful as the house, still rich with fruits and vegetables the birds and deer would eat. Dirt was still under my fingernails from picking squash the day before and I thought of the time and effort we all put into that wonderful garden. The wagon rounded the bend and my house, garden, and chickens were gone. My breath left me.

Survella and I hugged, for she was thinking the same thoughts. "We'll get through this, sister," she said. She rubbed my back. "We will."

Adele, Royal, and Gilmore were waiting for us where our paths met the main road, and our homeless group started south. We hadn't gone half a mile when, without a word, Papa turned Percy around and ran back down the road. "Papa!" Teague yelled. "What are you doing? Papa!" But Papa paid no attention. So Teague turned his feisty mare, Medea, around and ran after him.

"Don't move!" Mama said in a stern voice when I stood with the intention of jumping down and grabbing one of the mustangs tied to the wagon.

From the back of the wagon, Beula gave a large sigh as if she was bored. Nobody sighed that loud except on purpose. "Hush up, girl," Mama said. My sister got on everyone's nerves.

A few minutes later Papa loped back with Teague behind him. "Now we can go," he said. Teague wiped his eyes with his sleeve.

"Teague?" I asked at the same time that Survella looked back toward our house and said, "Where's that smoke from?"

"Our farm," Papa said. "No one will live in it and no one will eat my garden."

Mama kept the blanket over her head.

Then Beula said, "And what's that smoke there?"

Gray smoke snaked upwards over Adele and Royal's farm. Adele didn't turn around and Royal said nothing. They burned their place, too. I knew then we weren't going back.

"Where do we meet Ellis?" sniffed Teague.

"We aren't meeting him," Mama said in a whisper.

"When's he coming west?"

"He's not, son."

"What about his brother Ruel? Can we meet him?"

"Ruel does what he wants, Teague. I don't know what he plans to do."

I was as disappointed as Teague, although I knew Ellis couldn't live anywhere else. She never told me how she knew Ellis was staying since we didn't get mail and there had been no messengers around for almost a year.

While we mulled over our predicament, our bodies stayed uncomfortable bouncing over rocks on seats with no padding. Saddles made me sore, too, but felt better than the bench. Survella had a hard time writing in her journals and Gilmore felt sick after reading pages that moved up and down, so they both gave up. Mama made us stop a lot to check Rebecca even though she never acted tired, just irritated that she couldn't stand still and eat all day.

"That damn cow is fine," Papa said when he rode up to the wagon.

"Damn *you*." Mama got harsher as the days went by. Papa rode off.

After two days my sickly brother James began sneezing and coughing. Mama covered him with all our blankets and he still got chilled. That night I dreamed James sickened. My bad dream woke me before the sun came up and I reached over to James and put my hand on his chest. He was breathing, although rough and watery. "James, don't leave us," I whispered to my sleeping brother. I couldn't convince myself that he would get better.

We finally reached Vicksburg a week later and joined other families who had missed the main group. They were as tired and depressed as we were. An old, bent woman in a calico dress that was finely made but dirty and torn from her travels walked over to us as we prepared for the night.

"Few days afore, almost three thousand of us left their belongings and got on them big steamers, the *Talma* and *Cleopatra*, that was s'posed to take them to the Red River," she said, shading her eyes from the bright setting sun. Her hair was white and her skin dark, but her eyes were blue-green. Her family started marrying whites a long time ago, I thought. What for? The same reason as Mama?

"What is all this?" Papa asked, gesturing to the wagons, furniture, and tools that littered the bank.

"Couldn't fit on the boats. People had to leave it. Nice things, but I cain't get any more onto my wagon. Luck to you." And she walked slowly away.

A couple of families were outfitted with teams of six horses each, covers on their wagons, and pack mules. Other families walked and didn't make it halfway to Indian Territory. Mama cried at the numbers of children who didn't have horses to ride.

We were a bit lucky; army men let us take our wagons and animals onto the *Triman*. I suspected they didn't like their job and felt sorry for us. One called all us females "ma'am" and tipped his hat. Still, they had guns and meant to see us to Indian Territory.

The Mississippi River was wide as a valley and deep in some places, although not where we departed. We watched the other steamer, the *Journeyman*, hit a sand island halfway across the river. The boat was only a hundred feet behind us and we heard people and animals scream. A wagon tied to a side deck fell off with the family still in it. We drifted farther away and couldn't stop to help. Horses and cows fell in as the *Journeyman* broke apart. Soon the people stopped struggling in the cold water to reach the shore. They drowned and their bodies caught in brush at the river's edge.

I've always wondered at God's reasoning. "What did God do that for, Papa?" I asked.

Papa gripped the railings while he stared at the ruined boat. "God has a reason for everything." He never could answer that question.

"But what could the reason be?"

"Sets other things in motion. Or, it could have been worse. If this had not happened, then something else might have." He rambled on with a few more ideas and I stopped listening. I believed in God, but couldn't reason why, if He loved us so much, He let bad things happen. The only thing I could think of was that God couldn't be everywhere at once and sometimes when He turned His head, Satan stepped in. No other explanation made sense to me, and still doesn't. Papa didn't like that philosophy because if it were true, then God was not all-powerful.

Our lonely boat kept on for twelve days when we joined the Red River. Then we traveled the Ouachita to Camden Post in Arkansas. We left the *Triman* and started in the wagon. It was still about 140 miles to Fort Towson and another sixty-five to Red Oak. Poor families, old and young people, walked and carried whatever they could. Some carried each other. Our torture really began here, either a punishment God exacted on us without letting us know why or He simply wasn't aware of us.

We crossed many streams in Arkansas. None as wide as the Mississippi, but most muddy and hard to ferry. The Saline River took a wagon, some cattle, and a family trying to cross in a spot that was calm on top and deep and fast underneath. They were gone before they could scream.

Then the weather turned. Cold rain soaked our clothes and we had no dry place to hide, much less dry wood. Water soaked through the crate that carried our clothes. All of us shivered.

James had been bundled up for weeks and couldn't get warm, so one cold, cloudy afternoon Adele wandered off to find a plant to help him. Within half an hour the snow and wind started. Papa took Percy to find Adele even though we couldn't see ten feet ahead of us.

"Papa, you want me to go?" Teague asked.

Gilmore was standing next to my brother and gestured loudly, "No, me. I want to go with you." He took a few steps forward. He tried to speak and couldn't. "Uncle William?"

"No, boys," Papa yelled through the wind. "Everybody else needs you. Do *not* come after me."

Gilmore stood with his arms still out. His hat blew off his head and hung down his back, held by the leather string. His mama was gone and he could do nothing. I watched Teague turn and put his arms around Gilmore and both boys, not yet in their teens, cried.

The wind screamed all night and Papa and Adele didn't return. Even though Mama and us girls huddled together inside the wagon with James in the middle, I recall the sharp sting of cold. Heavy, wet snow bent tree branches to the ground. My face and feet hurt, like a crawdaddy pinch. Two of my toes froze, turned black a week later, and then came off in my shoe after another week. Coyotes and wolves howled at night and I wondered if they were warm. Funny how in the heat of Mississippi summer I wished for ice to rub on me.

Gilmore and Royal sat together under their blankets all night, facing into the wind, the way Papa had gone. They fell asleep and were covered with snow by daybreak. The morning sun broke the clouds and brightness off the snow blinded our eyes and gave us headaches. Mid-morning, Papa rode in with Adele propped in front of him. Papa's blond beard was icy and his eyelids so frosted he could open them only halfway.

Papa said he found Adele in a creek. Her lips were blue as wilted cornflowers. We figured she tripped and fell down the creek bank. We put her in her wagon onto a bed of thin blankets and I rubbed her hands and Survella put Adele's cold feet under her clothes to warm them. "So cold," my sister said. "Like ice." But she didn't move her aunt's feet from under her dress. A deep gash on Adele's forehead didn't bleed and I wondered at that.

Adele never spoke. She stared at the sky and was cold as the ground. Ragged people came to the wagon with good intentions but none could help. They had troubles of their own. Many had already died from the cold and more coughed blood.

A couple of wagons broke their axles. The tools to fix them had long since been abandoned on the road. The day Papa found Adele, Teague sprained his wrist digging in the frozen ground while burying a baby and old lady. The shovel broke in half after getting just two feet down. That was how it was on our trip west. Two feet down.

Adele's eyes froze. She hadn't blinked since Papa brought her back.

"Aye," he said. "She was cold when I fetched her from the water. 'Del may have been dead then."

The weather was so unmerciful we couldn't tell the living from the dead.

Papa went to the wagon for the broken shovel. Mama sat on the cold ground and rocked back and forth. Royal stood by the wagon with his arms crossed, his once-thick belly flattened by the heavy weight of starvation and depression. I kept looking at my Aunt Adele to make certain she was dead. How could she be dead? I believed my aunt could do anything and would always be here.

Teague tugged on my sleeve and pointed to where Papa crouched, hitting his fist against a wheel spoke. That was the only time I saw Papa cry. Most thought he was crying for Adele, but someone else came to my mind like a lightning bolt.

I ran to the wagon and fell, splitting my chin. I looked in at James and he was still, staring toward the sky. Dead. I lost my breath and started to fall again, but Gilmore held me up and pressed my chin with a rag to stop the bleeding. It was the same cloth he'd used on Adele's forehead. The only blood on it was mine.

We buried James and Adele together in a creek bank where the ground was softer. I imagined that in the spring they'd wash away. While Papa and Teague dug graves, Survella closed my chin with the big needle we used to sew leather. Her fingers were cold and the needle went in deep. "Sorry, sister," she said. "Does it hurt?"

"No." I didn't feel a thing.

That evening we stood at the edge of the bank. Papa barely managed a prayer about giving us strength and taking care of our dead. Standing on the east bank I looked west and watched the sun set. All blue and pink. I wondered how many Indian people the sun had watched die.

I turned back to the wagon and saw the moon rising. I thought God played a mean joke to let us see the sun and moon so beautiful while we buried our dead family. Was it God's fault that Adele and James died? Or was it our fault for not fighting for our land? How could Papa ask for guidance from the being that let this happen? I stayed confused about God for a very long time.

We buried more people on that trail than I can remember. Mostly little ones. Old men and women froze too, but some young men died, like two army men who looked strong when we first saw them at Vicksburg. One with curly blond hair and a dimpled chin died from fever, and the other, who was terribly homely with a wayward left eye, cracked his head when his horse slipped on ice. I felt worse about him because he rode the line every day to ask how we were doing. Those white men were tired and sorry they came, but there wasn't any place for them to go except with us.

It was three weeks to Fort Towson and everyone was dying. Mama rode in the wagon, her head bobbing like she was asleep or stupid. When we stopped, she wandered around like she was looking for something but couldn't find it. Beula had a wide-eyed stare like a scared deer and her carefully arranged coils of hair hung straight. She'd stopped pushing it away from her eyes. She clenched her teeth so hard I thought they'd break.

I remember everything about the trip and wish I couldn't. Mama told me about when I was two and fell off the cedar chest in her and Papa's room and broke my collarbone. She said I cried for hours after Adele pulled my arm back to straighten it and could hardly stand having my shoulders tied back for two months. I don't recall. That's God's gift to very little ones. They don't remember the bad things, the pain. It's when we get older that the bad times stay with us, even when they're really long gone.

Rejected dogs that once were pets followed us like skulking, sick wolves, scared to come close but afraid not to. I felt bad for those shivering and hungry dogs, knowing that they used to be fat and happy, lying on a porch in the sun, chasing rabbits and squirrels because it was fun. Not like now. If they could find anything to chase, they couldn't catch it. Their lives depended on speed and they weren't fast enough to catch their dinner. So, like us, they slowly starved and froze, their thin, worn-out carcasses littering the trail.

One morning our rear axle broke and the crate holding Mama's china fell out. Mama screamed so loud we jumped.

"Noooo! It can't be," she wailed. We all looked at each other. I didn't know it meant so much to her. Every piece was broken save a little blue sugar bowl. Mama wrapped it with a piece of torn blanket and held it to her like a baby. "*Chuka, chuka*," she kept saying. *Home*. She was losing her mind. I figured it reminded Mama of our home. I still have that sugar bowl but keep it under the bed in a box so I won't have to recall what it reminds me of.

Papa worked on the wagon for hours, but it was ruined. "Cannot fix the axle." His head dropped, one of the first times I ever saw Papa look defeated. We loaded our few belongings into Royal's wagon and rode the tired horses. Mustangs are often smaller than other horses, and they can go farther, but after weeks of hunger and cold, ours fought to stay upright. Rebecca was thin but she kept on walking. Beula rode only because she had no strength to walk even a few steps.

People before us suffered similar problems. Clothes, silverware, dishes, and even a guitar and harmonica lay strewn along the road. Survella and I sobbed at the memory of James's awful harmonica playing. I kept crying and kicked my poor horse hard to make him run ahead of my family. Then I lifted my shredded skirt to my face and wailed for the first time in my life. I hurt everywhere, was hungry and cold.

"Billie," Survella said after she got her horse to catch up with me. She patted my back like she did when she said something important. "We can make it, Billie. It has been too hard to just stop. Look at Gilmore. He takes care of everyone even when he feels sick. Teague's trying, too. Don't let us down."

"Where are we going?" I asked her but stared straight ahead. "No house, no family. How bad will it be there?"

"Can't say, sister. We have to find out and make the best of it." I scratched my abused horse and we rode in silence.

We saw bodies that lay where they fell. Small families had no help in burying their dead. A few bodies were wedged between tree branches. The old Muscogees buried their dead in hollow trees, but these poor folks just wanted to keep wolves and coyotes from eating their loved ones.

We had traveled seven weeks by that time and I figured we'd spend the rest of our lives suffering. I couldn't remember being warm. We hoped for food and warm houses at Fort Towson. Instead we received cold biscuits and thin tents. "Is this all? I can't believe it," Teague asked very loudly to no one in particular.

"Come on, son," said Papa. "Nothing here for us." We took what was offered and went north to find a home.

Two weeks later we crossed the Fourche Maline, a thin river north of the Kiamichi Mountains. It was cold and windy and I don't recall Mama saying two words the whole way. We ate everything we had. Gilmore managed to shoot a few rabbits and once I found some old frozen meat on a dead porcupine. Papa had wanted to butcher Rebecca a month before, but after seeing that sideways look Mama gave him he stopped talking about it.

Finally we arrived where my house is now. After rounding that thicket of old oaks next to where the barn is now, Mama said, "I ain't goin' no more." Then she slid off her horse, limped over to the big rock by that outhouse, and sat. There was no other access here by wagon because of the large rocks and boulders that covered the area three acres around. Over time we moved most of the smaller rocks and made fence posts out of them, and years later other folks came to buy the pretty ones to make chimneys or rock houses.

Papa didn't rest. He took in all the trees and quickly decided which ones would stay for shade and which ones would be the house. He got the ax and started cutting and by dark he had shaped four big pecans and used their branches for shelter. Rebecca and the mustangs were too tired to wander and a small corral of brush kept them in.

My sad, spent Uncle Royal died during the night. Although he hadn't been sick, he decided to give up when Adele died. My cousin Gilmore then became my third brother. Teague, Survella, and I stood around our beloved deaf cousin as Papa prayed over him. I took Gilmore's hand and smiled. "Brother," Teague said, and Gilmore nodded. Papa put his hand on Gilmore's shoulder and squeezed. Papa was angry at Royal for not staying alive to take care of Gilmore and I never heard him mention Royal again.

We looked thin as rat tails and felt sick in our bodies and minds. If we didn't get some food we knew we'd die, so after two days Teague took three horses to find food at an army post that gave rations to arriving Choctaws. He rode in one evening loaded with goods. "What you got?" Survella asked. "Any notebooks?"

"A few blankets, flour, coffee, and salt pork. No paper. Sorry."

"Not enough," Papa said. Mama heard.

"He found all this, William," she said. "Be grateful for once."

They both were right. We hadn't eaten a fruit or vegetable in over two months and wanted garden food, but Teague did the best he could. Nobody had gone to the creek so one day I explored about a mile of it and was surprised to find fish about seven inches long. I made poles from tree branches, unraveled some string from my skirt, and made hooks out of two heavy sewing needles. Gilmore and I caught fish every day and felt good that we brought food to the family.

One day Teague came home with a thick canvas tent. At least it was one warm place to sleep and sit during the cold days. Papa and the boys slept outside in the brush house they made.

We stayed protected here and didn't see many people. A few times my brothers went to the main road to see who passed by, but not many people came. Those who did told us stories about the second removal. Seems most came the same way we did, but there was never enough food and they starved. Everyone we talked to lost someone. A few lost everyone. I just couldn't believe how many died. We were flat-out disappearing. Were all our people in the cold ground? How could we be a tribe if our numbers were down to nothing? Nobody had answers so we kept our thoughts on staying alive.

Mama's brother Burl and his wife made it, but their boy died of cholera. They came across a thawed pond and drank the dirty water without noticing the dead cows in the shallows. About 100 people out of 400 died that week. Burl lost some fingers to frostbite and his wife, Nannie, started drinking as soon as she found a bottle. They settled ten miles south, where Bengal is now.

Not all Choctaws came west. Some hid in the woods while others stayed in the homes of white people who didn't think it right to move us. Papa was angry after he found out that his brother Roger avoided removal by taking his family to Virginia. There was talk about Choctaw doctors who gave their kin medicine so they'd be invisible to soldiers. Would our lives be different if Ellis had made us invisible? We never saw him again to ask.

Mama and Beula had nightmares and Survella went off in the woods to cry by herself. She didn't sleep because she thought the Crows would get her. One evening Teague came back from the main road all out of breath because he saw the Crows. I figured those men made it here by taking what others had and, sure enough, army men told Papa later that the Crows had killed all along the way. They stole cows and horses and sold them to whites. I couldn't imagine anyone doing that to their own people.

Every day Teague and Gilmore helped Papa build the house from dawn to dusk. That was their way of forgetting what happened. Papa started on the chimney one morning and finished two days later. They nailed the roof on the next day, and after three weeks we had a house to live in. The mud in between the chimney stones was still wet but we lit a fire anyway. Mama and Survella took turns standing guard with the musket in case the Crows came around while our men were busy. When she wasn't watching for the Crows, Survella wrote in her diary.

I worked the garden. I wanted to see life growing so I staked the rows and marked the rocks. The ground was too hard and cold to plant, but that didn't stop me. I used a heavy pick to break up dirt and strained my back so bad I could hardly stand. I tore my nails, broke a finger, went to sleep filthy, and I didn't care.

By spring we had a house, a garden, and a frame for the barn. It didn't feel like home for a long time. Mama cried by the grave markers in the cemetery we staked out. Beula almost stopped eating and looked like a walking stick. Papa hardly talked and Teague stayed busy building the barn. Gilmore made enough rabbit sticks to kill every rabbit in Indian Territory and split enough wood to last for ten years.

James, Adele, and Royal weren't here to make our lives complete. They always lived in my memory, but that hasn't been good enough. I'm here and they aren't. It isn't fair.

Clyde Lee

SURVELLA

On the road to Talihina. 1838.

You ready, sister?" I asked.

"I guess so," Billie said with a sigh. "We don't have much choice."

When I was twenty and Billie fourteen, our parents sent us to the Mather Mission Boarding School in Talihina. Neither one of us was excited about going since our other school experience was with missionaries and they didn't know a thing about Indians, much less about our tribe. Beula would've liked it, but she ran off with her music teacher the year before. At least we didn't have to stay around the house with Mama, who was still depressed about our move.

"Survella. Billie. Time to go," said Papa.

Since we left late in the day and the traveling was slow because rocks stuck out of the road everywhere, we spent the night by the road. Mama filled our dinner and breakfast basket to overflowing with more food than we could eat in a week. "I love you girls and I'll write every day," she said.

That night we camped by a stream and ate chicken legs and boiled potatoes. Billie wasn't scared of anything except snakes and she insisted on laying a rope around her to keep snakes away. We told her that if snakes can climb trees they could surely crawl over a rope on the ground. She wouldn't listen and kept arranging her rope into an almost perfect circle around her.

We slept as long as Papa let us, until the sun shone across the water. "Twenty miles to go, girls. Hurry up." Looking dazed, Billie sat up for a few minutes. She always acted dizzy in the mornings until she drank coffee. We ate biscuits and crushed raspberries that had spilled out of their jar onto Mama's white napkins. "Oh, me," said Papa as he rolled his blanket. "I hope there's a store along the way."

We arrived at the school shortly before lunch. The yard had five buildings and a barn that stood next to the classrooms. We smelled those animals all day, but I didn't mind it except for the pig stink. Anyways, Billie and I looked around for an older Choctaw that might be a teacher.

"The only dark skin I see's on that cook standing in the kitchen doorway," Billie said. It was Jotty, the Negro cook.

"Looks like all the teachers are white and the students are Indians. Again." I was disappointed. "Won't be doing much learning about Indians here."

"Listen to me, both of you," said Papa. "You're to learn to read and write and you better not give your teachers any lip."

Billie and I looked at each other and giggled.

"It's not funny. I am serious. Here comes the principal, I think."

Sure enough. The principal's name was Mr. Burlingame. He was a tall, thin man with a nose that looked like it had been broke and fixed wrong. He wore the same black clothes every day and smelled of whiskey and horehound candy.

"What are your names?" he asked, looking at his notebook. He didn't say hello or offer his hand to Papa.

"The McKenneys," I said. "I'm Survella and that's Billie."

"Follow me to my office. I need more information." Then he turned around and walked into the building with fast little steps, like his shoelaces were tied together.

We followed him into his office. The only things in the room were a desk with nothing on it, his chair, and an awful wall picture of bloody Christ nailed to a cross. There were no chairs for visitors. "Have your girls been sick lately?" he asked Papa.

"No, they don't usually get sick."

"Have they been scratching themselves?"

"Well, no." Papa looked at us. Billie shook her head. "No. No scratching."

"Are they baptized?"

It angered Papa that Mama refused to baptize us Catholic. In this case, however, he figured it would go better for us with Burlingame if we were baptized in something. "Yes. Baptized Presbyterian when they were three."

Burlingame's wife walked in. Billie elbowed me and smiled. She looked us up and down and walked to her husband's side. Mrs. Burlingame was as wrinkly and unfriendly as him. She always wore a black dress and a white bonnet so we never saw her hair. She reminded me of pictures I'd seen of skinny Puritans with pencil necks.

"These are the McKenney girls," Mr. Burlingame said to his wife. She hardly looked at us. "You can take your things to your room," she said. "Upstairs, second on the left, east side." Then they bowed their heads and read the notebook together, which meant we were to leave.

After we took our trunks to our room we went with Papa to the wagon. "Now be good and do what you're supposed to," he said.

"Always, Papa," said Billie with that smart grin she wore when lying.

With a look that meant he didn't believe her, Papa kissed us and started home. I think he wondered if he should've left us there. We went back inside for supper and a look-see at our classmates.

We entered a large dining room furnished with long checker-cloth-covered tables. "Got themselves organized, don't you think?" asked Billie after she surveyed the crowd of faces. "The poor fulls are over by the window. Next to them are half-bloods who look Indian, and the older half-blood girls who look more white than Indian are by the door sizing us up."

Billie was almost right. The white half-bloods were looking at me. I was light in color and the whole year those girls tried to get me to join their group, but I wasn't interested. Billie was darker so they never talked to her much.

"Where you want to sit?" I asked.

"With the little ones."

After dinner we went to our room to unpack. When we almost finished, two cousins from Doaksville walked in. They appeared to be fourteen, half-bloods, and more Choctaw than us. The older one, Clyde Lee, wasn't pretty but had a distinctive look. Her eyes tilted down at the ends and her nose was round with big nostrils. One top tooth was missing and she had a peculiar way of sucking her bottom lip under her top one.

I shouldn't talk about appearances, though. Papa and Billie always say I look serious and mean even though I don't feel that way. I do have straight teeth, however, and none of them hurt.

"What's your name?" was the first thing I heard Clyde Lee say.

"Who?" asked Billie.

"Who what?"

"Who are you talking to?"

"You is who."

We all laughed. "I'm Billie and this here's my sister Survella."

"Survella? Never heard that. Maybe I'll call you Sur. Or Vella. Billie sounds like a boy's name. That's not short for anything, is it?"

"Billie Lou," my sister shrugged.

"Two boy names. Was your daddy wanting a boy and got you instead, like me?"

We had never thought of that. "Nothing he could do about it," Billie said.

Clyde was tougher than a bald owl. She said what she thought and wasn't shy about a thing. She said she lost her tooth in a fight and at first I didn't believe her, but after I got to know her I surely did.

"This is my cousin Lucy. She's stupid," Clyde said about the girl still standing in the doorway with her mouth open so wide she could've been catching flies. Lucy had enormous cheekbones that just about took up her face. She had a dullard personality and followed Clyde Lee around like a shadow. I thought she was interesting in that she couldn't think for herself. Clyde treated her like the village idiot and Lucy didn't seem to mind.

"Time for bed." Mrs. Burlingame opened our door without knocking. "If I hear any noise whatsoever you will receive demerits."

"Demerits? What's that?" asked Clyde as she folded her clothes.

"Demerits are punishment for disobeying orders."

"And so what'll happen? Do we get spanked?" Clyde acted like she couldn't care less.

"Yes."

"By whom, may I ask?" She said it better than Billie could have.

"By my husband." Her voice got louder.

"I bet he likes it."

Mrs. Burlingame tried to ignore that but couldn't. "*And* you will stay in a room by yourself for a week. Now go to bed." Then she slammed the door.

"She looks like a turkey," said Clyde.

"No. A goose," said Billie.

We got into our beds and talked late into the night. Clyde told us about her family, her farm, and what she wanted to do with herself when she grew older. She never said so, but I suspected that her family had money. Turns out they had one of the largest horse and cattle ranches in the Choctaw Nation. Her daddy made her speak Choctaw at home and they went to political and religious meetings. Clyde was Indian and looked it, but she also knew a lot about whites and wasn't confused about her place in the world. I knew I had made a friend.

That next morning we dressed quickly and I went to the outhouse that was behind the kitchen. I never understood why they put it there since we smelled it during mealtimes and flies buzzed everywhere. Anyways, when I got back to the room Mrs. Burlingame came and told us to follow her to the dining hall.

Breakfast was typical of what we always had: milk, biscuits or bread, scrambled eggs, and hot mushy cereal that I hated. Sometimes it was pancakes with maple syrup and butter. I always wanted more of that even though it gave me a bellyache. We weren't allowed to drink coffee, but once a week we had fruit juice and everyone drank as many glasses as we could get. The only time I had pineapple juice was at that school. Mrs. Burlingame made us take a spoonful of cod liver oil when we walked in the dining hall at lunch but I always spit it out under a table.

After breakfast we took a short writing test. Billie, Clyde Lee, and I were assigned to eighth grade. Lucy was put into the first grade even though she was fourteen. Seven children in our class were fulls and they weren't happy about being there. The fulls in our district weren't too interested in white schools, and most of the children were half-bloods who looked like us. Their parents thought that because whites were everyplace in the Choctaw Nation, there wasn't any choice but to learn what they were about.

Our first class began at eight o'clock with a prayer I don't remember. We sat on wooden seats attached to a flat desk with room inside for our tablets and slate pencils. My seat had a piece of wood sticking up and it kept poking me, so when nobody was looking I switched my desk with someone else's. In the first few weeks that desk made its way around the room until it ended up in the back row with nobody in it.

We studied the basics like arithmetic and grammar, along with science, French, and Shakespeare. My favorite class was mathematics. We also read the Choctaw Constitution and the tribal laws. The only reason we did was because Burlingame wanted to compare our tribal laws to the United States laws and to make sure we knew ours were inferior. Billie drew a lot of pictures, mainly of the full-bloods because she thought they had the best faces.

Outsiders came to visit the mission and praised the teachers for all the "miracle work" they did, teaching us heathens to read and write. I didn't understand why they were so proud of themselves. School wasn't that difficult. The fulls just didn't like being away from home. Some didn't stay long. They were poor and came to school with raggedy clothes and head lice. They looked miserable and wanted to leave as soon as they got there. Around planting time they went home, came back, then left again to harvest. They came and went so often I wonder how they could learn anything. Not everyone was nice to them, either. Day school teachers had always been nice to Beula, though. That was because she tried so hard to be like them.

When it came time for the Burlingames to say our prayers for us, those fulls would hang their heads and stare at their hands. I did the same thing and still do. I can pray for myself.

We hungered for knowledge about our tribe. Mama and Adele had told us all the stories and Choctaw words they knew and it was up to us to piece together what everything meant. The Burlingames wouldn't allow talk of our religion, so at night and during recess we talked to each other in Choctaw. Billie and I didn't know the words as good as Clyde and Lucy, but after a few months of concentrating hard I could talk to the fulls.

Clyde's uncle was on the tribal council, and once a month he sent a letter of goings-on in the Nation. The traditional girls passed the letters around until the papers tattered. After class we played outside. We had to stay clean so we couldn't do much except throw the balls back and forth and play jacks. The fulls stayed together during the break, usually under the pecans in the north yard where the mules were penned. I sat with them several times a week to hear stories their families told them, but Billie thought that through their eyes we were too much like the whites so she didn't come with me much. If the Burlingames came to see what we were doing we changed the conversation to a discussion of Shakespeare.

Burlingame was a mean, dark man. Strange, too. Sometimes when he preached, bugs floated around his face and he'd not take notice when gnats flew in his mouth and up his crooked nose. Every day we saw him walk around the yard and look up at the sky and talk.

"Who's he talking to?" asked Billie.

"No one around. Must be talking to God," Clyde reasoned.

"Why would God talk to him?" I wondered.

"I didn't say God was talking to Burlingame," said Clyde. "I said Burlingame was talking to God. The Almighty's got better things to do than talk to that fool."

After a few days everyone knew who Clyde Lee was. She was the most talkative of any other girl and wasn't afraid to sass teachers.

The second evening she asked me to explore the mission.

"When, after dinner?"

"No, after dark so they can't see us."

After Mrs. Burlingame patrolled the halls and told us to go to sleep we snuck out. We went to the kitchen first and stole sweet rolls. The next morning at breakfast, Jotty's wife, Regine, came by our table and asked if we liked them. I still have no idea how she knew we stole some, but she always did. She was worse than my mother when it came to reading my thoughts and having that third eye in the back of her head. She cooked better than Mama, however, and she had a way of telling us we were wrong without scolding. Regine's parents were slaves in the Cherokee Nation and she didn't think much of Indians or whites. Still, she had a good nature and was kind to us girls.

Then we came to the Burlingames' room. Clyde stopped at the door. "I bet they're lying in bed three feet apart with covers up to their chins," she said. Then she turned around, hiked up her skirt, pulled down her britches, and bent over. Right at that second Mr. Burlingame opened the door.

He stood there in his red long johns and black socks and his eyes got big as plates. There was Clyde, still bent over. Lucy and I ran and he didn't see me since I turned the corner first, but he saw Lucy. Clyde finally ran and we hurried to the yard and climbed the trellis to our room.

We never got in trouble for that. The only people who knew about our adventure was us girls, Regine, and the Burlingames. Afterwards Mr. Burlingame made a point not to speak to Clyde directly, but I saw him stare at her from a distance. Clyde never looked at him.

"What's going on with him? How come he keeps looking at you?" I asked Clyde one day after I caught Burlingame watching her.

"Nothing's wrong."

"Clyde. Tell me."

"Don't you tell a soul, Survella." I knew she was serious since she never called me by my full name. "That next day Burlingame called me to his office. He didn't say anything, he just walked behind me and put his hands on my shoulders and before they moved any further down my front I slapped him, and told him to keep his monkey hands off me." She looked down at her feet and I didn't ask her anything else.

Over the next months other girls told us of Burlingame calling them to his office for no important reason, then he'd stand close and touch them. One evening a girl named Cinder cried after she met with him. Her family didn't live far and she walked home that night.

Her papa came to the school the next morning and went right to Burlingame's office. We heard a WHACK and a thump, like someone fell on the floor. Mr. Burlingame tried to hide it, but he had a bruise on his face for the next two weeks.

Cinder told her daddy about her situation and he took care of it, but Clyde didn't tell her folks. She just got mad, like a rode horse who got put away wet. And, oh lordy, she got back at him. Clyde made his life miserable. She pulled the heads off his chickens and burned down the chapel and the corn crop.

One year, probably 1839 because I remember talking about President Van Buren in class, all of us got sick, even the teachers. We were too weak to run to the outhouse so we'd crap in glass jars that would sit sometimes for two days before they got thrown out.

A white doctor from Tuskahoma gave us quinine and hot whiskey that made me feel worse. He bled some of the children and two died. I never understood why he'd make a sick person bleed. Papa came to take us home as soon as he heard of the sickness. Mama made us eat oats and rice and as much water as we could hold. In a week I felt well enough to walk around the yard and feed the chickens.

After we got over our sickness, poor Teague caught smallpox at his school. A hundred boys and teachers got sick and twenty died. Mama and Papa were scared and made him come home. Papa and Gilmore stayed in the barn so they wouldn't catch it, and for two weeks Mama set their food and clean clothes on the porch so they didn't have to come in the house. Teague kept a few scars on his back and on his face where he scratched the pox.

We went back to school at the start of the next term and some of the children didn't come back. Poor Lucy died from her sickness, which made Clyde even angrier at the Burlingames. She locked their door from the outside so they couldn't get to the outhouse. Then she'd look down from our window at them and laugh when they tried to climb out of theirs and fell five feet to the ground. We had an outbreak of scabies the next year that made our heads itch all day and night. The doctor put turpentine on our heads and burned the sheets and clothes. Clyde thought and thought about how she could put that itch in the Burlingames' underwear, but she never came up with any good ideas.

The Burlingames' daughter Carla was the youngest girl in my class and she was a snotty little thing. Her attitude was that her daddy was privy to the word of God and us dumb Indians were supposed to learn it from him. She led the prayers at the start of each class, and if she saw us looking at our hands instead of keeping our eyes shut she'd start over and make the prayer last twice as long.

Clyde detested Carla and one day put mustard on her chair seat. Another time she blew her nose in Carla's Bible and the pages stuck together.

Clyde wasn't the only one who could put a body in their place. So could Billie. One day in cooking class Carla went on about how light skin looked prettier than dark skin. Considering that everyone in the room had one shade or the other of brown skin, Carla insulted the whole class.

"Brown skin looks so dirty, don't you think?" Carla said to one of the dark full-blood girls who was trying to roll out biscuits. That little girl was shy and didn't know what to say.

"You know, Carla," said Billie, who was standing behind her with her bowl of cake mix, "that the Devil himself is red." We had been outside most of the day before in the garden and Carla's arms were burned pink. Billie touched Carla's sore forearm and asked, "Are you sure you aren't related to him?"

Carla's eyes got big and her cheeks puffed, then she went to her daddy's room to tattle. A few minutes later Mr. Burlingame stood at the door and told Billie to come to his office. Billie took off her apron and walked down the hall with her chin high. Clyde and I ran behind and put our ears to the door in case we needed to run in and save my sister.

We didn't have to. Billie came out less than two minutes later with a grin on her face. She made a fisticuffs motion to me as she passed by. Papa taught us girls how to fight and it seems she was ready to demonstrate her left to Mr. Burlingame. He never spoke to her again. Or to me.

Shortly afterwards, Billie fell off a pile of logs and knocked her shoulder out of joint. The Burlingames didn't know what to do, but Clyde put Billie on a table facedown with her arm over the side. Billie held a bucket while we filled it with rocks and when it was heavy enough the weight popped her shoulder back in.

"Learn something new every day, huh?" Clyde asked the Burlingames, who stood there watching.

Around that time Clyde planned another nighttime adventure. "Got a project I need to finish. Want to help?" she asked during Regine's dessert of sweet potato pie.

"Sure, what now?"

"You'll see. Wear old clothes." I knew it'd be good.

Around ten we left our room and climbed out through the parlor window. We went to the outhouse where she picked up a burlap sack hidden in the bushes. It smelled nasty.

"What the heck's in this, Clyde?"

"Be patient." Then she pulled out an empty box and a big jar of what I thought was water. Then we went to Burlingame's room where she emptied the bag into the box. Clyde had collected all kinds of manure, from the chicken coop, the horse corral, and the barn where the cows stayed. Droppings from the pigs smelled the worst. Then she opened the jar—oh my. It was full of her water.

"Clyde! You peed in here!"

"Is that what it is? I forgot."

She propped the box and jar up against the Burlingames' door. Then she knocked, grabbed my arm, and whispered "Run!"

Burlingame opened the door and all that crap fell into his room. I reminded Clyde that it was her doing we got to smell it for the rest of the time we stayed at the school. The Burlingames, however, never accused Clyde because they couldn't catch her doing anything.

That next year the Burlingames left and I'm sure it was because of us. We never gave them a moment's peace. Their replacements weren't much better, but at least they were dumber.

Mr. and Mrs. Hampton were of considerable size. They looked like each other in the way a lot of husbands and wives do after living together a long time. Both had blond hair and plump rosy cheeks. Mr. Hampton was a fat man with a chest like a woman's and a voice that stayed the same volume in conversation as it did when he was preaching. His hair was cut so short it stood straight up. He wheezed through his nose when he breathed. "Girls and boys," he'd say, "it's time for prayer." Then he'd squeeze his eyes shut tight and pray while we watched his chin wiggle.

Mrs. Hampton was built the same way, with big bosoms and a belly that seemed bigger because of the apron she wore tied up above it. She wore her hair in a tight bun wrapped with a white bow. She had a funny walk, her toes pointed out like a duck, her chest stuck out and shoulders back. When she walked past I just knew her big legs were rashed.

Those Hamptons were impatient with the fulls and treated them like they couldn't be smart if they tried. None of us were allowed to speak Indian and they kept an eye on us. Some of the girls who carried medicine things had them taken away. The Hamptons weren't as mean as some missionaries, but they made it clear that the Indian way was the worst way.

One time an Indian girl named Amy—they called her that because they refused to learn how to say Ameahtubbee—wouldn't speak English to Mr. Hampton during recess. Those Hamptons got in an uproar and got up close to her like they were trying to scare her into acting right. Mr. Hampton slapped her across the face hard enough to knock her down. She left an hour later and we didn't see her again.

It rained hard all that day and when Amy tried to cross the creek she fell in and drowned. The water washed her five miles downstream where a church congregation found her during a baptism. The Hamptons never mentioned it. Luckily, they never looked at me close enough to find the medicine bundle Ellis gave me. I'd have run away like Amy did.

Even with the bad happenings, Clyde, Billie, and I had gotten used to school. We didn't mind it because we never knew when we'd see something interesting. Like the time the Hamptons took us to a revival a few miles away. There wasn't enough room on the wagons for every child so just twelve of us got to go, including me, Clyde, and Billie.

After eight miles we came to the edge of a valley and heard singing. From a distance the crowd looked like folks picnicking, but they were doing something stranger than that.

About a hundred white folks and Indians stood together in a crowd swaying back and forth with their eyes closed, nodding their heads up and down so hard I thought their necks would break. It was like a crowd all excited at an *ishtaboli* game, but these folks had their minds set on something else, that was for sure.

When they stopped singing, an old man dressed in black clothes and a black hat started preaching. He said his sermon so fast it was hard to follow. "Welcome, brothers and sisters. Welcome," he yelled at us when we got within earshot. His flock turned to look our way. They watched the preacher like he was doing a strip.

"Hurry and git down," said Mr. Hampton. We scurried off the wagon and stood together. All of us were scared except Clyde Lee. She had her eye on the tables of food and started inching over that way.

That old preacher yelled about God, Satan, and hell, and at the end of every word he hung on to the last letter a second. He'd say "Brotherssss," "sinnnn," and on like that. It was interesting to hear but got tiresome in a hurry. The crowd in front seemed to know when to start singing and once they got going, everyone did. I never heard "Amazing Grace" sung so loud.

When they finished singing, a man younger than Papa got up to talk. He was the strangest-looking person I ever saw. His skin and hair were white as milk and he had no color to his eyes or eyebrows. He dressed in black like the old preacher, which made him look even more whitewashed. That boy's hair was cut short all around and left long on top so the front part covered his eyes. Every time he nodded his head back and forth, that hair shot up away from his head. He got the crowd waving their arms and saying "Amen" after every sentence. Then a lady fell and started rolling around and nobody made a move to help her.

After she dropped, others started falling and flopping around like caught fish. A few people shook their bodies real hard and one man ran to the oak grove and howled and barked like a dog. The Hamptons held hands with two other folks, husband and wife probably, and kept walking in a little circle with their eyes closed. I thought they'd fall down but they stayed upright.

The other students took it in as hard as me. They stood as close together as they could get. Two boys cried, and one girl, Donelda, studied the wagon like she was trying to figure out how to escape. We heard horses running and turned to see some Indians who had come at the preacher's invitation heading out of the valley like ghosts were after them. Clyde Lee acted like nothing bothered her. She just chewed bread and pickles and watched the crazy people.

After an hour the crowd quieted down and the lying-down people sat up to take water from helpers who brought water buckets and cool rags. After recovering, they made their way to the picnic table like nothing had happened. By then, Clyde was full and came to sit with Billie and me.

One old lady brought us a plate of cookies. Up close she looked normal, but a few minutes before she'd been rolling on the ground and still had buffalo grass and yellow dandelion petals in her hair. I was afraid to eat a cookie, figuring that there was something in their food to make them act strange.

Mr. Hampton came over, all hot and sweaty, and told us to line up. One by one them people shook our hands. Most didn't say anything, they just smiled like they were half asleep. A few said "I'll pray for you," and one said, "There's hope for heathens, you young 'uns. It's in God Almighty's hands." Clyde and I looked at each other and wiped our hands on our skirts. I wanted to wash up after touching those people.

We got in the wagons and none of us wanted to talk to the Hamptons about what we had seen. Those two were all smiles and for the next few days they preached louder than normal.

"White people can sure act crazy," my sister said that night. "Choctaws would never do that."

"How do you know they don't?" asked Clyde.

"I just do. Indians aren't like that. Did you see those Choctaws ride out of there?"

"Lots of other Choctaws are Christians," Clyde said.

"And? So?" Billie turned in her bed to face Clyde in the dark. "Not all Christians roll on the ground."

"Some in my family do. Now shut up, Billie Lou, and forget it."

From then on we avoided talks about crazy white people and Indians.

Two years later Clyde, Billie, and I left the mission. It never occurred to us that we wouldn't be together. We taught in the same school for thirty years. I taught math, Clyde taught literature, and Billie was the science teacher. All of us married and had children. Billie and I lived three miles east of the school and Clyde moved three miles west. We met "in the middle" at work and on the weekends we took turns visiting each other and watching our children grow.

Clyde Lee, Billie, and I made the best of a bad situation. We were Indians and there was nothing the Burlingames or Hamptons could do about it. We read all the books and newspapers in the library and even though we hated missionaries we paid close attention to their lessons. We didn't learn about our culture from the teachers, so we taught each other at night when the missionaries thought we were asleep.

We got an education, good jobs, then *we* did the teaching.

Our Lost Sister

BILLIE

1846.

Teague, Survella, and I went to our first mission boarding school in 1836 when I was twelve. What I remember most about school, besides the teachers who didn't know a thing about Indians, was getting headaches from eating too much snow ice cream and that my sister Beula started to disappear for wanting to become white. She was so frustrated that she only ate enough to stay alive and nobody could get her to eat more. She was born unhappy and was never proud of who she was. I enjoyed attending the Mather school later in large part because Beula wasn't there.

Beula hated school because she didn't want to be around Choctaws and she read numbers and letters backwards and got assigned to the class with young full-bloods. There she was, having to spend her days with the people she tried to escape. It almost made her crazy.

Toward the end of the first semester a new piano teacher arrived. Clancy Bernard was twenty with curly brown hair and he wore a big silver ring on his right hand. He dressed in black suits with white shirts underneath and cuff links on the wrists.

Beula liked him right off. She sashayed past him whenever she got the chance and he noticed. One night they took a wagon and one of the mules and ran off together. Clancy even left his piano behind.

Papa talked about tracking down and killing Clancy, but he didn't know where to look. So he stayed mad the rest of his life, which was just a few more years. Mama mentioned Beula at least once a day until she died. I got tired of hearing about her and it had been a relief to go back to school in 1838.

Nine years after Beula disappeared we received a letter from Clancy addressed to our dead mama saying that Beula was fine, married, and had three children. Clancy didn't tell us where they lived but the postmark said Independence. I was twenty-one and Teague was nineteen. We had saved some money and thought it might be fun to travel.

Missouri was different from what I thought it'd be. Pigs and mangy dogs ran through the streets between three-foot-deep mud holes. The slaughterhouses smelled worse than a fish market on a hot day and flies buzzed in our faces and ears.

We found out where Beula lived through the post office. We rented a wagon and horse and drove three miles to her plantation. It was pleasant outside the city. Instead of breathing the stink of dead animals, we smelled fruit tree blossoms and wet grass. Farmhouses dotted the landscape like islands in the ocean.

At the three-mile mark we arrived at the Bernards'. They grew acres of corn and cotton, and hundreds of cattle grazed in the 1,000-acre pasture that was partially closed-in by a white fence. Tall, old trees shaded the two-story house. Beula was living big.

We knocked and my sister opened the door. There she stood, dressed in creamy colors with her hair piled up. Her face was plump and her corset barely managed to hold her middle into a hefty hourglass shape. My once-scrawny sister had found her appetite.

She looked at us like we were Satan and his helper. I thought she'd want to hug us. Instead, she spat a hurtful "What are you two doing here?"

Teague, of course, barbed her back. "What do you think you're doing, sister?" he asked.

Clancy came to see who was at the door and didn't recognize me. "Who's this, dear?"

"Brother Teague and sister Billie." She glared and didn't ask us in. Clancy did.

That house looked like a museum. Vases and paintings lined the long hallway. Bushes trimmed to look like animals glistened with morning dew outside the stained glass windows.

Beula and Clancy had three boys who favored their mother. The oldest boy, Quincey, about eight, who was dressed in a black suit with white ruffly shirt like his daddy's, took one look at Teague with his long hair and yelled, "Indians! Indians, Daddy!"

The child was only excited, though, and after Clancy invited us to stay for dinner, the youngster pulled me by my arm to the dining hall. Beula was riled at Clancy for letting us in. She looked like she'd hold her breath and turn purple like she did when having fits as a child.

Clancy opened a bottle of wine, the first time I tasted another liquor besides whiskey. The dry, purple wine gave me a headache, but the more I drank the more I handled the situation. Teague never drank because it slowed his running.

We watched Beula act like the people who took our land in Mississippi. She ordered around her two darkies like they were dogs.

"How's life, Beula?" I finally asked.

"Fine," Beula says, sawing her Cornish hen with a knife and fork even though it was tender enough for just the fork. I kept looking at her fancy hair and dress and wondered how long it took her to fix herself. She had help with that hairdo, I tell you. All I did was bend over and twist my hair in a knot.

We weren't going to get any conversation out of Beula while her husband and children were around so I drank wine and questioned Clancy about Missouri. Quincey kept asking us about Indians. "Sing us a song," he said. "Where're your feathers?"

Finally Teague said, "Ask your mother. She's an Indian."

The little one, Harrison, yelled, "My mother's not an Indian!"

It was amazing to me that Beula hadn't told them about her family and ancestors.

Beula dropped her fork, stood up, and says all uppity like, "Dinner is over and our guests are leaving." She stomped to the front door and held it open. She was breathing so hard I thought her bosoms might rip through her dress.

Clancy walked out with us. "Say, now. Look," he said. "Beula was sad in Indian Territory. I just want to make her happy." He kept smiling. "My family accepts her and no one talks about Indians." He dabbed at the corners of his pretty mouth with his fancy napkin.

"Not sure what to say about us? Or you think Indians aren't worth talking about?" Teague asked.

The corners of Clancy's mouth dropped. "For our children's sake, don't come back."

I thought Teague'd hit him. Instead, he got in the wagon and I followed him. Clancy wasn't worth dealing with, and at that moment I realized Beula wasn't, either. My brother-in-law, who was a stranger to me, started back to the house.

We rode through the gate when Beula yelled at us. She passed her husband on her march to the wagon, arms swinging hard. Clancy watched her. "Why did you come?" She wasn't asking. "I've been happy without you," she almost hissed like a snake.

"Beula," said Teague, "you may try to forget who you are, but we know. You left your family and haven't asked about them. Why Clancy brought you here is a question I have to ponder a while."

"He loves me and can forget about me being an Indian." She shaded her eyes with her hand, the one with the diamond ring the size of a green sweet pea on her third finger.

"That's his problem."

I didn't feel like saying anything so I clicked to the horses and we trotted back to town.

Once we got home, I kept hoping Clancy'd tell the children about us, or that they'd be curious enough to write us letters. Survella said she'd surely love for them to come visit, but the years rolled by and we never saw Beula or her children again.

My family knew that Beula wasn't content around us. She couldn't be a Choctaw. We hoped she'd find happiness, but I never thought she'd leave her family to get it. Mama died thinking her daughter saw her as trash.

What a family I had. Beula pretended she was all white, Survella pretended she was all Indian, and Teague and I weren't sure. Papa tried to make us white, Adele taught us to be Indian, and Mama thought we should think about being both. After all, we were.

Teague and I agreed that sometimes we felt like wads of rainbow taffy stretched every which way, and from then on, whenever I acted confused, he called me "Candy."

Corsets and Husbands

BILLIE

The start of every spring is marked by something special. Trees bud out, baby birds sing, and the cold gives way to the more comfortable warmth. By the end of April one year, my big hen that I named Trixie had been sitting on thirteen eggs for three weeks. They weren't all hers; we had twenty hens and one rooster who fathered all the babies in the eggs and she was the only hen who wanted to set. Baby chicks break through their shells after twenty-one days and I was getting worried about Trixie.

I hadn't seen her eat or drink in weeks, although I knew she had to be getting water when I wasn't looking. Otherwise she'd be dead. But she sat still as a rock day after day in that warm henhouse. One morning when I went to check on her, there was movement under her breast. She pecked me when I moved her and I saw six babies. That evening there were six more. I figured that the last egg was bad and was about to throw it away two days later when a small hole opened. I held it close and felt a tiny movement. I put the egg in a box by the cup shelf in the sunshine and watched a chick trying to get itself born.

It couldn't do it alone and I peeled away some of the shell. At the end of the day the fuzzy baby was out, but it lay still, panting and weak. I didn't have the heart to kill it so I fed it sugar water and kept it in my warm shirt pocket. Days went by with no improvement and I almost gave up, but one morning I heard chirping loud enough to wake us.

"Billie Lou, I told you to put that animal outside," yelled Papa. I was eighteen, but since I still lived at home Papa talked to me like I was a child.

"It's just a sick baby, Papa."

"Well, kill it then, You have no time to spend on puny chickens."

Then he got dressed and went outside. I figured I could hide the baby a few more days if I needed to.

I looked in and my baby was standing up in his box and wanted food. I put it outside with the others and it wasn't long before there was no telling it apart from the others.

Adele always said if we treat animals with respect and kindness we all will be happy and healthy. I watched those thirteen babies run around the yard following their mama and knew she was right.

That same spring my sister Survella married Jincy Wilson, who lived three miles away on a good-sized farm. Papa didn't like him at first because he was a full-blood, but since Jincy could read and made good money with his cattle, he shined a little. Papa had stipulations to them marrying. Jincy had to support Survella, never lay a fist to her, educate the children, go to church, things like that.

Jincy kept his promise. They went to the Presbyterian mission, at least until Papa died. They also taught their four children to speak Indian and went to tribal functions. Their boys Skarloey and Pulsey—everyone called him Corn—went to boarding school.

Soon after Survella married, Mama lost weight and hurt all over, especially in her belly. She faded away just like the melting snowmen did in our yard during the warm winter days. All of us stood around Mama's bed during those last minutes trying to comfort her. A traveling white doctor had given her a drink of what he called "elixir," said she'd be better in the morning, and that we owed him half a dollar. Another white man from Krebs gave her everything from quinine to hot toddies, but nothing made her feel better. There weren't any *alikchis* nearby. Teague and Survella felt that Mama would've been cured if one treated her.

The last thing she said before closing her eyes for the last time was "Beula."

Teague dropped her hand. "That damn Beula," he said.

Papa grabbed my brother—who was by that time bigger than Papa—by his shirt and threw him against his holy fireplace hearth. "That's enough about your sister," he yelled. Without even looking at his dead wife, he pushed open the front door, took up the metal pail, and went to relieve our grumpy new milk cow, Athena. Us kids buried Mama.

After Mama died Papa went about his daily business, although he moved faster than usual. He stayed outside most of the time, tinkering on the barn, the roof, the garden fence.

After Mama's death Papa started to change his mind about Indians. Or at least he talked about Indians differently. We figured it was because Mama wasn't there to argue with him, or maybe he felt that he needed to support us better. At any rate, Burl decided to invite him to the Council House and after talking Papa into it, all of us traveled to Nanih Waiya, about seventeen miles from here. The Council House was a log cabin and the center of our government. We were impressed with the meeting room and the oak table big enough for sixteen people. After seeing those shelves of books and documents Papa decided we should stay a day longer.

That night the council met. We walked through the door and when Papa saw all those dark faces looking at him, he began fidgeting. Then one short councilman stood up and offered his hand to my father and asked him to sit. The rest of the council except for a few smiled. Their friendliness surprised Papa. He thought all Choctaws hated him, including his family. He was mostly right. The meeting started and Papa listened intently for three hours. Teague was thrilled to be there and didn't miss a word.

I could tell that Papa was deep in thought on our way home because he didn't say much except, "Education is a tool and a weapon," and "I forgot to ask about the next meeting."

I always hoped that he'd realize that we couldn't become white people because we were Indians. It was too late to find out for sure what he thought because less than a week later, as Papa was adjusting an eave on the barn, the ladder slipped. He reached for the gutter and missed. He fell twenty feet without a sound, as easily as a rag doll dropping off my bed to the floor. He landed on his head, breaking his neck.

Teague and I stood on the porch, watching him fall, and couldn't do anything about it. My brother had told Papa to wait, that after lunch he'd help. As usual, Papa was in a hurry to repair something that didn't need fixing.

My brother and I ran to him, but already knew he was dead from the way he hit the ground. We both cried, and couldn't believe Papa was lying in the dirt, crumpled and dead. How could a strong man die so easy?

Gilmore had been in the back room finishing a blowgun. He didn't hear what happened, of course, but he saw us standing over Papa through the kitchen window. He walked up behind us, looked down at his uncle, and then walked into the barn to get a shovel. We never said so to each other, but Teague, Survella, Gilmore, and I were relieved that Papa was gone.

After Papa died it was just Teague, Gilmore, and me at home for a year. Survella and I taught school along with our friend Clyde Lee, who lived three miles on the other side of school while Survella lived a shorter distance to the north. Those kids didn't like to sit still and we had a heck of a time teaching them. So many came and went depending on crop planting and picking that it was hard to keep everyone caught up to the same level.

Teague married a full-blood named Dicey Meashintubby and lived with her family, but came to visit almost every afternoon. Dicey and her brother were the only ones in her family to come west. The rest of her family hid with the Muscogees in Alabama during removal so they could stay.

My brother also became a Lighthorseman. Most trouble was caused by white men or half-bloods who had no loyalty to their tribe or families. Teague liked to boss white men, but not the fulls. Not even those drinking themselves to death.

"You gotta tell them what to do, brother," I said one night after a dinner of catfish and greens with vinegar. "Those ones drinking don't know anything and if you don't help them out, nobody will. Their families sure don't."

"Yeah, I know," he said, pushing strawberries around his plate. "But I feel like I'm nosing in."

"It's not nosing in, Teague," said Dicey. She was a small, dark girl with no education, but a lot of horse sense. "White men brought that liquor to us and it makes us weak and feel like we're stupid. Cain't get strong again unless they throw those bottles away and find something else to occupy their time."

Not all those white men were bad, of course, but they still made their livings from Indians. A few opened successful trading posts, like Thomas Edwards. He came from New Zealand in 1850 and built a store four miles north of here called Edwards' Store. Different kinds of people traded there and I liked going, especially before the war when the Butterfield Stage had Edwards' Store as one of its stops.

Teague agreed to talk to some of the bad drunks although I never heard him talk about any in his conversations. I suspected he kept his focus on the whites and left the Choctaws alone.

I got married for the first time shortly after my brother, in 1844. Teague brought some of his Lighthorsemen friends home for dinner one spring and I got to visiting with one, Peter Bohanan. His daddy was a half-blood and left Peter and his two sisters some money. He wasn't all that smart and I couldn't make up my mind if I wanted to be married to him. That'd mean I'd have to be around him a lot. He knew Ellis back in Mississippi and I thought that a good sign, so I agreed to marry him. We stayed here since his older sister lived at his place. I didn't want to leave my house anyways.

Around the time I married Peter, Gilmore married a schoolteacher. Alexandra—we called her Alli—was white and she upset her parents so bad by marrying an Indian, and a deaf one at that, that they never spoke to her again. Gilmore's problem didn't seem to bother her and they got along fine for forty years.

I never knew any other white woman who married an Indian man. Alli was a tall girl with flaming red hair and Gilmore stood about six feet. The contrast between his dark color and her pale skin, combined with their handsome faces, made everyone stare when they walked past.

A couple of Alli's students were deaf and their parents thought they were retarded or crazy, but Alli knew better. She had read a book about a lunatic asylum in New York and wanted to make sure the children weren't mistaken for insane and sent away, so Gilmore helped her teach the children to talk with their hands. Those kids hung on Gilmore like he was a big playtoy. He and Alli had two boys, Matthias and Ziah, and a daughter, Reby.

Cousin Gilmore still read his books and made blowguns. He was an expert blowgun and rabbit-stick maker and before he was twelve, Choctaws from all around southeastern Indian Territory bought his goods. Shortly after we moved from Mississippi, he made enough money to buy a horse named Chully, whose owner had no idea about the sort of horse he had; he merely thought the animal too small and ornery and sold him to my cousin for $10. Gilmore knew what he had bought because Papa raised Spanish mustangs.

A breeder from Oklahoma City passed by our farm one day and offered Gilmore $300 for Chully's stud services. Over the next decade Gilmore and Papa made almost $4,000 from their horses, and when Gilmore turned sixteen he could afford to attend an institution for the deaf in southern Illinois for a year. He didn't get his hearing back, but he learned how to talk without yelling. He also learned to use sign language. Afterwards he attended a mission school.

Gilmore was determined to practice law, even though he'd be one of the few Indian lawyers in Indian Territory. With the help of the Methodist church minister, whose brother was the president of the University of Missouri, Gilmore entered law school. Nobody made it easy on him, but he passed all the tests and earned his law degree. He came back home for a year until he decided to open a business in Red Oak, and later, Wilburton. Alli kept their children with her at school in the mornings then packed up and took them to help Gilmore in the afternoons.

I stayed busy too, teaching and drawing. My husband and I got along fine as long as I didn't start any deep conversations.

Peter was a tall, quiet man who was twenty years older than me. He was a handsome, feminine man, and not smart. I was forever explaining things to him. Peter made a good model, though; he sat still and had contrasting features that were easy to draw: long curly black eyelashes, full lips, and nice face bones. I did have to work some to make him look thoughtful, although I never told anyone that. He feared thunder and lightning and we didn't get much work done March through August since he thought it might rain.

One day we went for a ride and my horse John Ross tripped on a downed branch. He fell, then got up and dragged me a quarter mile with my foot caught in the stirrup. Peter didn't know we fell until he missed us and turned around.

Peter unhooked me and I lay on the road. My lower back felt as if I was stung by red ants and squeezed at the same time. I bled from a cut on my leg where John Ross pulled me over a branch and a lump grew on my head. I looked over to my horse and was angry to see him standing under a large pecan tree across the road, ignoring me and asleep in the manner of horses, head down and back foot cocked. I always believed that his mane kept him from seeing so I braided his hair with ribbon that hung down to the tip of his nose. Peter kept telling me that horses lived for thousands of years with hair in their eyes and would I please leave him alone. Peter got me on his horse and started home.

A white man happened on the road and Peter stopped him when he recognized the black doctor's bag on his saddle. That doctor scolded Peter for hauling me like a sack of feed. We didn't have whiskey to ease the pain of him sewing my leg up, so I bit on a stick until I fainted.

That first week I hurt and vomited all day and night. Peter thought I'd die and I wanted to. I'd never wanted my Aunt Adele as much as I did then. And I never hated Beula more.

I was still mad Adele died and that Beula left. I was angry that she complained about everything even though she was healthy, while my brother James always smiled and never wanted to trouble us. He'd say, "That's okay, Mama, I can do it," even though he could barely breathe, while Beula'd whine. "It's not fair," she'd pout. "God made me an Indian." Then she'd stomp her foot.

Beula is one of those unpleasant memories I put in a room in my head. I keep the door shut so as not to think about her. Being Indian taught me that. We have lots of rooms, lots of closed doors.

Peter quit the Lighthorsemen to stay home with me and his mother moved in to help. Hortence wasn't satisfied with white doctors and got an *alikchi* to look at me. That doctor was tattered and thin like Ellis and had a tattoo on his arm. He sang a song then burned a plant. He felt of my belly and back, all the while talking so fast I didn't understand. Then he gave Hortence a jar filled with leaves and brown water that stank and told her to wipe some on me twice a day.

When he got to the door, he turned and raised his hand in farewell. He looked just like Ellis. I almost sat straight up. "Ellis," I yelled, but he shook his head. I cried myself to sleep.

The next morning the pain was not as bad. I felt tingling in my legs after a couple of weeks, which gave me hope. A Lighthorseman fell off his horse a year later and broke his back. He never got feeling in his legs again.

I got to depending on a stiff pink corset that Hortence found in town and I've worn one ever since. A month after I fell I could walk to the creek. I was lucky with my back, but not with my husbands.

One morning a group of Lighthorsemen stopped on their way to a raid on a loggery across the Red River in Texas where Choctaws in the southern part of the Nation bought whiskey. Peter hated what liquor did to our people, so he decided to join them and got shot in the head even before he got to the border.

Dew Crow had been at Survella's the day before, but we had no way of knowing that. He walked through her front door one morning after Jincy had gone outside. He sat down at the table and mopped his face with that red kerchief he always wore around his neck. Then he started talking about him and Survella going off together. Survella said he never stopped staring at her with those owl eyes. She made her way to the door and ran out, yelling for Jincy. When they came back to the house from the barn, Crow was riding away.

Survella saw him again that evening out by her garden, standing in between the corn rows. "Dew Crow stood there for half an hour not moving," she said. "He was covered with dust that made him look golden in the sun. I was so mad!" And she hit the table hard with her hands. "Why can't he leave us alone?" Survella rarely showed her temper, but when she did, we stayed ready to duck in case she threw something. "I was so tired, had to piss, and that damn plug-ugly Crow made me and Jincy stay up all night with our rifles ready." Survella was angry and frustrated and I didn't blame her. Dew was the Crow who killed my husband.

The Lighthorsemen brought Peter home to me. He was tied down across his horse, blood from his head wound pouring all over that poor animal's legs and leaving a trail and smell behind them. Peter's buried out back.

My second husband was a white man, a merchant who sold feed in McAlester.

"You can't be serious, sister," said Survella, upon hearing of my plans to marry Monte Brown. "You're just marrying him because Peter died."

I looked at Teague, who sat on the other side of the table making a show of eating his potatoes and green beans. He didn't say anything, but his eyebrows went up whenever he agreed with Survella.

"Billie," she said loudly. "You feeling all right? He's old and mean. You got nothing in common."

"Yes we do. We can talk about. . . ."

"Nothing."

My sister was right about everything except me being upset about Peter. I wasn't all that out of sorts about him dying, I just thought I should be married. At the time I married Monte Brown, I knew I didn't love him. I tried to convince myself that he was a good man. He appeared to be of good nature because his thin upper lip didn't cover the length of his top teeth, which gave the appearance of smiling when he wasn't.

The nagging feeling that I had done something wrong became more clear at the wedding.

Monte wanted us to have a Christian wedding. I didn't mind mainly because I can usually ignore the Bible parts I disagree with. We hadn't talked about vows and when the preacher said, "Billie Lou, do you take this man to love, obey. . . ." I didn't let him finish.

"No, not obey, but I'll help out when he's sick," I said.

That preacher almost dropped his teeth. He looked at me, then looked at Monte, then back to me, like he wasn't sure what to do next. Survella was standing opposite me and started laughing. I looked over at Teague, who was looking down, shaking his head and trying not to snort. Monte had a surprised look on his face and after a pause said, "Uh, go ahead."

After we were done, our families lined up so we could walk down the aisle between them. I could tell that the Browns thought they were all superior to us Indians, but if you looked at the two groups, it was plain that we were a whole lot better put together than them. My family stood straight and strong, the women with pretty, decorated hair and flowers in their hands, and the men wore shiny boots and clean pants and jackets. Brown's family looked like they tried to look nice, but they were really fat, unhealthy people who couldn't be pretty just by taking a bath and wearing new clothes.

Monte Brown owned a big ugly house outside of town that I hated but I moved there anyways. The trees weren't tall enough for shade and there was no creek, just a dry bed that flooded. He was nice as a peach before we married, but darkies slaved for him and I didn't like Monte ordering them around. Monte said, "So what? They're ignorant."

His house sat in a hollow and one August night it rained and flooded the property. One of Monte's black men tied a rope from the porch to the barn so we could cross the yard. The water was up to my knees and I managed to save a few chickens. I struggled up the stairs with two hens under each arm and a large rooster on my shoulder. Three dogs and a pig followed me. The horses naturally ran up the hill behind the house, but two cows stood their ground and got washed away. Monte was lazy and never did any physical labor so he didn't save anything.

Monte bought some useless furniture from back east, like the little sofa he called a "love seat" that was too hard to sit on. I didn't care that it got ruined. I never drew his picture and divorced him and moved back here. The only things I brought with me were my clothes, a hundred dollars, and three dogs and a pig, who didn't like Monte either. I was glad to be home. In general, I hadn't really set my cap for Monte, he just happened to be there.

Sim Perry was my third husband. He also was a Lighthorseman and a half-blood who attended the Choctaw Academy in Kentucky. He believed in education and served as a school trustee for our district. He was a smart man who liked to read and learn, a real different sort from Peter and Monte.

Sim could be Indian and white, depending on his need, although everyone saw him as Indian. He was smart enough to know that sometimes he had to imitate whites even if his full-blood friends didn't like it. He kept his hair short and we went to the Baptist church every now and then. Sim had been an excellent stickball player when he was young, and then got thrown from a horse and broke his hip and scarred his face. His face and limp embarrassed him but he rode better than anyone.

"Does my limp look funny?" he asked me one day after walking back from the barn.

I sat on the porch nailing together a birdhouse. "What limp?" I asked back at him.

"That's not funny, B."

"I'm not laughing. No, it doesn't look funny. Nobody notices but you."

"They have to notice. Even my face looks funny."

"Even if it does, who cares. You think nobody else has problems? You just can't see them."

"Easy for you to say. You don't have any. Neither did that other husband of yours. I seen his picture in the box."

"Sim! Peter got shot in the head."

He ignored me and instead of coming up the porch steps he went to the garden. I watched him take the basket from the gate and walk to the blackberry vines that were heavy with fruit.

What he said about me not having problems pained me because not only did my back hurt all the time, my mind did too. Family that I cared about were dead or gone. Just when I thought I could tuck all that away in one of my brain rooms, someone had to drag it out again.

We had four children: Rufus, twins Dawson and Ollie, and Tish. Gilmore designed a pregnancy corset for me with slats on the side and extra material that expanded when I grew. Being pregnant while wearing a corset was not pleasant, but I would've done anything for my children.

Sim was away when I birthed Rufus. I was raking pecan tassels when I felt a warm gush of water down my leg. I barely got to bed when the pain started. Some tears were from fear since a young schoolteacher died the year before while having her baby. Rufus came out easily, though, and about that time cousin Gilmore came visiting.

Being deaf, Gilmore couldn't hear me cry, so he walked through the house to find us. When he saw me with little Rufus wrapped up in bloody sheets his mouth got as big around as a pie. "Billie, Billie, what?" he yelled. That was the only time Gilmore wasn't sure what to do. He read up on birthing and was here to help when my three other babies were born while Sim sat on the porch and bit his fingernails.

My boys grew to be tall and rangy, like Sim and my brother Teague. They were active and happy although Rufus had a terrible temper that worried us.

Ollie was shy and scared, while Tish, my youngest, hung upside down by her knees from the barn rafters at age three. Ollie wasn't fond of water or of getting dirty while Tish was rarely clean. Ollie and Tish both were pretty little girls, smart too, although Ollie was too quiet and often didn't speak up during times when she needed to defend herself. She couldn't read people well, either, a trait that later caused us all grief.

Iyup: The Son-in-Law

GILMORE

1862.

Ollie's husband was mean. She married Andrew before she finished school at New Hope Seminary mainly because he was polite and helped his family make money selling cattle. When his father died, Andrew stopped working, lost the business, and began drinking days and into the nights. I believed fifteen was too young an age for a girl to marry, especially to a man who was thirty, but Billie and Sim gave their permission.

I thought that Andrew treated Ollie bad because she was educated and he was not. My nephew Rufus said that Andrew was like other fulls who felt inferior because white people called them uncivilized. So he took his anger out on his wife, who happened to be part white. That sounds about right.

We did not know Andrew beat Ollie for a whole year. He stayed away from hitting her face except once before they came for supper at Billie's. An eye was swollen shut and her nose did not stop bleeding all evening. She could not stand without holding on to something.

After that dinner Billie decided that she and Sim needed to talk to Andrew about what was going on in his house, but Sim did not want to, saying that what goes on between married people was their business. Even though I cannot talk well, I said that I would do it if Sim would not, which of course made Sim change his mind. Two days later, Sim and Billie took Teague, Rufus, and me with them to cook catfish for Ollie. Sim promised he would talk to his son-in-law after we ate.

Andrew returned from gambling in time to eat and was pleasant enough until he wanted coffee. Ollie did not make it fast enough and when Sim went to use the outhouse, Andrew hit her straight in the face, splitting her left eyebrow.

I started to jump Andrew first, but Rufus was closer. Rufus happened to be standing behind Andrew when he hit Ollie, so Rufus dropped his plate and grabbed Andrew around the middle. He pulled on him so hard and fast they broke through the porch door and rolled across the dirt to the barn. They did not pause between punches to think about their next move like boxers do; they just swung and kicked at each other as furiously as two mountain lions might claw and bite over a kill. Both snarled and showed their teeth like animals. I was surprised at the strength and anger in Rufus, who was only seventeen.

Finally, when Andrew tried to butt Rufus with his head, my nephew stepped back slightly, taking the force out of Andrew's charge. Rufus kneed Andrew in the belly, then hit him twice in the face and once in the ribs. Rufus cut open Andrew's cheek, split his bottom lip, and appeared to have broken a few ribs. Andrew stood up slowly and wiped blood off his face and pushed his long hair back behind his ears. Then he staggered into the barn.

Sim walked over to Rufus and patted him on the back.

"That will take care of him for a while, son," Sim said as he picked up a long piece of straw and put it in his mouth.

We thought Andrew was ashamed and would stay in the barn, but instead he came out with a rifle and pointed it at Rufus.

"My God. Son!" I could see that Billie was screaming.

Teague caught my eye. He was running toward Andrew to stop him from shooting, yelling, "No!" but he was too far away.

Rufus was breathing hard and stopped tucking in his shirttail. He put his arms up, his hands across his face. Rufus knew he was about to be shot and turned his head the other way, but I could not look anywhere else.

Then Andrew pulled the trigger and missed. I do not know how since he was only ten feet from the target. He cursed something and aimed again.

Billie and I were standing by Teague's horse Osceola. We both saw the shotgun in the boot, but she quickly pulled the gun out and shot Andrew in the chest with both barrels. His blood and insides sprayed all over the barn right before he flew backwards five feet. Rufus ran over to Andrew to see if he was dead.

Teague was shocked and did not move. Rufus looked Andrew over and looked up at Billie. "You sure as dang got him, Mother."

Sim took the shotgun from Billie and put it back in the boot.

"You all right, B?" he asked.

She nodded yes and did not move. Teague put his arm around her and neither one said anything.

Ollie had crawled to the porch and sat with her back to the wall and her legs stretched out while she watched her mother kill her husband. Sim carried Ollie to her room and she fell asleep.

We wrapped Andrew's body in a blanket and put him in the cool barn. Teague rode to Andrew's mother's house four miles away to tell her what happened while I cleaned and wrapped Rufus's skinned knuckles. Teague was still a Lighthorseman and later told people he shot Andrew in self-defense. Most folks knew of Andrew's temper so his explanation made sense to everyone, including Andrew's family. A few hours later Andrew's mother and her daughter that looked as old as her came in their wagon pulled by two large mules to get the ruined Andrew.

Sim offered to help her bury her son, but the woman replied, "No, we can do it. After we pick the garden in the morning I'll decide what to do with him. I can't blame you none. If he hadn't married your girl he would've beat us." Then they drove off.

"I guess that's one reason to marry off your kid," Teague said. Then he walked back into the house.

After some berries and milk, we all decided it was best to stay the night. Sim brought blankets from the wagon and barn. I wrote on a pad that I read someplace a person hit on the head should be awakened every few hours. We did not understand why that was a good idea, but we feared Andrew had cracked Ollie's skull, so Billie and I took turns throughout the night gently shaking Ollie and making her open her eyes.

The next morning I awoke early and watched Billie bake two peach pies and her specialty: strawberry cobbler with a doughy sweet crust. She learned that cobbler dish from Regine at the boarding school and we liked the crust almost better than the fruit. Then she made coffee and two skillets of eggs, squash, and onions—one with hot peppers for her, and one with just salt and regular ground black pepper for everyone else.

Ollie kept her pantry full of flour, canned peaches, cornmeal, and all sorts of dried meat and fruit so she had plenty to cook with. Andrew always insisted that the food storage stay perfectly clean and arranged so that the labels faced outwards and nothing touched the item next to it. Andrew made Ollie clean the house every day whether it needed it or not, and both had to wash their hands with lye soap every time they came in from outside. He was even stranger in that he never took baths. At least his fingernails stayed clean.

Billie checked on Ollie and was satisfied at hearing her steady breathing. At supper, I suggested that Billie sit at the head of the smooth shiny table where Andrew used to eat. Sim sat at the other end. In the middle was the wooden bear that Billie carved for Ollie when she turned thirteen. I always liked that bear because she looked at me no matter where I stood in the room. Bear had a look on her face like she was smelling something, or was curious. Billie caught me looking at Bear.

"I still dream about her, you know," Billie said, reaching out to touch Bear's nose with a finger.

"I hope so," I said.

Everyone was quiet because we worried about Billie. Rufus was the first to talk.

"Mama, how come you always make the same amount for you as for everybody else, even when there are five other people, and you don't get fat?" He was nervous. "I can't understand that. When I get full, you're still eating. Look at you. You're so skinny you have to run around in the rain to get wet."

"It's a gift, son," she smiled. "I can eat a whole pie after dinner and not get a bellyache. The problem is, when I need to eat I have to right then. If there's no food I get out of sorts. Some people can go without breakfast and even lunch, but not me."

"Like on the trail?" he asked.

She put down her fork full of fluffy golden eggs. Many children starved on that removal and here she was eating enough for half a dozen people. Billie often said that she felt guilty about living when so many died and she tried not to think about it.

"That was different, Rufus," said Teague, looking at his sister. "Everyone was hungry all the time and we got used to it. There was no choice.

When there is plenty of food around we have a choice as to what to eat and how much."

"Sorry, Mama." Rufus began to cry, something he had not done since he was a small child. The events of the past day caught up to him and he had wanted to outrun them. "I just. . . ."

"Son, son." Billie stood and walked to where he sat. "My baby boy. This wasn't your fault. It happened. It would have happened sometime. Your sister's safe now." She said something close to his ear and I could not understand, but he took her hand and kissed it.

"I would have done it, yes sir," Sim said. "It was coming." Then he put his head down and ate so fast I thought he would choke. Sim wasn't good at smoothing things over.

"Let's finish breakfast and then see to Ollie," she said, stroking Rufus's black hair. "I love you."

Rufus nodded and played with his eggs and I wished my mother was alive to say she loved me.

After breakfast we checked on Ollie. She was awake, sitting up and looking out the window that was surrounded by light blue lacy curtains. Her hair usually looked brown, but the sunlight pouring through the window made it glow a light red. She was the only one in our family with curly hair. She let it grow to her waist and the pull of the heavy hair gave it a wave. Billie often said she wished she had hair like her daughter's.

Ollie drank a few sips of water then laid back down and closed her eyes without speaking. Billie covered her with the soft white sheet and patchwork quilt that Survella sewed for her wedding present.

I made a third pot of coffee and Billie swept the floor. "What will Ollie do now?" she asked me. "Should she come home with us?" She put the broom away and poured coffee for Teague.

"Let her decide, B," I said. "She'll get better."

"I hope you're right. Here's your cup, Teague." Then she picked up hers.

I wanted some water and while pouring a dipper from the bucket on the sink, I saw Teague nudge Billie's arm, making her spill her coffee. Billie took great pains to mix the right amount of sugar and cream in the strong black drink and I knew she would be mad to start over.

"Look," Teague said. I turned to see what he was gaping at and standing at the porch door was an old Indian with matted hair and patched clothes and carrying a cloth bag. It was the bonepicker we saw years before in Mississippi.

Teague and Billie were too surprised to speak and I just looked. Sim and Rufus came out from the back room and saw our guest. "What's wrong with you three?" Sim asked. Then he walked to the door and let the rugged old man in.

Now that we saw him up close, it was clear that he was a man and not all that old, except for his droopy eyelids that swallowed his eyelashes. The picker said in English that he lived across the field and knew what happened to Ollie. Rufus and Sim took that messy picker, who looked like he would smell bad but did not, by the arms and led him to Ollie. Billie, Teague, and I followed. He felt Ollie's head, put some corn and what looked like red dirt on her pillow, and said she would wake up soon. Then he started out the door.

"Wait," Billie said. "Here, take a pie." It sounded silly, but she could not manage anything else. Billie always gets nervous around old Choctaws, especially the ones that may have powers.

The picker smiled and showed us straight, snow-white teeth. I expected brown teeth, or no teeth. He took the pie, said *yokoke*, then left. Teague watched him walk through the field until he disappeared.

"He lives that way," Teague said, looking south.

Billie was excited and wanted to ask the picker questions. "He doesn't seem dangerous and tried to help us, didn't he?" she asked after he left. She talked through supper about what he may be like and I said that the only way to find out is to ask him.

During our supper everyone looked up at once toward Ollie's door. I turned to watch Ollie say, "*Hohchafot sa taha*—I am hungry."

Billie jumped up. "Here, baby, sit down."

Ollie had on a white long-sleeved shirt and brown skirt and no shoes. She combed her hair straight back and tied it with a red ribbon. She walked to the table slowly, her arms outstretched as if she expected to fall and catch herself.

Her Uncle Teague leaned over and kissed her cheek. "Have some of this gravy. I made it this time." Then he poured the thick lumpy gravy that tasted of smoked bacon on top of a browned biscuit and handed her a fork. Everyone watched her.

"Well, what do you all want for dinner?" Billie asked, wiping her hands on her bright red apron.

Teague laughed. "I'm not done with this yet, sister."

"Okay then, we'll have stew from that salt pork in the pantry. I better get to cooking so it'll be tender." Then she set out to fix dinner that was not for another six hours.

That afternoon Ollie sat in her room with her father and brother while Teague, Billie, and I rode across the wheatfield to tell the picker that Ollie was awake, but we could find no house.

"Told you I'd find a way to see that picker again, sister," Teague said.

Billie looked puzzled. "Well, I can't see how you planned it. At least he didn't take your skin."

Teague craned his neck looking all around the field. "Wonder where he went to. There's no house. Where's his house?"

Teague was right. There was no house and no footprints in the soft dirt to tell us where the man went. He was gone.

"Forget it, Teague," said Billie.

"He does what he wants," I said. "He is one of those."

Teague continued to turn his horse around, shading his eyes while searching for an old gray man that would not be found. "Maybe."

In the next few days Billie used up a foot-high stack of papers drawing that picker. She was never satisfied with what she sketched and for years she drew what her memory told her, until the pictures of the picker did not look a thing like what I thought I had seen.

I knew Teague wondered about that bonepicker man the rest of his life.

Ollie got over the shocks of being hurt by spending time by the creek or riding horses. Watson Glenn, a white man who had taught school with Survella, came by for eggs one afternoon and talked with her. They visited every afternoon for a month and soon got married. All of us were happy that Ollie married Watson. He was solid and we knew he could make her happy. But life changed for us soon after that.

One afternoon the Crows came to see Survella. Jincy told us the day afterwards at Billie's kitchen table that Survella and their boy Skarloey were out in the garden picking beans to take to his new wife. The older son, Corn, was in the barn stacking hay. The Crows rode into the yard and Dew asked where she was.

"Time for her to come on with me," Dew Crow said. Jincy recalled that his voice was like a whisper, but at the same time loud like a regular voice. He had not heard anything like it before.

"Go on, get outta here," Jincy yelled. He was scared and was not sure he could make them leave. Corn ran out of the barn with a pitchfork and tried to spear one of them, but that pitchfork handle reared back by itself and hit him between the eyes and knocked him cold.

Then all four Crows got off their horses.

"Was so strange," Jincy said, shaking his head. "Their right feet hit the ground at the same time. The three older Crows just stood still while Dew came up the porch steps then stared at me with those yellow eyes. I didn't remember anything until I woke up and was lying on my face in the flowers."

Jincy could hardly talk to us after that for crying. He wept so hard he had to throw up. After he drank some water and wiped his face with a wet cloth, he told us that after he came to, he ran to the garden where he knew Survella was and found her and Skarloey dead, their throats cut.

"Don't know how long I stood there looking at them," he said after his second crying spell. His chest rose and fell with the deep breaths he took. Crying takes a lot out of a person. "I got Corn into the house. Laid him down with a rag on his head for a while. Then we came here."

After hearing Jincy's story, Teague went to find some Lighthorsemen who found the Crows and surrounded them, but said later that those weird men did not act worried or afraid.

Stone Gray, one of the Lighthorsemen, recalled that Dew stood, tossed his drink into the fire, and explained about Survella, saying, "She didn't want to come with me. 'Get away!' she screamed like a caught rabbit. So I had to kill her. I'll find another. Happens."

Then a big wind came through the trees so hard that dust swirled and blinded the Lighthorsemen. When the wind died, the Crows were gone and so were all the tracks. No one saw them again. That night the running stars were out and we could only look at them a short while before coming in and locking the doors.

Stone and his men came back to Billie's house. "Never saw anything like them men," said Stone. "They had yellow eyes that were too big for their heads. They weren't men. I feel sick. I need to go see that *alikchi*, Ruel Battiest, to get my head clear."

Ruel was our great-uncle who did not come over on the trail with the tribe. He came years later during warm weather and settled where McAlester is now. Billie and Teague had sorely wanted to meet him, but were afraid to, I think.

All of us were sick after Survella and Skarloey died. We missed our sister and her son, who as a child always wanted to sit next to me at mealtimes. Billie ached the most and spent a lot of time drawing pictures of them.

"Know what?" she asked one day after riding to my house. "I have to see Ruel. Are you coming?" Billie, Teague, Jincy, and I quickly packed our wagon and went to see Ruel in hopes that he could make us feel better.

"You sure this is the right way, Gilmore?" Teague asked when we were almost there. We had a badly drawn map that Burl made for us. Lines and arrows went everywhere.

"Hard to describe how to get there," our uncle told us. "The house is, well, different. It's two stories with stairs on the outside."

"Should be close," I said. "The map shows a small hill and it's probably that one over there." I was right. As we rounded the hill, the house slowly showed itself. It was painted yellow and looked very bright with the gray sky behind it. From a quarter-mile distance, it was huge and I could not help wondering why the stairs were built on the outside.

"Never saw a house like that. Big house for a medicine man," Billie said.

Teague squinted. "What's he got in there, I wonder?"

Our mustangs pulled us to the dirt yard full of chickens and ducks. There was a garden bigger than Billie's surrounded by a short yellow picket fence, but no flowers, birdhouses, or porch for a swing. There only were a few trees, but they were full of plums and peaches. "Where's the creek?" Jincy asked. "There's gotta be water somewhere."

As we climbed down, a tall, very black man wearing brown overalls and heavy boots and carrying a vegetable basket climbed out of the root cellar.

All of us took in a breath because he had no nose. Just two holes in his face where a nose should be.

"Hiddy," I think he said. He smiled big. "Ruel's comin'. Name's No Nose." And he extended his big hand to all of us. Then he walked past us to the garden and pulled onions. We all turned to watch him, like a herd of cows turn to watch their master when their feed is coming.

"How'd he lose his nose?" Teague asked.

"Don't ask me," Billie said. "Maybe he never had one."

The door at the top of the stairs opened. Out stepped a man who looked like Uncle Ellis, except shorter and more filled out. And he was cleaner in a white shirt, dark pants, and boots like No Nose. His long hair was tied neatly back with red and blue ribbons. He looked us over and stepped down the stairs like he was gliding on ice. His body did not seem to pause after each step and he grew bigger and taller as he got closer, but when he stood in front of us, he became shorter again. I blinked and looked at Billie and Teague and they stared at him, too. My head pounded.

"Uncle Ruel," Billie started. "We. . . ."

"I know. The Crows are powerful witches and they kill hard. They make you sick here, too." He pointed to his head and to Jincy. Then he looked to Billie. "Survella's fine." That was an odd thing to say considering she was dead. "Come on." We followed him up the stairs. The steps were strange, almost twice the size of normal steps, as if they were made for very long feet. I glanced back to the ground when we reached the landing and the garden appeared to be ten stories down, not two. I staggered and grabbed the rail for balance.

We entered the house and were surprised at how bright and colorful the front room was. The yellow curtains, red and white checkered tablecloth, and red chair seats came from a woman's hand, I thought. Bowls of blueberries, raspberries, and strawberries sat on the table. The colorful throw rugs on the polished wood floor looked new. Wildflowers in glasses sat on every windowsill and table, and the walls were whitewashed and covered with animal skins. Dishes on the kitchen counter were of all colors, as were the cups. Nothing looked like it cost much; it was in the way the room was put together that made it seem rich.

The room smelled funny, though, like a just-washed dog, but there was no sign of any animal except the dried-out skins. It was also peculiar to see a small table and six chairs in the kitchen corner set with small dishes and cups. It must be a child's table, I believed, but whose children?

"Where's Merly?" Billie asked. Merly was Ruel's wife whom we had never met.

"She lives downstairs. Now, let me see what Ellis gave you."

We didn't know what to make of his wife living downstairs, but said nothing. Billie, Teague, and I took off our small medicine bundles and gave them to Ruel. "You buried Survella's with her, didn't you?" Jincy nodded. "Good. I'll be back. Those berries are for you." Then he went into the next room and shut the door.

We all looked at each other. "Nice house," said Teague. "Look at those fox and wolf hides." He took a mouthful of blueberries. His eyebrows shot up. "Perfect."

"Everything looks new," said Billie.

"Except those brown pots over the fireplace," I said. "They look like old Indian pots from out west. I have seen them in books."

"And that old bench there by the door," Jincy noticed. The seat and footstool underneath were fixed for someone ten feet tall. "Does Ruel have children?" Jincy asked. We looked to the small table as Ruel came from the other room.

"I like to make my friends happy and comfortable," said Ruel as he shut the door behind him, referring to our questions about his furniture. "Here." He handed us our pouches back. My little bag was heavy as a rock. "They'll lighten up after a while," he said. "Jincy, wear this. Remember you're never alone. Your family is with you." Billie's head jerked up. Ellis had told us the same thing years ago and Ruel knew it. He smiled at her. "Berries are ripe." We took handfuls of the juicy fruit like he wanted us to.

"Will these bags protect us from the Crows?" asked Teague.

Ruel looked out his south window to his garden then turned back around. "No," he said. Teague cocked his head. He thought Ruel could save us. "The Crows can kill you. The medicine will save you any pain the Crows may cause. Or you can choose to die before they kill you. That is all I can do for now."

"You mean, you can't kill them?" Billie was hopeful.

"No, Billie Louise. Not in this time. Not in your lifetime."

"But, why not? Are they so evil that nobody can kill them?"

"My power simply isn't strong enough now. It grows over time." He looked at each of us in turn. "A very long time. That is why our family is so important. You have to stay together and you must teach your children about our family. It is the most important lesson you can give them. If you had not come to see me, I would have come to you in the next year just to tell you that."

I made out every word Ruel said, but did not get the meaning. What did our family have to do with his power and killing the Crows?

"As my power grows, so does the Crows' power," he said.

"What are they?" Teague asked. "They look like *opa*-men."

"They are just that: owls and men. Both at the same time." He held his hand up when Billie started to ask the obvious question. "I do not know how they came to be, but I see how it is possible. Evil has been around a long time and takes many forms: human, animal, wind. We cannot see all evil, but we feel it sometimes. We can see and feel the Crows. Sit and rest."

After we ate all the berries and asked questions Ruel could not, or would not, answer, we followed him back down the strange stairs. "Have you seen Ellis?" Billie asked him, hopeful.

"Ellis is fine," said Ruel.

That could mean alive or dead, I thought. Billie accepted his answer.

Before we got back in the wagon, Ruel took each of our hands in his. His were smooth and very warm, almost hot. Then he walked back to his house.

"Bye-dee now," waved No Nose, who turned back to his onion-pulling.

"Ruel was almost like Ellis," Billie said after we had gone several miles. "Teague?"

"A little. They both have secrets and are older than they look. Ruel's got more power than Ellis, I think. No Nose is real old, too. I saw his hands."

I agreed with Teague. We were all thinking, feeling peaceful.

"Maybe Papa was right in thinking that God does everything for a reason," Billie said. "Life is a circle, too, like Ruel said, and what goes around, comes around. Survella and Skarloey die, but others are born. Ruel said they were fine, so there must be another place to live after we die, not just in the ground. And we'll get to see them again. The Crows'll get what's coming to them someday."

"You'll get a headache thinking all that, sister," said Teague. Billie usually did when she thought hard. "Still, makes sense."

"I have to stay strong for my children," said Jincy. "I can do it now." And he squeezed Billie's hand. "I just wish Ruel could do something about the Crows."

We all did.

"I guess this is what we wanted from Ruel," I said. "Peace." Everyone nodded and we went home.

Teague had three boys. Arie became the sheriff of McAlester, and Colbert, who is straight and healthy, reads well and breaks horses like Teague did. He can't get along with people, so he runs every day, although nobody's sure if he is trying to get away from something, or just looking. During those years during and after the war, none of us were sure about ourselves, either.

Two years into the war, Teague's youngest boy, Romy, was hung for murder. Romy was terribly bowlegged at birth and his legs never straightened out. Although he could read and write, he was not very bright and made poor decisions. He did not kill animals like some bad people did, and he did not talk badly to girls, but his temper was quick like his Uncle Sim's.

Romy started drinking when he turned a teenager and that liquor brought out his bad side. Teague never could figure out where Romy got his whiskey and he hid it well out in the woods. When Romy turned twenty, he killed his friend one night with a pickax over an argument about a boxing match in Wilburton. After he sobered up the next morning, he did not remember what happened, but it was too late. Romy got a quick trial and immediate hanging—even before Teague could arrive to represent him.

Teague was ashamed, not just from his boy's hanging, but also because he believed it was his fault that Romy was ignorant and did things without considering what might happen afterwards. After he died, the family talked about him as if he was out of town, not hung and buried.

The funeral was attended by all of Teague's Lighthorsemen friends.

They were sorry for Teague and afraid—like all parents are—that one of their boys might go bad, too. After the crowd drifted away from Billie's house, Teague and his tired family went home. Watson, Ollie, Billie, and I sat on the porch and watched the bluebirds bring little pieces of straw and grass to their nest. Billie had nailed the blue-painted box to the big pecan next to the porch years before and the bird family returned every spring. Within weeks of making their soft bed, there would be babies wanting bugs for breakfast.

"Finally over," said Ollie as she sat on the porch-long bench. She sipped her cup of water. "I knew Romy would kill someone."

"For sure, nothing Teague could do," Billie said as she fanned herself with one of her sketch papers. It was very warm on the porch with the setting sun shining on us. Romy was hard to control and no amount of punishment could straighten him out. All of us had talked to him at some point about being responsible, but our discussions made no difference. "That boy was a few sandwiches short of a picnic." Billie did not mean to be funny. I imagined that his brain was small and did not fill his head.

Before going to bed, Billie said what we all worried about: "I hope God will not be mad at Romy for being a fool."

Ghosts of War

BILLIE

Sim, our boys Dawson and Rufus, and Gilmore's son Matthias fought for the South. A lot of the white men who married Choctaw women used Negro slaves, and some half-bloods also owned some, but we didn't believe in making other people work for us.

A lot of Choctaws were afraid of Republicans since they were itching to get our land, so they reasoned that fighting for what might be taken away from us seemed the thing to do. All four fought for the Choctaw-Chickasaw Mounted Rifles even though Dawson and Rufus really didn't know what the fighting was about. Their daddy went off to war in the last part of 1862, so they did, too.

Waiting out that war was as hard as having children. My girl Tish, who was three when the war started, stayed with me, so I wasn't lonely. Gilmore came by a couple times a week. We wanted to know how the war was going, but no letters came. I liked to worry myself sick about Ollie even though I knew she was safe with Watson.

It was a strange time. We didn't leave home so we left no tracks. Sometimes I'd wait in the bushes for a traveler to come by who could tell us news. Other than those few people, we saw nobody. Our world stopped at the edge of the trees and nobody knew about us. My house sat off the main road like it does now, surrounded by thick trees and bushes that were heavy and green in the warm weather and gray and quiet in the winter. Gilmore, Alli, and their kids always came through the back field so nobody would see them.

We had quite a bit of smoked meat at the beginning of the war and it lasted the first winter. Then I caught fish in the creek and the garden grew like it knew we needed the food. I planted corn right up to the porch steps and there was a heavy crop of pecans, peaches, and apples each fall. Rains came on time, giving us grass for the milk cow and mustangs. The chickens ate leftovers. Those animals stayed strong for us.

When the wind blew toward the house, we heard wagons on the military roads from Fort Smith. I thought that at any minute a regiment would come through and take everything. If I'd known they'd never come I would've enjoyed those years more.

Gilmore and Alli didn't have the same luck we did. Their house was out in the open and it seemed that everyone who went past there begged or tried to steal something. Finally those northern troops burned their place at the end of the third year. Luckily Gilmore brought their books and blowguns over to my place before they got lost. They moved Ziah and Reby here the last year then they moved to Wilburton instead of rebuilding.

I was especially afraid of the creek. I walked way upstream to fish, so the old path covered up. It was hard to get to my new fishing place, but I couldn't be seen from the other bank. That trail got pounded in deep from me walking on it every day. After sixty years the trail's still there, but I can't climb it anymore.

One cool fall evening we heard a hoot, then a brown owl flew across the yard not twenty feet from us. It didn't swoop down to pick up a mouse, it just flew by. We heard it hoot a few more times in the trees and then it was silent. Locusts got quiet, then a few minutes later started up again.

We went in the house and told Gilmore what I'd seen.

"The Crows?" he asked.

"No, I don't think so. This was a real bird-owl."

Gilmore pondered a minute. "Still. We need to be careful. Owls around mean something."

He said to lock the door. Then we walked around trying to figure out what might happen. I checked Tish for fever then looked at the fireplace to make sure a cinder wouldn't pop out. I went to bed thinking the owl was there because I caught a cold the week before and believed that my sickness would kill me. Ellis told me I'd have my bundle for a long time and I thought thirty years was what he meant. Before we slept, Gilmore said not to worry about the owl even though he looked concerned, checked the rifles, and put one by the door and one next to his bed.

Deep in the night I woke up and saw Ellis dressed in bright clothes, leaning over me. He was the same age as when I last saw him, except that he had large white teeth and wasn't as thin.

He said the same thing to me he did before: "Billie Lou, you will have this a long time."

Then Ruel stepped in front of his brother. "You will never be alone," he said.

Adele, James, Survella, and Skarloey stood behind my great-uncles, smiling and nodding. I fell asleep wondering if my family was happy. I felt rested that morning and forgot about the owl.

A week later, Uncle Burl brought us a wagon full of newspapers and a letter. It was the first time we had seen him in almost four years. The letter was addressed to me and written by a surgeon. "Almost opened it, Bill," he said. From the return address, I understood why he wanted to read it.

I read aloud to my family that Rufus got hit by a cannonball and died at Muddy Boggy after losing a leg. The doctor didn't think him losing a leg would kill him, but the gangrene that set in did. He died the day we saw the owl.

Losing a child is impossible to bear. And I had to bear it. I had lost a brother, sister, a nephew, aunt, uncle, and both parents, but their deaths were different, somehow. All my fears and nightmares of my baby Rufus falling into the creek or putting something in his mouth that could choke him were behind me. What was the use of all that worrying? My baby was gone, and I was here.

Alli rushed toward me as I fell. She caught me before my head hit the floor, but still, I was hard hit. She sat beside me on the floor and Gilmore sat on my other side. I recall sitting on the cold wood, my daughter in my lap, talking about Rufus and Dawson to Gilmore, Alli, and Burl all night. Ziah and Reby slept by the fire. I did not want to sleep, for I knew that waking would be a nightmare. It was, eventually. But I got through it, thinking that Ruel would have told me "Rufus is fine."

Sim returned home a few days after that. He rode into the yard while I was in the garden and the sun was behind him. He sat in the saddle wrong, slumped and holding his arm. As he got closer I realized that he wasn't holding the arm because his arm was gone. He was scrawny, almost starved, and probably hadn't slept in a week. Gilmore helped him down and led him up the porch steps by his remaining arm to the rocker by the fire.

"Got whiskey, B?" My husband's voice was cracked and old.

"A little." I used it for cuts, not drinking.

"Got shot two weeks before and the surgeon sawed my arm off," he told us as he looked down at the bloody bandage that needed changing, then took a large drink from the bottle. Watching him made me wince. I'd never seen my husband drink before. "Told that sawbones I didn't want to lose it, but he only knew to cut off body parts, not save them. He cut off arms and legs all day. Piles of 'em. At the end of the day, they either got burned or buried, depending on how much work his helpers wanted to do." He stared into the flames. Then he took a small vial out of his shirt pocket and sipped from it.

Gilmore sat behind Sim and signed with his hands what Sim was taking: morphine. It was a new medicine that helped to ease pain. I later heard that many men with hurts from the war took morphine. Problem was, the more they took morphine, the more they wanted and needed it.

"Does it hurt, Papa?" asked Tish. She was standing in front of Sim, reaching out to touch his hurt.

"Yes, girl. Don't touch me."

That stung, and Tish went to the kitchen table bench with Gilmore and Alli and watched her sick papa from a safe distance. We all knew something was wrong with Sim besides his lost arm.

"Didn't see the boys after the last fight. Figured they'd be here. I need to see my boys. Where are they?"

I gave him the letter about Rufus and after reading it he started talking very quietly. "We started out fighting together." He smiled. "That morning we talked about building the new room to the house when we got home." He fingered the letter. "It was a hard fight. The boys were supposed to stay close to me."

He pounded his leg with his one fist. "I couldn't find them after." He started hitting his leg harder.

"Sim, we'll get through this all right," I said. Survella had always said that to me in hopes of making me feel better. Alli took Tish outside.

"Noooo! It's not all right! It will never be all right!"

The look he gave me was of pure fury. Then he stood and pushed the chair over. He dropped the letter and stomped on it. "Not all right. Not all right."

Then his mind shifted and he cried until his heart broke.

I followed him to the creek and heard him crying so I came back to the house. He stayed down by the creek all night. Tish wouldn't go near him.

Dawson came home two days later, and even though he wasn't hurt he had the same look as his father. He didn't say much when he hugged all of us. He picked up Tish and looked at her and held her so hard she squealed. He put her down and went to bed. After I told him about his brother and showed him the letter, he nodded and didn't mention Rufus for a long time. Instead of staying up late like Sim, he went to sleep early and stayed there until lunch. He worked hard all day or took a horse out to run. The horse came back lathered and hot, and Dawson just took off the saddle and put him in the barn without caring for him.

I was all cried out and knew that Sim needed time to get over his grief. I thought we'd talk about it, but never did. Our whole world was changed with that war. The fighting was over but Sim wasn't ever the same. He always thought that someone was behind him about to shoot him in the back, so he kept turning around to look. One night when he was sleeping, I got into bed and startled him. He pulled a pistol from under the pillow and pointed it at my forehead. I slept with Tish after that.

Sim had a hard time getting in his saddle and doing chores. I cinched his saddle and took it off when he came back. He couldn't dress very well and needed help doing everything. I knew he hated me for it.

Matthias came home a few weeks after Dawson. He got hit in the elbow with grapeshot and a piece of scrap lodged between the bones, which kept his elbow from straightening. He kept it bent in a sling under his coat.

"Told that old doctor I'd kill him if he tried to take my arm," Matt said. "I'd rather have it than not, even if it don't work."

So many boys came home missing an arm, a leg, or both. One who lived down the road lost his eyes and shot himself with his mama's shotgun. In town we'd see men all broken down. I don't know how they got through it.

We were lucky, though. There were a lot of Indians from other tribes that stayed in our Nation and didn't have much to eat. Bad characters came from everywhere looking for people to steal from. A lot of Choctaws lost their farms and homes and the whole Nation lost schools, stores, bridges—something of everything. Every neighbor lost their cattle and horses to rustlers. After the war all kinds of white people started moving into our Nation and built railroads, towns, coal mines, and houses all over the place. Luckily, not many came around us.

Even people outside the war had a hard time. Gilmore's wife Alli brought over a newspaper that talked about Cheyennes getting killed in Colorado by some creek. Then the cavalry went after those poor people again four years later over on the Washita. Indians had lots of troubles before the war, but afterwards it seemed that everything went wrong for tribes everywhere. Even at my house.

One evening as I poked at logs in the fireplace, one rolled onto the rug. I pushed it back and burned my hands. Sim sat in the chair and watched without moving or saying a word. Not when I ran for the water to put my hands in, and not when I put butter on my palms and wrapped them in rags. By that time it was clear that he was tore up in his head, and I knew we'd lost him.

The next morning he managed to saddle his black stallion Pope and leave us. I thought he was going to check on the cows like he always did, but he didn't come back.

Teague said a friend of his saw Sim a year later over in the Creek Nation during a stomp dance. We had a brand on Pope and Teague saw him at a horse sale in McAlester, but nobody knew a thing about the owner. Teague was thoughtful and bought the horse back for me. After a few years Gilmore helped me get Sim declared dead and I put a marker for him out back.

After I told Tish what I'd done, she took my hand in her small ones and said in a very grown-up way, "It's a good thing, Mama."

My boy Dawson never said much after his daddy and brother were gone, but he did start drinking. One night he fell headfirst into a rain barrel and almost drowned. He was too heavy for me to lift, so I pushed the barrel over with him in it.

"What in hell's the matter with you?!" I screamed. Then I pulled him upright so he was sitting, stale rainwater pouring down his face. He looked like he was trying to sweat out his anger.

"Mama. Mama, let me go." He was crying like his daddy did, and it made me madder.

I slapped him again. I was so angry I scared myself, but my sense was that this had to happen.

"No, you're not going to be this way, Dawson. You've got your life. Others don't. You made it. They didn't. We're here and they aren't." I realized I was talking about myself as well as my boy. Then I fell to my son's side and cried while he sat staring at the slimy silt at the bottom of the empty rain barrel.

Dawson straightened out after a few months. He went to Jones Academy for two years then came back and was appointed secretary to Chief Coleman Cole. He married the daughter of a sub-chief and moved to the capital in Doaksville. It was moved up to Tuskahoma a few years after.

Matthias married a Cherokee girl named Bette and opened a store up north in Muskogee. He got some money from Gilmore's law earnings and he made money selling tack shipped in from New England. After saving enough money, he went to the same law school in Missouri as his papa, then came back and became a judge over in McAlester.

Matt got to be friends with Jackson McCurtain during the war and when McCurtain was elected chief in 1880, Matt acted as his adviser on things like the railroad that came from Arkansas across Choctaw land to Texas. Matt also advised him on expanding the Indian police. There were so many cattle thieves and murderers here that McCurtain had to do something. It was the worst problem the Nation had. McCurtain was so strong about punishing outlaws that he had feared for his family and moved south of the Kiamichis.

After the war, the Lighthorsemen's jobs got harder, what with all the lowlife moving into Indian Territory. There was lots of trouble in Red Oak but folks had their share over in Wilburton and Caddo. Even more troublemakers moved in after the railroads were built. I was proud of my brother for wanting to enforce the laws, but it was dangerous work and I worried about him.

In 1870, I married my last husband, Rolland Watchman. He was a half-blood farmer I met one afternoon when Dawson and I went to buy supplies and we came across Rolland fixing a broken wagon wheel. Rolland was a widower with no children and lived with his parents in McAlester. He was the same age as me, forty-six, when we married in 1870.

Rolland was a kind person and didn't talk much. No schooling and didn't want any. His daddy was white and Rolland didn't like him. Seems he was a lot like my papa, always telling the Indians what to do. I liked him the best of all my husbands. Too bad he killed himself ten years after we married.

One evening after dinner while we watched the sky, Rolland bit down on a pecan shell and cracked a tooth. Several days later he got a pain in his jaw and by night couldn't hardly stand the hurt. He tried to numb it by drinking the whiskey I kept for treating cuts, but it made him sick. The boiled rags I put on his face didn't help much and neither did morphine. It just made him sicker. After two weeks of suffering, he finally decided to see the white dentist in town.

"Doesn't look good, I tell you," said the white-haired man with huge silver muttonchops. "Should've come in earlier."

Then he cut the gum to drain the poison and pulled the tooth, but the infection had gotten into Rolland's head. That socket didn't close over and he was in such pain he didn't recognize the people around him. He just went crazy from hurt and fever. At least he had manners enough to stand in the creek when he used my shotgun to blow his head off his shoulders.

He's buried out back next to Peter and the marker for Sim. I figure my dead husbands don't mind, and even if they did, there's nothing they can do about it.

That year Tish, my baby who was twenty-two, married a Cherokee farmer named Biff Walkingstick who thought enough of her to move from Park Hill in the Cherokee Nation to McAlester.

The years went by and things was tough for Indians everywhere. Tribes all over Indian Territory lost more land and by the time of allotment there weren't as many Choctaws around here as before. A lot had moved to Broken Bow or the capital, so the only ones left were my family and a few others we didn't know well. There were so many white people coming in that Indians started to clear out.

I thought we were going to disappear. Things changed so fast we could hardly keep up, and allotment made it worse. Still, I found a lot of ways to stay happy. I went to fights over in Krebs one year and saw a fight between "Gentleman" Tom Abbott of McAlester and "Mysterious" Billie Ross from Seattle. The next year I watched fights in Bartlesville where Elmo Harjo, the "Fast Feet Creek," fought "Smoking Henkel," a white man who did his bag training with a cigar in his mouth. That was a bloody one. They wore those leather gloves that cut and both men were a bloody mess. Little kids got right up there close to the ropes and nobody moved them off. I keep all my newspaper fight clippings in a box under my bed next to my drawings.

Wasn't long after allotment that Oklahoma was made a state. Statehood didn't go over well with most Indians like me, but here we are. I like the name *Oklahoma*; it's made of Choctaw words. *Okla* means men and *humma* means red. Sounds like the state belongs to Choctaws, but it doesn't.

About the only things us Indians get to keep for ourselves are our memories and our pride. Many Indians have been beaten down so hard they don't have pride anymore. Mama, Adele, and Survella, especially, the women of my family, taught me to be proud. I am proud of me, proud of my family, and of my people. Those are things white people can't ever take away.

Bad Luck

Krebs, Southeastern Oklahoma. 1892.

That it?" the rangy Corn Wilson yelled to his foreman. Even though his light brown skin was covered with black dust, one could see the muscle definition in his forearms. Corn was like his Aunt Billie, who could eat as much as she wanted but not gain weight. Corn also liked beer with his food and the added calories didn't affect him.

The last coal car came out ahead of the two dozen men who had finished their shift. After ten hours underground their faces were almost unrecognizable under coal dust. Some changed clothes and washed in the rain barrels before going home; others just dusted off and then went to Big Tom's for a few rounds of Choc Beer. The beer wasn't that good, but it was made in town so residents said it tasted better than other brands. The federal government outlawed Choc Beer in 1895, but now, three years before its demise, the suppliers made hefty profits.

Krebs was a coal mining town and some of the people seen on its main street were Indians. Most were white, however, many of them Italians. This particular summer evening, a Muscogee man, Andrew Jackson Harjo, walked into Big Tom's.

His mother had named him Andrew Jackson so that he and his family wouldn't forget the destruction the president did to their tribe. Her son didn't think kindly of her reasoning. It would've been fine just to hear the removal story and not be burdened with such a name. So he went by Jack.

He was a stout man with straight black hair trimmed straight across at the middle of his back. His light blue button-down shirt and brown pants were clean, as were his heel-worn boots. Jack was traveling to Poteau to visit a cousin and he stopped in Krebs for the night.

Jack noticed that coal miners took up half the tables. Three Indians, all

Choctaws, sat at one. Jack took his beer to their table. One man was full-blood, but it was hard to be certain because of the coal dust.

"Join you?" asked Jack.

The three men looked at him and knew he was Muscogee. "Sure, have a sit," said Flynn Noah. Flynn liked to talk.

"Jack," he said, taking in their body odor. He held his hand out to each man in turn then took off his hat and sat.

"On your way?" asked Flynn.

"Over to Poteau. You miners?"

They nodded their heads.

"Dangerous business, huh?" asked Jack.

"Yeah, it's a job, though," said Kenny Wilson, a pudgy half-blood with a lisp. Jack could see that Kenny's right ear was filled with coal dust and wondered how he'd clean it.

"Get lung sickness?"

"That's the least of it. Our foreman's son got killed a few months back when his mine exploded. Him and a hundred other workers got blowed up. Got buried together because they couldn't tell who was who."

Corn Wilson, son of Jincy and Survella and who also was Flynn's brother-in-law, took a long pull at his beer. "Explosions they make on purpose are called windy shots. They're supposed to knock down dirt so we can get the coal, but sometimes there's too much gas in the shaft and the whole mine blows with everyone in it. Them boys got kilt by a worker who started the blast before everyone was out."

"Who owns the mines around here?" asked Jack.

"A white lady named Hattie Lane owns the one we work in, but I run it. Or I'm supposed to. She keeps buttin' in."

"A woman in a mine is bad luck," said Hugh Powers, an eavesdropping white man at the next table. "Lane's always around to watch what we bring out. Nobody likes her bein' there."

"She's gonna get someone killed," coughed skinny, pale Prod Baker.

Hugh nodded. "Hattie's unlikable. She dresses like a man and cuts her hair real short. She swears worse'n me, and tells jokes makin' fun of Indians, Italians, and everyone else differ'nt from her. She don't have concern for nobody's feelings. She just wants money."

"An' so do I," laughed Prod. He had swallowed four beers in a short time and would turn obnoxious if he drank another.

"An accident happens almost every time she goes in, but she just hires more workers and tongue-lashes 'em," said Hugh.

"Why a body would want to work underground, all dark and damp," Jack said as he shook his head.

"Gotta do somethin' for money," said Corn.

"Gittin' late," said Flynn. "Gotta git home to supper."

"Hey, mind if I come out tomorrow and take a look?" asked Jack. "I never seen a mine."

"Yeah, sure," said Kenny. "It's just outta town a quarter mile east."

The 6:00 A.M. train whistle woke Jack. The big man splashed his sweaty face in the water bowl, dressed, then visited the ivy-covered outhouse. Pages from the new Sears and Roebuck catalog covered the inside walls. A bucket painted red with blue flowers and filled with ashes sat in the corner. Jack read a few pages, then sprinkled ashes into the pit.

He walked to the main street and headed for the other hotel in town, the expensive one that served breakfast. Jack saw only white people as he passed the town bank, post office, drugstore, and funeral home. When he thought that maybe no Indians came into town, two short, dark-haired men emerged from behind the train depot. One had hair cut above his ears and the other wore his in a ponytail. The three men nodded as they passed each other on the tree-shaded sidewalk.

The coolness of the hotel was a contrast to the heat outside. A plump, half-blood Indian woman, adorned by a dress from a Sears and Roebuck page that Jack had seen on the outhouse wall, led Jack to his table. She brought hot coffee and cold cream and said that the number three meal was best.

After ordering, Jack pondered two paintings that hung near his table. One featured a Cherokee and the other a Choctaw, both dying in the snow. *Reminders of the removal. Now why would white people let those pictures in here?* he wondered.

After a breakfast of strawberries, hot buttered biscuits, and greasy gravy, Jack walked to the mine. It was a cloudless, hot July day. His steps stirred the dust and his scalp itched. *Need to wash my head.*

Grasshoppers and other insects flew out of the sparse meadow as he walked past. Soon he reached a dark, forty-foot passageway created by the branches of enormous pecan trees. Vines wrapped around the trunks combined with bushes and undergrowth made the tunnel damp and cool. Birds and squirrels jabbered in the dense green canopy. Trickles of water fell to earth and darkened the road. Jack closed his eyes and enjoyed the cool breeze that rushed through the tunnel.

Jack exited the odd passage into the heat. The mine entrance was only a short distance away. Trees and ground cover had disappeared, leaving broken carts scattered among piles of rock. Puddles of mule piss simmered, stinking in the heat. The men he met the night before argued with a white man who gestured dramatically to the mine entrance. As Jack got closer, he saw that the man was actually a woman dressed as a man. This was probably Hattie Lane, and the men clearly did not want to go in the mine.

"I told you sons a' bitches to git your arses in there," she yelled in a deep, hoarse voice.

"We won't. It's a bad sign," said Flynn. He was as dirty as when Jack met him the night before.

Corn walked over. Jack appreciated that he had washed. His face was tanned brown and his short hair was shiny red-brown, not coal black. Corn looked to be about fifty. "Heard an owl this morning," Corn said.

Jack nodded, understanding.

"Knew it meant trouble and sure enough one of them 'talians fell and broke his leg right inside the hole. I ain't goin'."

Prod overheard them talking. "Not owls again. Owls ain't got nothin' to do with it. You Indi'ns got some strange ideas."

"Then why don't you go in?" asked Hugh.

Suddenly, the hoot of an owl came from the oak grove behind the wagon. A group of Indians glanced at each other, alarm in their faces. They quickly walked away, ignoring Hattie's profanity.

"You stupid asshole heathen Indians. It's just an owl and a bird can't do nothin'." Spit flew out of Hattie's mouth when she yelled. "I'll show ya."

She marched to the mine entrance and called for the miners to come with her. There were a dozen non-Indian miners, but only two volunteered. "Start it up, dumb-asses. We're goin' to the end an' back."

"She may go to the end," Corn said, "but not back. That's for sure." Then he turned and walked to the rockpile and stood behind the barrier, waiting for what he knew would happen.

The two Italians pushed the cars into the mine. Hattie and the men disappeared into the shadows. Everyone outside the mine stood quietly, waiting. Locusts stopped humming. The owl hooted then emerged from the grove. It swooped past the men then vanished out of sight.

Seconds later, an explosion within the mine caused the ground to rise. The men ran away from the tunnel as fast as they could, knowing that support beams would fly from the entrance with such force they could impale a mule.

After the dust settled, everyone looked toward the collapsed entrance. Rocks and beams were heaped together. If Hattie and the two men were alive, they would surely suffocate before the debris could be moved. None of the men approached it.

The entire episode only took three minutes and Jack was breathless. "Well, glad I got to see a mine," Jack panted to the men crouched behind a pile of broken mining cars. He stood and brushed himself off. "Good meeting you."

Then he jogged back to town and waited impatiently for the Missouri-Kansas-Texas line to arrive and take him to Poteau.

Hattie's daughter, Lily, inherited her mother's three mines. No more accidents occurred until two years later when Lily walked thirty feet into one of the mines and an explosion killed her and five workers. Flynn, Corn, and Kenny witnessed the collapse of that mine and they, as well as Prod and Hugh, saw the owl soar past before it blew.

The evening after the blast the miners drank beer at Big Tom's. The Indians sat at one table and the white men at another. The Indians remained quiet and listened to Prod and Hugh talk loudly about the explosion.

"It was Lily, I tell you," said Prod. "Bad as her mama."

"Shouldn't have let her go in there," said Hugh. "Women are trouble around mines."

"Hey, Flynn," said Prod. "A woman in the mines is bad luck, huh?"

Corn downed the last of his warm beer. "If you say so."

Corn, Flynn, and Kenny looked at each other without expression.

"Time for supper," said Kenny.

"Yeah," yawned Corn. "See ya tomorrow."

All three Indians got up to leave. Prod and Hugh watched them walk out the door.

"Yep, a woman in the mine is bad luck." Then Prod scratched his head and looked at his empty bottle. He looked puzzled. "Ain't she?"

The Deaf Lawyer

Wilburton, Oklahoma. 1875.

After the family rebuilt their house and farm in Red Oak after removal, and their sharp grief settled into acceptance, Gilmore Lamb spent his days working the property, playing with his cousins, and making his blowguns and rabbit sticks. He was deaf, but he completed law school and was confident and knew that he could succeed as well as white people.

All his adult years Gilmore tried to make a living as a lawyer. He was smarter than most people in Indian Territory, but not many wanted to hire a deaf Choctaw. Some people called Gilmore a dumb Indian and others ignored him. Still, he had paperwork cases and his wife Alli taught school, so they made enough money to buy food and to keep their house shingled.

Gilmore and Alli were good at their professions, but now, in 1875 and in their fifties, they struggled with his failing law office.

One summer afternoon a small, elderly white lady with cotton hair came to Gilmore's office. That Gilmore was deaf did not bother Mila White in the least.

"That R. and C. Company out of Missouri built my house over there by Edwards' Store," Mila said. In 1850, Thomas Edwards moved from New Zealand to Indian Territory and built a trading post about fifteen miles east of Wilburton. Prior to the Civil War, the Butterfield Stage made Edwards' Store one of its stops and helped to make Edwards a wealthy man.

"Two days after we moved in," Mila explained, "that was about two months ago, the roof fell. The builders didn't use support beams. Can you imagine? Killed my husband and my cat and broke my furniture."

Gilmore appraised the little woman and decided that she was probably poor. He needed money and couldn't afford to take her case, but he also felt sorry for her. He signed his thoughts to Alli, who signed back, "I agree."

After discussing the case procedure, Mila said, "I've got three hundred dollars to get you started. I'm staying at the hotel across the street. Room 218. I'll be there most of the time. Come get me if need be." She got up and left.

Alli stopped teaching to help Gilmore with Mila's case. They traveled to Missouri, but the courts wouldn't work with Gilmore since he was from Indian Territory. Even though it appeared to be a dead case, Gilmore was determined to keep trying.

After they returned from Missouri, Alli met with Mila in Gilmore's office. "We can't win in court because no judge wants to hear the case," Alli told her, "but we did tell the R. and C. Company that Gilmore would put notice in papers throughout Missouri and Oklahoma about the accident. Reporters from Oklahoma City and Kansas City are coming to interview you next week."

She smiled big and hoped the little woman would accept their strategy. It cost them $200 to entice the reporters and now they had no money at all. Alli stood wringing her hands.

"Well, tell me when they get here, dear," Mila said.

Alli watched Mila through the window as she slowly walked across the street to the hotel. Then she put her head in her hands and fought back the tears.

For five weeks Gilmore and Alli wrote to newspapers to share the story of Mila White. To their surprise, ten stories were printed. Nevertheless, Gilmore knew that he would lose his office within the month. Alli returned to teaching but her small salary was not enough to pay rent on his building.

During the second week of August, Gilmore received a letter from the R. and C. Company. He stared at it, believing the envelope held a letter threatening to sue if he persisted in spreading Mila's story. When Gilmore opened it, however, he found a check for $60,000. He ran to the hotel to find Mila.

"Well, that settles it," she said after listening carefully to Gilmore's strained speech. "I am so happy I came to see you, Gilmore. What a fine lawyer you are." She sipped her tea. "And that money is yours to keep."

"Thirty percent," Gilmore said.

"It's the principle of the thing," Mila said. "I don't need another penny. I got too much money anyways."

Gilmore walked toward her, intending to protest. "My dear," said Mila, "now that this is over I'm going back to New York. I own four clothing factories there, and I need to make sure my son-in-law isn't messing up business."

Gilmore looked at the papers scattered around her room. She straightened the pile on her nightstand. "My dress designs. Anyway, all this quiet keeps me awake at night."

She stood on her toes and kissed his cheek. "You go on home now." Seeing that he was hesitant to go, she said, "Dear, I'm worth a hundred times that check in your hand." Then she went to the bed and lay down, her back to Gilmore.

When Gilmore returned to his office he found three white men waiting for him. One sat in Gilmore's chair and the other two leaned on his desk.

"Name's Richard Olsen," the heavy-set, balding man said, extending his hand. "These are my partners, Ted Roosen and Roger Small. I own the Olsen Sawmills. Mila White told us about you. We got a problem and wanna hire you. Know anything about corporate law?"

Gilmore raised his eyebrows and said quite clearly, "It's my specialty."

The Death of Matthias Lamb

McAlester, Indian Territory. 1895.

Sheriff Arie McKenney, oldest son of Dicey and Lighthorseman Teague McKenney, kneeled behind a rain barrel outside the house where Wirt Crow hid. Arie and his three partners had chased the Crows for two years, ever since they killed the Bail family over in Wilburton. Arie heard that Mac and Parson Crow were shot a few days before in Hartshorne by a farmer, but until he saw the bodies Arie thought it best to assume they were alive.

Some people, not just the old-timers, said the Crows were the same men who killed Lewis Wilson and thirty others back in Mississippi. Others said no, they were the grandchildren. Another rumor said that the older Crows were killed during the Civil War by Curly Johanson, a Swedish woman who shot all five men after they skinned her cat. Not everyone believed it but it made for good conversation.

"Come on out, Wirt," yelled Arie.

"Go ta hell."

"Wirt, there's three other people out here in the trees. You can't get anywheres."

"You gonna shoot?"

"No, you gotta go ta trial."

Silence.

"Wirt?"

"Okay, I'm comin' out. No shootin'."

Wirt threw out a pistol, then walked onto the porch. Lighthorseman Impson Wilks came out from behind a large pecan tree with his rifle barrel pointed downwards.

Wirt pulled another pistol from his belt and shot twice—one bullet hit Arie's stallion, Archie, in the forehead. The other hit Imp in the chest. Four shots from Wing Homer and Pete Ervin knocked Wirt backwards into the house.

"Son of a bitch," said Arie. He ran to Imp. His eyes were open, staring. Next he looked at his still horse. Arie was sorrier for Archie than he was for Imp. He'd raised Archie from a foal after his mama died and he doted on the big black mustang. Arie's eyes began to water.

"Who's gonna tell Ludie 'bout Imp?" asked Wing.

"I'll do it," said Arie, walking toward the house. "Let's go see about Wirt."

Wirt had blood in his throat and was holding his belly.

"Now what?" asked Wing.

"He ain't gonna make it," said Arie. He thought that Wirt's owl face was ugly.

"Got yur horse. He's dead, too. Like yur friend." Wirt laughed. "I cain't die."

Arie, Pete, and Wing looked down at the bleeding man. They had not decided if they believed him.

"Hellfire, look at that." Pete pointed to Archie.

Arie turned to see his horse standing, a hole the size of a silver dollar in his forehead. He ran over and grabbed the reins. Arie saw bone pieces sticking out from the edges through the skin. Archie's eyes were alert and he was breathing normally.

"Well, I never saw nothin' like that," shouted Wing.

"God Almighty, Archie," said Arie. He took his bandanna from his pocket but couldn't figure a way to wrap it on his horse. So he tied the reins to a tree and went back to the porch.

Wirt looked at where Archie stood. "He's supposed ta be dead," he said evenly. "Has to be."

"Happy to disappoint you." Arie jerked Wirt to his feet. *Light as a feather*, he thought.

Three days later Wirt Crow sat in his McAlester prison cell eating fried chicken. The doctor could not explain his recovery, but many residents of

McAlester, both Indian and non-Indian, believed that his wounds were healed because he was a witch.

"Told ya," Wirt said when he saw Arie through the cell bars.

"You ain't a witch."

Wirt slowly chewed a biscuit and looked at Arie without blinking. "Cain't beat us."

Arie turned and walked out.

"You cain't beat us, Arie boy. We're everywheres," Wirt yelled after him.

On the day that Wirt was to be tried, another member of his gang was caught. Dixon Crow, brother of Wirt's, raped and killed a young girl who'd gone to use the outhouse during a church service in McAlester. Two women saw him attack the girl from the Sunday school window. One, the young widow Callie Russer, ran outside with the fireplace poker to stop him and got shot in the arm for her trouble. Then Dixon shot the girl in the face, took her hair and ears, then rode off. His horse broke a leg a mile from town and he was caught by a group of ex-Lighthorsemen who'd been in town for Wirt's trial.

On that day, Corn Wilson brought his aunt Billie Watchman to visit Matt, and Billie happened to know the woman who was shot. She stood by Russer's bed holding her good hand while the lady doctor tried to set the shattered bone without starting the blood flowing again. She used a hot brand from the livery across the street to get it to quit spurting from the brachial artery, but it didn't want to stop running.

After two hours of struggling, Dr. Moira Banks wrapped the arm tightly, gave Russer morphine because the laudanum didn't ease the pain, then let the lady rest.

"It's a mess," said Banks. The short, strong woman wiped her bloodied hands with a damp cloth. "Can't say for sure if it'll heal right since the bullet broke the bone in several places. I need to rest a minute."

"I'll watch her," said Billie. "Go and clean up. Corn," she looked to her nephew who had been watching the surgery with interest, "go on over and see your cousin."

Corn stood but didn't leave. He had never seen the widow Callie Russer before and found that even though she had been screaming, was covered with blood, and most likely would not have use of her arm again, he wanted to stay and tend to her.

"Corn! Go on, boy," Billie urged him. "I'll introduce you when she feels like it."

Billie had patience and much experience in dealing with the sick and dying and she knew the doctor did all she could. Banks was a good physician who knew more about medicine than anyone she'd met. The year before, she fixed Matt's arm that had been crippled in the war by removing the piece of metal that kept his elbow from straightening. Matt was leery about allowing a woman doctor to work on him, but his wife, Bette, insisted.

Matt tried for months to get his strength back. First he lifted a bridle or horseshoe a half-dozen times twice a day for three days. Then he curled a rifle, books, and filled canteens and whiskey bottles. Soon he could lift a bag of flour and now, a year later, Matt had almost full use of the arm he once thought was useless. He was a complete man again and was sorry he doubted the good doctor Moira Banks.

He never questioned his judgment of criminals, however. A few men had suggested that the Crows be taken over to Fort Smith in Arkansas so the "hanging judge" Parker could hear the case. Murderers and thieves, they argued, didn't stand a chance in Parker's court.

"And what do you think they'll get in mine?" Matt asked his sheriffs and lawyers.

It was decided among the lawyers that with two of the Crows in custody, they should be tried together and in Lamb's courtroom. Two days after catching Dixon Crow, the trial was held and the jury deliberated. Matt was sure of the verdict.

"All right. Order," said Judge Matthias Lamb, son of Gilmore and Alli and cousin to Arie McKenney and Corn Wilson. Half the courtroom was filled with people related to victims of the defendants and they would not keep quiet. Outside vendors sold lemonade and cake and some men started a horse race. A group of church people had been singing hymns all morning. A group led by the father of the murdered girl had a noose and horse ready to hang Dixon, if only they could get to him.

Billie sat with the wounded Callie. She had become delirious and yelled for her dead mother. Her cousins in Arkansas had been wired that Callie's situation was bad and they answered that they were on their way.

"Order, I say." Matt was a good judge, intolerant of transgressors, but known for his fairness. Whites called him "that Indian judge," but they liked him. Matt was a fixture in McAlester. He always wore a long black coat and high-heeled boots, and fixed his hair just right, long to his shoulders and short in the front. Matt was the only one in his family who could grow a mustache and he wore it thick over his top lip. His wife Bette thought it amazing that he could eat without getting food on it.

"Has the jury reached a verdict?" Matt asked.

"Yes, your honor." Scat Watson, the foreman, had to speak loudly. Then everything was quiet. "Guilty."

The crowd roared. After Matt ordered the two smiling men to hang they were taken to jail through the back door. He made certain enough guards escorted Wirt and Dixon Crow so they would live to die later.

That evening Matthias ate dinner with Corn and friends at the hotel. They drank whiskey, even though liquor wasn't allowed in town. Matt being the judge, nobody told him he couldn't have it. Every few minutes someone passed by the table and slapped him on the back.

"Savage as meat axes, both of 'em," said Ross Wyly, the postmaster.

"Should make them suffer," said Ruger McIntosh, a half-blood Muscogee from Okmulgee who moved to McAlester to build wagons. "Never heard of such things. Oughta string them up by their peeters and see how they like it."

"No, pull out their nose hairs and toenails first. Little things like that hurt," said Wyly after a loud belch.

"Most heathen bunch of clients I ever had. Wouldn't even talk to me. How could I defend no-good sumbitches like them?" asked Don Smith, the defense attorney. "In the old days, if a Choctaw killed someone, everyone expected him to come in and take his punishment, like Silon Lewis did."

"Didn't hear," said Wyly.

"Happened after the election of 1892 when the Progressive and the National Parties ran against each other," Smith said, throwing another handful of peanuts into his mouth. "Lewis was a National and he and some others killed a few Progressives because the Progressives wanted statehood and to allot the tribal land. Couldn't kill everyone they wanted to so they surrendered. Lewis got caught and was released 'cause they knew he'd come back for his execution in November. Sure enough, he made his will and came in. Lewis wasn't no scoundrel. He used to be sheriff of Gaines County east of here."

"I saw that execution," said Matt in his deep, slow voice. "Lewis sat on a blanket and opened his shirt so the sheriff could draw a white circle on his chest. The bullet went clear through him and he didn't die after he laid there and bled for an hour. Finally the sheriff put a handkerchief over his mouth and suffocated him. Some of the Choctaws there said that was murder."

"Murder? How could an execution be murder?" asked McIntosh. "He was a killer and got executed."

"Not the point," Matt said slowly. "Lewis was supposed to die by a bullet. It liked to make me sick."

Wyly nodded his head. "A man comes in all honorable-like and he needs a quick death, not suffering."

"Are you upset, Don?" laughed fat William Perky, the prosecutor. "Did you want them Crows to come riding in and say they done it so it'd look honorable? You can't defend people like that. I won, but anyone in my position would have." The two attorneys often discussed cases afterwards and were usually competitive, but this was different. "Hey, Matt, can we burn down the jail with them in it? An accident, you know."

"I got an office in there, smart-ass." Matt reached out with his healed arm for a bottle. It was a gift that he could pour a drink with both hands now, he thought. "Wish we could do all of that, boys. But wouldn't be right. They gotta swing."

"Those men," Corn said as he looked at each man in turn, "ain't men. You can hang 'em all day till their heads pull off, but they'll be back." He paused and nobody said a word. "They always come back."

Loud voices from the restaurant floated between the six men. They tried to consider if Corn was right, but were too drunk to think clearly. They offered further ideas for torture and it was decided that hanging was best, but the Crows should slide slowly off the platform, not drop fast and feel only a second of pain.

After the men ate a dinner of pot roast and carrots and shared three full bottles of strong whiskey, Matt said he needed to go home. He shook hands with Corn then went to the livery.

Matt lifted his saddle onto his brown mare Willow, but asked McIntosh to cinch it because he was too drunk and saw more than one strap. He got on and swayed in the saddle. "Tomorrow," he said to McIntosh, the last decent man he would ever see.

Matt lived less than a mile from town. He felt sick and was irritated with himself for drinking so much. He'd feel very bad in the morning. With his house in sight, he leaned over to vomit and then felt better.

As he drank water from his canteen and wiped the beads from his mustache, he realized how quiet it was. If Matt had not been drinking, he would have noticed the silence earlier. Then he heard an owl hoot. He was wary of owls, but he was also drunk and did not see the men waiting quietly behind a thick oak grove. The owl hooted again above Matt's head. As he looked up to find the owl, he saw three bright stars streak across the sky.

"Well, I'll be damned," he said aloud.

Two shots knocked him from Willow. A dozen more hit him while he lay on the ground. Then, after he could feel no pain, two men emerged from the shadows into the moonlight, pulled their long knives, and hacked Matthias apart. Willow bolted, turned once to look at her master, then ran home.

The boy fishing in the creek for channel cats heard the commotion and looked through the bushes. Because of the moonlight he saw the killers. Bo Casey sat still until the men left, then he sprinted home to his family, who heard the story in between hiccups. He managed to say that the men looked like *opas*. Like a family of owls.

At four in the morning Arie answered the loud knocking at his door. It was his cousin Tish Walkingstick, her nightgown tucked into a pair of her husband Biff's pants. Her long, dark brown hair swirled around her face. "It's cousin Matt. He's dead," she said steadily. "Murdered. Jolene Casey came over just now," she continued. "Bo saw it happen. It was the Crows."

"Crows? It can't be. Jeke was spotted up in Tahlequah just two days ago and Parson and Mac are dead."

Tish took a step toward him, challenging. "How do you know, Arie? You know how they are. They're like the wind. You can't see them but they're all around."

She wasn't panicked. Arie admired that of her. He had a crush on his cousin, just like every other man did. She was thirty-eight, but looked twenty. Tish was uncommonly pretty, and smart. She was educated, raised two happy, healthy children, and loved target shooting. Arie never did understand why she married a soft Cherokee farmer like that uneducated Biff, unless it was because he was handsome, intelligent, and endlessly patient with her.

"All right. I'll see to it. You go on home."

Not a chance, thought Tish as she watched her cousin pull on his boots.

The three sets of tracks were easy to follow, which worried Arie. *Are Mac and Parson alive?* He followed them to the east side of Krebs, to one of the coal mines. As he rounded a corner, he stopped and watched one of the Crows ride off toward the south. The other two Crows were setting up camp inside the mine entrance.

A rifle shot sounded behind him and a Crow at the tunnel fell. Before Arie turned to see who killed him, he leveled his rifle at the other Crow and pulled the trigger. Arie then looked around and saw Tish, who held one of his rifles and wore his coat. Of course. He had left her at his house with his guns. He was mad that she followed but also somewhat relieved. She was a better shot than him and tenacious as hell.

Under cover from his cousin, Arie went to the cave and found Jeke Crow shot in the shoulder. The other man lay dead. They looked alike except the dead man's skin was covered with bloody sores. Arie heard that Mac had bad skin.

Jeke smiled big, showing brown teeth. "Can't kill me. Not really."

"Hush."

Jeke stopped smiling and opened his eyes wide. "There's more of us now."

Arie and Tish looked around quickly. There had been three pairs of tracks. Where was the other Crow?

Despite Jeke's broken shoulder, Arie tied the Crow's hands behind him and shoved him outside. The horses were tied in the partial shade of a blackjack oak. Scalps and ears hung from their manes and tails. Some were fresh and some looked very old. Arie wondered if any were Survella and Skarloey's. He put Jeke out in front on his horse and followed him while Tish held the reins of the horse carrying the body of Mac Crow.

For six miles nobody said a word. The riders heard water sloshing in the horses' stomachs. Tish noticed how quiet it was; no birds sang and no locusts hummed around them, but she heard them in the distance. It was as if everything stopped and watched Jeke Crow pass by, then resumed their chatter after he was safely gone.

Tish stared at the back of Crow's misshapen head. She wondered where men like the Crows came from. Did God make them knowing they'd behave poorly, or did He not know how they'd turn out? Did He have no control over them? Mama Billie always said that we can't blame God for the bad things that happen. He just has too many things going on, can't tend to all His creatures at once, and some of the bad ones take advantage of His inattention.

Billie didn't have an explanation as to why God created evil ones in the first place. This question troubled Tish because she figured God wouldn't have to worry about His beloved people if He made everyone good.

Considering what Billie had told her, that God can't tend to all His flock, she made a decision. If she didn't do something, who's to say this man won't escape and start killing again? Two miles from town, Tish exhaled sharply through her nose, dropped her reins, and rode up behind her cousin, who was behind Crow. She hit Arie in the back of the head with her rifle butt and caught his arm so he wouldn't hit the ground hard. Jeke Crow swiveled his odd head to look.

"Turn back around," said Tish.

"Can't kill us, girlie." Jeke smiled and showed brown teeth as he looked her up and down. Tish thought he probably ate nasty things. "Wirt and Dixon got away from jail. We'll always be here."

"You won't." Then she shot him twice in the back. He lurched forward over his horse's neck then dropped to the dirt. Tish noticed how softly and slowly he fell, like one of Billie's sketch papers. Then she dismounted and walked quickly to him while putting two more shells into the chamber. His scarred white horse stood still, breathing hard. *He'd be pretty if you hadn't have beaten him*, she thought. She took a deep breath and wiped away her tears.

"Wirt and Dixon got out? How'd you know that?" she asked the dead man with copper eyes and brown teeth.

After dinner Arie sat on his porch with a cool rag on his neck. He told his wife Opal that he killed Jeke Crow, who was trying to escape, then he fell and hit a rock.

Dixon and Wirt had indeed escaped from prison, but nobody knew how. The deputies guarding the jailhouse said they didn't see anyone leave. *They flew out*, reasoned Arie. After all, a pile of clothes was left behind.

"You need to rest," said Opal.

Arie felt his head. It hurt but he gave Tish credit for doing the right thing. "I'll be in directly. Gonna check on the horses."

Archie looked fit except for the hole in his head. Arie fished out the bullet, covered the hole with a mesh cloth to keep bugs out, and hoped for the best. Jeke's bay had so many ears and hairs knotted into her mane that Arie shaved it off. Tish took Mac's gelding and guns for herself and the bay for her husband.

The night was all warm air. Arie sat in his porch rocker and held the English-made pistol that had belonged to Matt. "Matthias, how could this happen to you?" he asked quietly.

Arie watched the stars that dotted the clear sky for an hour and none moved. He reached for one of the bottles of whiskey Bette had given him from Matt's large cache, swallowed two large, burning mouthfuls, and looked up again. The sky was still. Then he went inside to bed.

As soon as the door shut, five stars ran across the horizon, and none fell.

Some of the townspeople, interestingly mostly white, had objected to burying the killers, arguing that they should be burned and their ashes disposed of by a medicine man. Most only knew him by reputation, but they insisted that Ruel Battiest, brother of Ellis Toshaway Battiest, oversee the cremation. They were surprised when he came riding into town one morning, just as their two spokesmen were about to ride to his place and ask him to perform the ceremony.

"Got 'em wrapped in burlap over at the jail," said LaVelle Lewis, the blacksmith.

"Doesn't matter," said the slow-talking Ruel as he walked to the office where his great-nephew used to work.

Eager to please, LaVelle added, "Without their boots."

Ruel laughed. "Thanks for telling me." *You could strip them naked, put lipstick on them, or cover them with horseshit. It doesn't matter. I'm just making you people feel better,* he thought. Then he walked faster, leaving LaVelle to lose his breath chasing him.

The Crows were burned in a large pyre, and their ashes raked into a large bucket. The contents were dumped into one deep hole in the small cemetery outside of town reserved for executed criminals. Battiest stood by the grave a long time, singing and burning specific plants, a combination he could only hope would contain the Crows.

After the ceremony, Ruel and his wife Merly moved to Tuskahoma, forty miles away. Because the medicine man left so quickly, the townspeople figured that he knew something they didn't and probably it was that Jeke and Mac's ashes would somehow rise from the hole in the ground and start killing again. They decided to cover the grave with heavy rocks to keep the witches from emerging, and when the group of determined men and women arrived the next day, they saw many tiny footprints in the soft dirt surrounding the grave.

"What were kids doing here?" LaVelle asked.

"Don't know," answered Roy Englehardt, "but they left a lot of feathers and leaves and leather bags all over it. Take 'em off. Might be witch things."

And as the years passed, more rocks were piled onto the grave until the mound was twelve feet high.

1907. Twelve years later.

It had not rained in three months, an excruciatingly long time. Cattle and crops shriveled and died. Dust blew like rain.

Around the twelve-foot-high pile of rocks under which the Crows' ashes were deeply buried, thistles grew in abundance. Poison ivy that apparently needed no water snaked its way around the base of the thistles but did not strangle the plants. No one came to the burial on a regular basis, save one.

Tish had seen the green life emerging around the rocks and began talking to people about witches and owls.

"We need to get Ruel Battiest back here," said LaVelle.

Many townspeople volunteered to find him. They left on the afternoon train and came back the next day, saying they found his strange house but that old man Battiest wasn't there. People began to worry. Stories about the Crows spread, and old-timers said that they were the cause of the dry spell and that everyone should get ready for trouble.

One afternoon at the Crows' grave, when the locusts were too weary to sing, a forty-pound rock that lay under half a ton of other rocks shifted, like a sleeper trying to find a more comfortable position. A minute later, the rock moved slightly in the other direction. Then it began rocking back and forth. Like a sleeper wanting to wake up.

"So, are you coming in anytime soon?" Biff yelled to Tish. His wife had been in the corral all afternoon training one of Archie's colts. She had him by a long tether, encouraging him to calm down and learn to pay attention to her while he alternately trotted and bucked in a circle. The horse was getting hot and bored and frustrated and she knew she'd better stop for the day.

"Almost done."

Archie had lived another twelve years with the hole in his head. Arie had been afraid to ride him and put him to pasture where he sired twenty or so foals. Tish kept four of the mares to breed and this was the best colt she'd had in years.

She dipped her scarf into the almost-empty rain barrel and wiped her face. Biff thought she was as beautiful and elegant as the day he met her, only she looked tired. She always wore a hat and had few wrinkles from the sun, although she was thin, which caused fine lines all over her face. "I'm going into town."

"Tish," said Biff, walking toward her, arms outstretched. "Honey, you can't keep going to that grave. They're dead." He held her close, trying to convince her to stay home, knowing that he couldn't. She rode to the grave almost every afternoon.

Tish hugged him back. "Something's happening. I know it." Then she let him go and stepped away. "I'll be back to make dinner."

Biff stood with his hands in his pockets as he watched his wife ride off to see the grave of dead, evil men.

"Who are you?" Tish asked the silent mound of dirt and rocks.

A mourning dove cooed in the shade of the oaks behind her, echoing her question.

"Who are you?" she asked again, louder this time. "I know you hear me."

Tish waited for an answer while her horse stood behind her. The old horse once belonged to Mac Crow. Considering who the animal once carried, Tish had almost killed him, but after spending time with the gelding she found the horse to be a good one. He thrived in the peaceful setting of her farm and her gentle hand.

Tish stepped closer to the rockpile. "Who are you?" she whispered loudly. A warm breeze blew Tish's dark hair across her beautiful face. Then a hotter, fouler air blew directly on her neck. The horse whinnied and rolled his eyes. Tish turned and saw no one, but she knew they were there.

McAlester.

That same week, Dicey McKenney decided to go back to Mississippi to visit her sister Ursa, who was suffering from the same painful breast ailment that killed their mother and two sisters. Teague took his wife to the McAlester train depot and kissed her good-bye for the summer.

"'Member to do something with that rooster, Teague. He's gonna hurt my hens even more. The two grays got bad cuts and you need to clean 'em." Dicey was concerned about the big red-and-green rooster that kept raping her hens. He'd bite their necks and hold them down so hard with his sharp talons that he'd rip open their skin.

"Lute said he'd take him," he nodded to their friend who stood by the depot waiting for Dicey to leave so he and Teague could go to Tish's birthday party, then fishing. "Don't worry about it. I love you. Got your pills?"

"Everything I need." Then she entered the train and found a good window seat. She took off the bonnet that Billie had given her and waved to Teague.

"Ready?" Teague asked his friend. "I'm ready to catch some big ones."

The depot was empty and nobody was on the platform when the train started to pull away. Teague walked down to the adjoining track to wave good-bye while Lute got the wagon. Movement on the platform caught his eye and when he looked to the south end of the depot, he saw Jackson Crow standing in the shade, smiling. Teague looked at him and wondered how he got there.

He looks so young, thought Teague. *How can it be so many years and he hasn't changed any?*

"Teague!" he heard Lute yelling at him. He'd answer him in a minute.

Why is he here? How come he's smiling at me? Teague stood on the track, unmoving and transfixed by the owl-man, who just leaned against the brick building and grinned.

"Teague!" Lute's voice was louder. So was the rumbling on the track.

An owl hooted directly overhead and Teague glanced up to see it hovering, like a kite.

This means something bad's going to happen. Wait, isn't Jackson supposed to be de—, and his thought was interrupted by the train that hit him.

"What's this, a present?" Tish asked Lute when he drove the wagon into her yard. "Where's Teague?" It was her birthday party and she had seen Lute driving down her road. There were two crates in the back and she figured Teague had something in store for her.

When Biff looked across the yard to his wife and Lute, he saw Lute telling her something with large arm motions. Tish shook her head, like she was saying "no," then she fell to her knees and put her hands over her face.

Red Oak.

Every plant was dry and the garden was struggling. Even the creek water was sparse and muddy. Clouds darkened the sky and no rain fell. Thin lightning bolts started fires for miles around Billie's house. Smoke from the burning grass was thick and Billie had to tie a wet cloth around her face. Deer ran through the yard trying to escape the heat.

Incredibly, rain fell just as the fire reached the rock field behind Billie's home. Farms around her burned, but it did not touch her fence. "God is either trying to make up to me, or He has control of the situation and knows what He's doing," Billie said to Jincy, who was visiting. Survella's husband never remarried and he came to visit Billie at least three times a week.

They worried about the fire and did not think to check on Ollie and Watson until their four horses appeared at Billie's barn, wild-eyed and lathered. "Oh, no," Billie said. Then she ran to the corral and caught her stallion, Sitting Bull. She pulled him to the fence so she could climb on, and off she ran without a saddle.

"Billie, wait," yelled Jincy. "Let me come, too." Billie was eighty-three years old, and she had just ridden away on a spirited horse without a saddle. Jincy had to settle for riding the old, half-blind mustang Biswack, the only animal he could catch.

Jincy and Biswack found Billie standing over the smoldering remains of Ollie and Watson. They were lying together down the hill from their corral, which was as far as they could go in outrunning the fire. Billie cried on Jincy's shoulder.

That night, after burying them in the cemetery, Jincy tapped Billie's arm and pointed to the sky. Together, they saw stars running back and forth, like they were happy with what happened. Jincy took his pouch from under his shirt and said to Billie, "Remember Ruel. Ollie and Watson may be dead, but they are fine." Billie barely nodded.

He watched Billie all night while she sat by the grave of her daughter and son-in-law. The next day, a sad but wise Billie prepared breakfast, dinner, and supper for the dozens of people who came to visit her.

Wilburton.

The case that Gilmore Lamb won for Olsen Sawmills brought him and Alli twice as much money as the White case. Gilmore's success drove out the other lawyers in town and he took on four partners—all Indian lawyers—to handle the load. By the time Gilmore retired, his children were grown and married and split the $20,000 their parents had earmarked for their education.

Their son Ziah built his home next to Gilmore's allotment. He made his living selling peaches and pumpkins and occasionally filed his friends' income taxes. Their daughter, Reby, earned her degree in nursing, bought some bulls, and married a wealthy cattleman, Curtis Enders, from Kentucky. Gilmore and Alli worked in their half-acre garden in the mornings, and because Gilmore wanted his grandchildren and great-grandchildren to know the tribal stories his parents had told him, he wrote stories in both Choctaw and English in the afternoons.

After Alli died at age seventy-three, Gilmore filled his days by writing a novel about their life together. On the last page he wrote: "My darling Alli opened my eyes and my ears. She was my grace and my happiness. I have had a good life."

On the morning that Gilmore turned eighty-seven, the day his cousin-brother Teague was killed and Ollie and Watson burned, he walked to the porch rocker. He sat, leaned back, and sighed. As he watched the blue jays splash in their birdbath, he heard something for the first time since he was five years old.

For sure, Gilmore thought, *owl hooting. The Crows.*

Gilmore sat still as the birds glided past; all five turned their heads to look at him with great yellow eyes.

The deaf lawyer only smiled. "You can't hurt me," he signed. "I'm going only because I want to."

An hour later, his nine-year-old great-grandson Scott found Gilmore in his porch chair, his eyes closed. Gilmore had a smile on his face and a rabbit stick in his hand. The child took the stick, gently kissed his great-grandfather's cold hand, and then ran back into the house.

My Life

BILLIE

1926.

The graveyard is perimeter-fenced with three horizontal rows of barbed wire. The tombstones are set in a low area about fifty by fifty feet and it's always quiet. Sunlight filters through the branches of two elm trees and the twisted vines. Some poison ivy tangles itself in the fence and Tom pulls the creepers away from the headstones every month in the summer. Without maintenance, the yard will become covered by the green life that is determined to prove that the living dominate the dead.

Half the graves are marked by two-foot headstones and the other half by flat markers. The stone nearest the gate is old. The chiseled inscription has faded, but I can still read it:

ROYAL LAMB 1788–1836
BELOVED HUSBAND AND FATHER

ADELE LAMB 1801–1835
BELOVED WIFE AND MOTHER

Adele is not here.

To the south of Royal and Adele's markers are my parents, Danny and William. There's a marker for James, who is buried next to his aunt in a creek bank between here and Mississippi. All the names are here: Survella, Teague, Romy, Gilmore, Matthias, Skarloey, my husbands and children.

In the west corner is a space for me. I often wonder if, after I'm in the ground, I will see the living from a distant place.

I'd heard once that time heals all wounds. Maybe not completely. I think that time allows us to rearrange our thoughts so we can understand our situation. All the ones who meant the most to me are dead, but they are not gone forever. I just haven't seen them in a while, and I will see them again.

Even if they aren't here, I'm still my family. Then and now, everything I saw them do and heard them say makes me who I am. The ones buried in the cemetery still form my words. Ellis was right. I've traveled a lot of roads, but never alone. My relations are with me. Even the ones I didn't agree with, like Papa and Beula, are in my heart. There's nothing I can do about it. Even though we were different, we often traveled the same roads.

It's not easy being an Indian. It seems that as a half-blood I live around the edges of being Choctaw, like I can't quite get in. Just when I almost understand what the old people said to me, I lose the meaning. What I learned runs in my blood, except the thoughts go so fast I can't see them clearly. But they are inside me.

All my life, people who weren't Choctaws or who had white blood have told me that the old ways aren't worth knowing. After living for over a hundred years in both worlds and seeing how others try to, I'm sure that the traditions are not worthless. There's good and bad about both ways of living.

Knowing our language and learning the stories make me who I am. But at the same time I couldn't have managed without white clothes, books, and tools. If my family spoke only Choctaw we wouldn't have known about the world around us.

We didn't have control over a lot of things. My brothers and sisters couldn't help it that Mama married a white man, or that part of our blood was white. Some fulls looked at us like we were different from them. We were, but we couldn't change to please them. I couldn't have lived my life any other way. I'll be fine.

My Horse

RALPH

The home place, McAlester.

"You can have the horse you catch," Aunt Tish said.

"Catch? How?"

I was sixteen years old and had wanted one of my great-aunt's mustangs since I was nine. I loved to watch the herd run across Tish's creek-crossed allotment that nourished cottonwoods, oaks, and tall grasses hiding deer, antelope, turkeys, and coyotes. I imagined myself riding the lead horse, a dark brown mustang stallion with his mane in his face.

"How you catch one's up to you, Ralph," said my aunt. "They come when I have the bucket of sweet feed, but they're hard to rope."

Then she patted me on the back and said she was going to town. I walked to the garden fence and watched the horses graze.

The next day I followed the twenty horses. They ran from me morning till afternoon, surely wondering what I was doing. I was tired and hungry and came back to the house. But I did have a plan.

The next morning I chased the horses through a low spot in the creek that was bounded by a steep bank in hopes they'd slow down enough for me to rope one. All the horses ran through the bottleneck except one, a young brown mare with black spots on the left side of her rib cage. She tripped and fell in the mud at the edge of the creek. As she struggled to her feet I dropped the rope around her neck.

She stood and looked at me, then over her shoulder at the herd. With a panicked whinny she turned and ran through the creek, dragging me over the rocks. She finally stopped and faced me with wide eyes. Although she was scrawny, not exactly the horse I wanted to ride across the plains on, a bigger horse would have kept pulling me. "I'm not lettin' go," I said. I decided she would do.

I had to think of a name for my horse. Mosquito bites covered me by the time we got back to the barn so I named her Skeeter. I didn't know a thing about breaking a horse so for days I led her around by a rope with a blanket on her back. After a week I put Tish's old saddle on her, then slowly tightened the cinch.

A few days later I stepped into the saddle and after a few jumps and a run across the field Skeeter understood what I wanted. I rode her every day before and after school, down the roads, into town, across unfenced land. She ran with the other horses, but she came to me when I called her. My favorite picture is of me standing on Skeeter's back without my shirt, hands on hips. She wasn't moving, of course, but the way her front feet were placed made her look like she was. That's what I told everybody.

After my last year of high school my father died and his allotment outside of Tuskahoma became mine. When I entered the Marines in 1941, I moved Skeeter from Tish's land to ours. Tish sold her herd to an outfit that made me suspicious. I've always wondered what they did with those horses.

I leased my allotment to Orville Johnston, a cattleman who agreed to watch Skeeter. Six months after I left, Johnston wrote to say that Skeeter learned how to open the gate and to come get her. I told him to forget about renewing his lease unless he latched the gate better and took care of my horse. He agreed.

I returned home after the war and worked on Daddy's deteriorating house and found a job as a diesel mechanic for three years. I still rode Skeeter even though she was older and I was heavier. I married a girl named Ange, had two kids in four years, and under the relocation program moved my family to California in 1950. I had to leave Skeeter behind once again. She was sixteen and I called Johnston twice a month to check on her.

In June of 1954, we returned for Tish's funeral. She was ninety-four and never seemed to age except for those last weeks of her full life.

It had been four years since I had seen my horse. She was twenty years old and walked slowly. I let my son and daughter ride her but I was afraid my weight would hurt her back. For a week I walked around the home place with my children, fishing and watching for deer and turkeys. Skeeter followed me like a puppy.

Skeeter, my old horse, was a measure of my life. I was a boy when I captured and tamed her. Yet I watched her grow old at a distance and I felt guilt at not being with her. Tish had told me that the problem with pets is that we always outlive them.

Skeeter was older and so was I. The house I was born in looked smaller than I remembered. It creaked and groaned with each step across the floor. Wind found the open spaces to run through, bringing dirt and insects inside. The house was dying.

When we drove out the road back to California I saw Skeeter in the rearview mirror, standing at the fence, ears pricked. That was the last time I saw her.

That week Johnston called to say Skeeter was probably dead. At least he thought she was. He looked for five days and couldn't find her. I cried until I was sick.

We didn't like the noise and crowds of California, so a year later I moved my family back to Oklahoma. I had longed for the quiet of home and the activity of our tribe. We didn't live on the allotment as the house and barn were falling apart, and I let them go. We moved just a mile from the home place.

Johnston quit the cattle business and my allotment grew back to the way it looked before I was born. Now, seventy-five years after my father built his home, all that is left is rotting wood, with oaks and bushes growing up through the splintered beams. The fence lay where it fell, a rectangle of broken posts.

A few years later I received yet another parcel of land adjoining my land from my widowed, childless sister. Sitting on it is an old, solid house that once belonged to Ruel Battiest. Now I use the home place for hunting. I strung another set of barbed wire to keep out poachers, but sometimes they cut the fence and hunt my animals. Lots of Indians with allotments have the same problem.

Once while scouting on the home place, I stopped to rest and to eat juicy plums in the fruit orchard. It didn't take long to realize chiggers covered the thick green grass, so I sat on what appeared to be the leg bone of a deer.

The rest of the decayed and odorless carcass was still attached to the bone, held together by tough hide and tendons.

I moved the grass apart to look closer. The bones were bigger than a deer's. I turned the hide over and saw brown with black spots. My horse. I sat on the grass, knowing my ass would start to itch, but I cried for Skeeter anyway.

I buried the bones in the plum orchard. I thought of making a small cross but didn't know what good that would do so I did nothing except tell Skeeter good-bye.

Two weeks later I got a phone call from Johnston. He sounded a bit hesitant to tell me what he needed to.

"I never found your horse."

"I did. Under the plum trees."

"Well, I'd been over there a few times but didn't see nothin'. Hey, listen. I know I was just supposed to graze cattle, but I also ran a few horses over there."

"Yeah. And?"

"Two were stallions, and, well, your horse had a few colts. One every other year, actually. Do you want a couple? They look like Skeeter. One's pregnant."

I stood with the receiver to my ear, staring at the framed picture of me standing on Skeeter. It sat on the phone table next to the pictures of my children.

"I'll be there in five minutes," I said.

The Tamfuller Man

Red Oak, Oklahoma. 1922.

Corn and Callie Wilson sipped hot sugared coffee and rocked in twin chairs. From their covered porch they watched red fox squirrels run through the heavy pecan branches. In a month the squirrels would labor to fill their cheeks with hard-shelled nuts, but now they could play. Locusts hummed in the warm morning air, although they hum loudest in the hotter afternoons.

"What to do 'bout this, Cal?"

"This'll hurt him bad, Corn." Callie dabbed at her nose. She had been crying. Crying gave her headaches.

Corn held two papers, one a letter dated July 21, 1922. It was from their older child, Toshaway, who was about to graduate from Spaulding's Commercial College in Missouri. Corn read the parts that troubled him: "*Last week I was interviewed by a reporter from the Tulsa Times named Dan Draper. He came through here looking to write a story about Indians and the dean referred him to me. We discussed my course work and career goal to become a writer. You might see a copy before I do. Buy an extra for Billie.*"

The other paper was the August 2, 1922, edition of the *Tulsa Times*. "Listen to this again, Cal.: *'Me like school. Good for head,' said Toshaway Battiest, holding up a brawny fist to his copper-colored temple. 'Me think all Indians need book learnin'. White way the best way. Me try hard to be like whites.'*"

Corn let go of the paper. It fluttered to the porch floor. "Tosh doesn't talk like that. He's a smart boy. Who's Dan Draper? Mean thing to do."

"Maybe we oughta wait till he gets home next week." Callie watched scissortail flycatchers chase flying bugs over the garden. She knew that

Corn was proud that his corn, peas, potatoes, and climbing fruit were neatly planted in the same order of the garden his Aunt Billie started in 1836 after arriving in Indian Territory. The garden was easy to water because only a hundred feet away ran a creek that branched off the Fourche Maline.

Corn sipped his coffee. "Need to get some tamaters." He rose from his rocker to collect Better Beefsteaks to go with the eggs and biscuits Callie planned to make after she stopped crying.

Toshaway Wilson arrived in Red Oak a week later on the 6:04 Missouri-Kansas-Texas line. That evening he sat on one side of the kitchen table while his parents and sister, Isi, sat on the other. Tosh and Isi were one-eighth Choctaw but were called half-bloods nonetheless. Isi was light-skinned with brown hair. Her brother was dark and looked like the full-bloods.

Isi hated her color because she wished she was full-blood. Tosh, who was named after his great-great-grand-uncle Ellis Toshaway Battiest, did not want to become white, but he believed that to survive in the white world he had to act like whites, and secretly, he wished his skin was lighter. Tosh and Isi agreed on the importance of learning Choctaw traditions but argued over the need to learn about white people. Corn and Callie were frustrated because they wanted both children to be happy.

Tosh ate ham, sweet corn, fried okra, and wild green onions with scrambled duck eggs. Every Choctaw cooked wild onions. Callie pulled them from behind the barn and was careful not to touch the poison ivy.

Bits of corn caught in Tosh's teeth and his family saw yellow when he spoke. Tosh knew the corn was there but he was happy to get a plate of his father's garden and did not care. "I'm going to meet with the editor of the *Oklahoma City Sentinel* in a couple of weeks. He liked my essays and wants to hire me as sports editor. Pays good, too. I can travel and maybe buy a house."

"What about your allotment, son?" Corn was still resentful of the federal government's purported effort to make Indians "civilized" farmers. He could read, farm, and speak Choctaw and English, just like his parents before him. Didn't that make him civilized? The allotment of 160 acres given him twenty years ago only made him angry. When he and Callie passed on the children would inherit the entire allotment, but Corn had no intention of dying anytime soon.

"I want to lease it. I can do that, you know."

"Better be careful," said Isi. "Whites'll ruin it."

"Ott Anderson won't. He just has horses to graze, no cattle."

A team of mules pulled a wagon into the Wilsons' yard. "Ren's here." Corn watched through the screen door as his friend climbed down from his wagon. Ren limped ever since he had an argument with his wife and hid in a tree to drink a bottle of whiskey. He was too drunk to feel coyotes gnaw off his toes.

Corn set a strawberry pie on the table. The fruit grew next to the onions in the cemetery. "Good thing I made this." Ren ate a lot.

"Come in, Ren. *Chim a chuck ma?*" asked Corn.

"*Halito*. Brought catfish and *banaha* for Isi."

"Ooo, thanks." *Banaha*, made of cornmeal, potatoes, onions, and usually peas, but sometimes beans boiled in cornshucks, was Isi's favorite, especially since Ren's wife made it with peas.

"So you're back." Ren didn't look at Tosh when he said it. Ren knew that Tosh did not approve of Choctaws keeping their traditions without also attending school. Although Ren spoke English and used machinery and clothing made by whites, he never went to school and considered himself traditional.

"How you doing, Ren?" asked Tosh.

"Good."

Tosh then ignored him.

Callie had a mouth that drooped naturally at the corners but Tosh could tell something was bothering her. When Callie was upset she rubbed her sore arm that had been broken years ago by a shotgun blast. "What's wrong, Ma?" He speared the last four pieces of chopped okra onto his fork so they lined up like freight cars on a train track. He always ate okra that way.

Corn answered. "Son, we got that paper article last week."

"Beatin'! Where?"

Corn reached behind him to the shelves that displayed his collection of small animal skulls and pulled the folded paper out from under a fox's jaw.

Tosh pushed his plate to the center of the table. His grin faded as he read.

Corn took a tiny oak-wood bear from his pocket to whittle. Black bears were common in Mississippi. Corn's family had lived near Canton before the government moved them to Indian Territory in the march that killed thousands of Choctaws in the 1830s.

Tosh rubbed at his chin. "I don't understand. . . . I. . . ." He kept reading.

Warm wind blew through the screen door. It smelled damp. Late summer brought rains, some heavy. Everyone was quiet.

"'*Me eat tamfuller and deer. Kill deer with arrows.*' Tamfuller? I don't say 'tamfuller.' I only told him there were two ways to say it."

Tosh believed that those Choctaws lazy in their speech altered the word to sound like *tamfuller*. But Tosh was careful. He did not want to appear ignorant so he said it the old way.

"'*Kill deer*'?" Tosh fished but did not hunt. "Where did he get this? I never said any of this. I don't even eat *tanfula*."

Everyone at the table knew that Tosh was humiliated. He put the paper down. "Why did I bother to go to school? I wanted to become a writer. Now what good is reading and writing if it doesn't make me respectable like a white person?"

Isi laughed at him. "You're a sellout, brother. You try to be white and look what happens. You won't never be accepted by white people. Not in Oklahoma."

"Whites think we're stupid, Tosh," said Ren. He poured milk over his bowl of pie. "They make money off us. Buy our jewelry and baskets then turn around and sell 'em for more. They make money takin' our pictures and writin' stories like this one. What'd you expect? We need to find a way to make money off *them*."

"I'm going fishing with Kit early," said Tosh. "I better go to bed." Tears caused him to trip over his chair. He caught himself on the table then went to his room. Callie started to follow.

"Let him be, Cal. He's gotta learn sometime," said Isi, opening her bag of *banaha*.

Nine days later Tosh sat outside the office of Mr. Frank Tait, owner and publisher of the small *Oklahoma City Sentinel*. His four-hour train ride from Red Oak had been difficult. It was hot and Tosh felt sick and stupid, even though he wasn't stupid. He wondered ever since reading "Choctaw Indian Glad to Be Educated" if Tait had read it. What if others had?

Tosh thought back to when he was eleven at the Padgham Mission School where a teacher called him an ignorant heathen for mispronouncing *Gomorrah* while reading the Bible out loud. He promised himself that nobody would have cause to call him ignorant again. Now here he was, feeling ignorant, but he had done nothing to cause it. He considered changing his name.

Tait opened his office door. "Mr. Wilson! Come in." He was shorter than Tosh, about five foot six, with black hair, brown eyes, and light skin. His thick hair was cut short and Tosh could see a leather cord around his neck. What it held was hidden under his shirt.

Tosh looked around the office. Books lined three walls, which was nothing unusual for a writer, but he was most impressed by the stacks of papers, folders, and journals that were piled on top of the books, crammed into every available space on the shelves and floor, and stacked four feet high onto three of the four chairs in the room. Tait's desk was hopelessly cluttered, leaving room only for his typewriter. Notes and letters lay atop a pile of journals. Some of the bottom papers were dry and yellowed with age.

"Glad to see you, son. How was the trip?"

"Fine, sir," he lied as he shook Tait's hand.

"Well, good, good. Have a seat. I realized that I hired the wrong man as managing editor a couple of weeks ago. Don't care for him. I've read your stories about Oklahoma life and the old Indians and I relate to the way you think. Don't have a lotta use for Indian stories, but you can write about anything, right? I'm offering the position to you. All your teachers gave you the highest recommendation. Don't worry about making mistakes at first. You'll learn the job soon enough."

Tosh stared at him. "Managing editor?"

Tait nodded. "We're a small outfit. You'll have control over most of the stories and you'll give assignments to the cubs. Pays more than sports editor. What say?"

Dumbfounded, Tosh hesitated. "Well, yes sir. Yes sir."

"Here's the son of a bitch now. Get in here, Draper, you idiot."

Tosh turned to see Dan Draper, the man who had interviewed him. The two looked at each other, not speaking.

"Draper, I fail to appreciate your writing. This isn't a political paper. You can't call Indians savages. I don't like it; they don't like it. My mama's mama was Muscogee, that's Creek to you ignorants, and Grandpap was an interpreter in Georgia. Uncle Charlie's on the school board over in Okmulgee. One of Mama's friends was Choctaw and when I was a kid I ate over at her place."

Tait winked at Tosh. "See Joan and she'll give you two weeks' pay. You're through here."

"But, now wait a minute," he stammered.

"Outta here, Draper."

Dan Draper looked at Tosh again, opened his mouth, said nothing, then walked out and closed the door behind him.

Frank Tait walked over to the stunned Toshaway and slapped him on the back.

"Okay, let's get to work. We got stories to write."

Kowi Annukasha: The Little People

Tuskahoma, Oklahoma. 1996.

Three days after school was out for summer, Richard and Victoria Hallmark arrived at the home of Ange and Ralph Glenn, their father's distant cousins. Richard looked forward to nine weeks of scouting for deer on Ralph's allotment and Victoria was eager to visit with Cheri Meers, who lived next door.

Usually their parents stayed to visit, but this year Sam and Irene decided that their children were old enough to manage without them, so they dropped off Richard and Victoria and went fishing in Colorado.

Ange and Ralph still worked at the tribal complex, Ange as the assistant to the tribal registrar and Ralph as an accountant. Each Tuesday they ate beans and cornbread with friends while they played bridge and discussed political issues, such as the chief's sexual harassment hearings. Wednesdays they bingoed. On Sundays after church Ange made cakes for supper at the tribal center while Ralph fished with members of the tribal council.

After lunch Richard and Victoria unpacked their suitcases and went back to the kitchen for dessert. Ange was washing dishes. "Ricky, dear, are you going out to scout?"

Richard loved his old auntie and resisted a smart-ass remark. Of course he was going to scout. That's why he came. "Yeah. After I eat this." He spread butter thick as frosting on his spice cake.

"The Little People have been out lately. Close to Ralph's place. Shirley's boy Phil saw their lights."

Ange's Certificate of Degree of Indian Blood identified her as quarter-blood, but she was pale-skinned, red-haired, and freckled. She was deeply religious, attending the First United Methodist Church every Sunday, and clipped religious phrases of profound meaning from newspapers and magazines to send to relatives. Nobody minded because she wasn't pushy about Christianity, but because she also was a staunch believer in Choctaw stories, especially the religious ones, they were a bit confused by her. She didn't appear to be torn between cultures.

"Little People? Who're they?" asked Victoria.

"Well," Ange began in her quiet voice, "the *Kowi Annukasha*, or Little People, live in the woods where most people don't go. They're about two or three feet tall. If they find a Choctaw boy alone in the woods, the watcher—his name is Kwanokasha—takes him to the Little People's cave.

"Then the boy is offered three items: a knife, some poisonous herbs, and some herbs that cure. If he takes the knife, he grows to be an evil man. If he takes the bad herbs, he won't become a medicine man—a doctor—but if he takes the healing herbs he will. Boys who take the good plants are taught to cure with them.

"At night in the woods you might see a light through the trees. It's a doctor and a Little Person carrying a lantern, looking for plants. Sometimes Little People cause mischief at night, like keeping folks awake with strange noises."

Victoria looked out the window. "Little People are here?"

"The old-timers say the Little People stayed behind on Choctaws' homeland in Mississippi. They didn't come west on our Trail of Tears."

Victoria considered. "If they're not here, then how do doctors know what to do?"

"I don't know. Learn from the older medicine people maybe," answered Ange. "We sure need more medicine people," she added. "There's always a need."

Richard laughed. "Only whitetail deer and turkeys live in the woods and I'm going to scout right now."

"*Shampes*, too," Victoria said seriously. "Be careful."

Richard had heard about *shampes* all his life. They were supposed to be ugly giants that live in the woods and come out only at night. They smell terrible and make a whistle sound. When Richard was younger he and his father found tracks on Ralph's land, near the strange old house that overlooks the pond. The tracks were huge, bigger than bear tracks.

That night Richard dreamed of an ugly bear with an ogre's face. It paced back and forth on the porch while Richard slept. The ugly bear stood on his hind legs and as he broke down the front door came a crash of thunder.

Richard woke up and looked all around the room thinking the animal was inside, but the only bear he saw was in a picture on the wall, and the only sound was gentle rain. He looked for the tracks every summer but never saw them again.

"There's a thermos and a bag of sandwiches on the counter," said Ange, "and the keys to Ralph's Bronco and the gate. The beaver had babies. Maybe you'll see them. Oh, and do you mind bringing back some onions? The bag's in the trunk."

"No. I'll do it. Do you believe all this stuff you talk about?" Richard asked her.

"Yes. Yes I do, dear."

"How come, if you've never seen them?"

"I just do."

"If you say so. Later." He picked up the keys and food and hurried out the door.

Richard drove a mile to the property Ralph inherited from his father, who had received it after his parents, Ollie and Watson Glenn, perished in the 1907 prairie fire. The land during spring and early summer was a heavy green, crisscrossed by small creeks and inhabited by a variety of animals. Ralph made sure it stayed that way. Ten years ago poachers cut the fence on the south side and within a month killed almost all the turkeys, deer, and bobcat family living under the old barn.

Ralph double-fenced the remote parts of the property, covered the chain link with NO TRESPASSING signs, and patrolled the land every day on the four-wheeler. He also carried his 30-30, which was inserted into the homemade rifle boot he had welded to the ATV. He hired his friend's sons to drive the property three times a week during the night to chase away poachers.

After months of Ralph's constant vigil and threats to call the tribal police, the hunters realized they weren't going to get anywhere by trespassing so they passed the word that the Glenns' property was off-limits.

Richard unlocked the gate, drove through, parked his car in the shade of two oaks, then snapped shut the padlock. He put the sandwiches, thermos, and burlap bag for the onions in his small backpack and started walking.

Richard looked around, admiring the day. The road was lined with thick-leaved pecan, redbud, and oak trees. Purple and yellow flowers dotted the underbrush and foot-high stems with scarlet petals—Indian paint-brushes—were scattered in the grass or next to remnants of cottonwood trees, foot-high tree stumps with tops gnawed to points by beavers. Birds and locusts sang together out of tune.

He spent every summer of his life here, exploring the woods and fishing for catfish. This was the first time he scouted without his father and he felt slightly lonely.

After ten minutes Richard arrived at the pond. Lily pads floated along the surface. A warm breeze ruffled the tree leaves and caused little ripples in the water. A mound of sticks and branches stood up four feet from the water on one side of the pond. Richard looked south and noticed clouds billowing like curtains in front of an open window.

Birds flew across the pond and over the field of wildflowers. *This is beautiful.* He felt a sting on his forehead and after swatting himself found a wad of mosquito and blood on his palm.

He continued down the road and veered off into the tall grass. He bent his knees and pulled up a handful of onions with long green stems. Every ten feet he reached into the grass and pulled out another bunch, then dropped them in the burlap sack. Next to one clump of onions was a rabbit's nest, the babies small and pink and vulnerable. He hoped the coyotes wouldn't find them.

Richard heard a *slap* from the pond. He observed a brown head moving through the water leaving a V behind it. "Hello, Mama," he said to the beaver. He watched her swim into a bunch of green plants at one end of the pond and then walk onto the bank. She lumbered about then went back into the water and swam out of sight behind her house.

It was four o'clock and too early for deer to be out, but Richard didn't mind. He liked to wander. He walked and sat in various places until it began to sprinkle around 8:30. Satisfied that he had seen six does and a buck, he went home.

Each afternoon for two weeks Richard scouted the woods with his bag of insect repellent, toilet paper, olive loaf sandwiches, Ritz crackers, and thermos of cold Hawaiian Punch. One day he walked to the house built over a hundred years ago by his ancestor Ruel Battiest. The family hadn't maintained it and how it still stood was a mystery. Richard had gone inside once with his father seven years ago after he pestered Sam relentlessly to take him in. Now Richard stood outside the fencing that surrounded the silent house, remembering.

"We'll go in, but you have to stay close to me, got it?" said his father. "No wandering around and don't touch anything. I mean it."

"Okay, okay," Richard had answered, rolling his eyes.

After leaning their fishing gear on the gate they walked into the wildflower-covered yard. They entered the ground floor through the dilapidated front door. Richard was scared but entranced by the age of the place. Piles of dust shaped like sand dunes sat on the windowsills and atop the fireplace hearth.

There was no furniture, no rugs, just four empty gray rooms with warped floors that bowed upwards. Sam stood in the main room, arms crossed, watching his son. He had been here before.

"What's upstairs?" asked Richard. Then he looked around. There were no stairs.

"We can't get up there from inside," his dad sighed deeply. "I'll show you."

They walked back through the front door and around to the stairs. "This way," said Sam. He started up a flight of solidly built stairs that hugged the outside wall of the house. The steps were thick and strangely shaped, as if they were built for someone with abnormally long feet.

"So, Dad, how come the stairs are on the outside? Didn't they get rained on? This is weird."

"Your ancestors were different people, son."

"What do you mean?"

Sam didn't reply. The door at the top of the stairs was securely shut with two large padlocks, one a foot from the ground and the other six inches from the top of the doorsill. Sam took two keys from his top coat pocket and after a few minutes of wrestling with the old locks managed to click them open. He turned to Richard and said, "Ange keeps the keys."

He pushed open the door and stepped in. "Just a minute, son."

Sam held the butt of the pistol he always carried when on Ralph's land. He looked around the upper rooms for a few minutes. Satisfied with what he didn't find, he told Richard to come on.

When Richard stepped through the doorway, all outside noises stopped. It was so quiet Richard heard blood rush through his head. The room seemed to grow until it appeared to be twice the size as a minute before. He looked around, surprised at the brightness.

The floor was identical to the one below, except that it was as tidy and clean as the downstairs was dusty and aged. Two rugs adorned the sitting room and clean white lacy curtains hung in the windows. There was no dust. The resident might even be in the next room, he thought. He looked at his father, who shifted his feet nervously.

"Did something die in here? It smells gross."

Sam said nothing.

Richard wandered into a room that was eight by ten feet, large enough for a bed and a three-drawer nightstand. The walls were painted blue and long nails served as coat hangers. Richard looked up and saw that white clouds had been painted on the ceiling above the bed.

A painting hung over the dresser. It was a scene of a pine-forested hillside with a stream reflecting the sun and clouds. A buck and three does stood drinking at the bank. Looking closer, he saw a blue jay perched on a low branch. The bright blue sky and yellow wildflowers identified the summer morning.

Richard noticed a pile of books under the recently varnished nightstand and bent over to investigate. Original, worn copies of Jules Verne's *Journey to the Center of the Earth* and *20,000 Leagues under the Sea* and H. G. Wells's *The Time Machine* were stacked on top of a few issues of *Boy's Life* and *Godey's Lady's Book*. He laughed out loud. So where's *War of the Worlds*? he wondered.

Richard walked back to the living area, which had shrunk. There was no furniture, but three pots in the kitchen windowsill held brightly colored flowers. Puzzled, Richard reached over the sink for them.

"Don't touch anything!" his father yelled, and grabbed his son's hand. Sam was sweating. "We're leaving." He looked over his shoulder.

"Dad, wait. Who lives here?" Richard looked at the room again and it seemed to grow once more.

"No one," Sam answered in a panicked voice. "No one has lived here in almost ninety years. Not since Merly Battiest died and Ruel disappeared."

"What?" Richard asked as his dad took him by the shoulder and pulled him down the stairs. His father was breathing hard when they reached the ground. Then he ran back up the stairs and snapped shut the heavy padlocks.

"Now listen to me," Sam said in a stern voice Richard had not heard before. "Don't you ever, ever come to this house again. Do not even think about going in, and if you do, you will never visit your aunt and uncle again. Is that clear? *Is it?*"

"Yes sir," Richard answered. He almost cried.

His father remained agitated until the yard gate closed behind them. A train whistled in the distance. Thunder grumbled to the south but they couldn't see the clouds for the tall trees. A mourning dove's sad song filtered through the trees, sounding unhappy about the heat. Then Sam stood up straighter and patted Richard on the back. "How about some catfish for dinner?"

They walked 500 yards to a bridge that hovered six feet above a branch of the Red Oak Creek. They sat down gingerly on the old wood. "What are those tracks with the turned-in toes?" Richard asked.

Sam looked down at the prints leading to and from the creek. "Skunk."

They sat still for a while with their lines in the water. Scissortail flycatchers swooped over the water.

"Dad, who lives in the house?"

"Nobody, son. Nobody ever goes in."

"But the flowers. . . ."

"Look, son. There are some things we just don't understand. Ruel Battiest was a medicine man. So was his brother Ellis, but he stayed back east during removal. Ruel was always around—people saw him in town and on the roads—but nobody could remember much about him, not even the family. They said he was surrounded by magic. He had a black man helper named 'No Nose' because he didn't have one."

"Didn't have a nose?" asked Richard. "How can you not have a nose?"

"That's what we've heard, son. I don't think Billie ever drew him."

"I've never seen someone without a nose," said Richard. Not that he wanted to.

"Anyways, Ruel moved here from Mississippi after removal and built this house." Richard had heard the stories before in detail from Ange. He didn't mind hearing again his father's version of how the Crows murdered Billie's brother Teague, her sister Survella and her son Skarloey, Gilmore's son Matthias, and dozens of others.

"A family of bad men called the Crows started killing our family after the Civil War. Ruel was supposed to have made certain the executed Crows didn't come out of their graves, but back in 1907, they say the Crows came out and started killing again. Nobody could find Ruel."

"So he could stop them, but didn't?" asked Richard.

"We don't know, son. The Crows were real, but them being evil owls is just a story."

"You don't believe it?"

"I haven't thought much about it." Richard figured he really had.

"Anyways, Ruel and his wife Merly didn't get along, so she lived on the bottom floor and he lived up top. The stairs were built outside to keep them from having to see each other. They lived there until she died. Ruel disappeared that same day and nobody ever saw him again."

"Did he kill her?" Richard asked.

"No, he loved her. One summer Merly fell backwards over a log and got stung by hundreds of baby scorpions."

"Geez. But. . . ."

"That's all I know." Sam had a tug and occupied himself with bringing up a four-pound catfish.

That was still the strangest thing Richard ever heard so when Sam had given him the same orders to stay away from the place every year since then, he said yes sir, even though he desired to go back.

Seven years later, Richard stood outside the still, old house. His dad may say he didn't think much about the Crows being evil, but Richard sure had. His parents hadn't talked to him very much about religion or the Choctaws' past. Aunt Ange did, and he remembered everything she said.

He looked at the house. The bottom looked older and grayer while the top looked like it had recently had a new coat of paint. It didn't surprise him to see yellow flowers in the upstairs window. Last summer they were red.

On Wednesday night of the second week coyotes howled earlier than usual. By seven Richard had eaten the two sandwiches. For the next hour he sat still and saw Ralph's six spotted horses and a dozen squirrels but no deer. At 8:40 he started home since reruns of *Gilligan's Island* began at 9:00.

Richard passed the pond and heard frogs croak. As he moved away from the croaks he heard an owl hoot, which he had not heard before, and it scared him. He knew what it might mean. Then he heard children jabbering, but couldn't make out if they spoke English. Then he saw turkeys in a stand of oaks and he turned on his flashlight.

Instead of turkeys he saw four tiny people looking at him. They were dressed in regular clothes, pants and shirts, except they were small. Their faces were wrinkled, ancient. Each one wore a heavy necklace and earrings that hung to their shoulders. Three carried bundles. One carried a sack with grass, flowers, and feathers sticking out of the top. The one with the sack grinned.

Richard dropped his flashlight and ran to the car. He tripped over a fallen oak, got up and kept going. He reached the Bronco, started it, and backed over a small redbud tree. He sped home, not bothering to shut the gate. He sat in the driveway a moment, out of breath and hoping everyone was asleep.

Richard was still sweating when he entered the house.

"What's wrong, dear?" Ange stood in the hall in her robe. "Richard, honey, tell us what happened."

Richard opened his mouth but couldn't talk. He thought of what he saw. *Did I see Little People in the woods?*

"So what's wrong with you, o mighty hunter?" Victoria had been experimenting with new hairstyles and only half her hair was pinned up.

Normally Richard would have made a comment about it. "Uh, the bobcat spooked me," he said instead.

"You finally saw Bob," said Ralph. "I've only seen him once."

"Yeah, well, goodnight," Richard said quickly. Then he went into the bathroom and turned on the shower where he stood until the hot water turned cold. Then he went to his bed and listened to the locusts buzz through the soft hum of the water air cooler. Richard knew the Little People were real. Richard also knew that they wanted him to see them. He looked out the window at the bright moon until it climbed out of sight and he fell asleep.

The next morning when Richard came to breakfast Victoria was mixing honey and butter together in a bowl to put on her toast. "Still scared?"

Before Richard could answer Ralph walked in the front door. "Found this on the porch." Ralph held out the flashlight Richard had dropped in the woods. "Doesn't work without batteries, you know."

"What do you mean?"

"Look inside."

Richard unscrewed the tube and instead of batteries, it was filled with yellow flower petals, turkey pin feathers, and a deer tooth.

Victoria came over to look. "What's all that? Why'd you put that in there?"

"I didn't."

Ange took an old photograph down from the wall over the bookshelf. "This is Ruel and Merly Battiest," she said and handed the picture to Richard.

Richard had seen the picture before but never really looked at it. Merly stood behind her husband's chair, her face and body tense. She had a large smile, crooked teeth, and unsmiling, crossed eyes. Her knuckles looked white where they held the back of the chair. *She looks disturbed*, thought Richard. He figured this was not the time to ask about her. This family has secrets.

Then he looked at Ruel's face; the black eyes were the darkest part of the old maroonish photograph. Ruel Battiest was as compelling to him as the Little People. Richard looked closer and the face floated toward him. The mouth opened and tried to speak.

"Thought you'd go out again. Maybe for a few days." Ange's voice seemed far away.

Ruel's face suddenly returned to its frozen image. Richard felt dizzy. He put the photograph down and looked inside the sack his auntie handed him. She packed a dozen sandwiches, several boxes of crackers and cookies, and a few other items wrapped in foil. She also handed him a bag of clean clothes.

Richard stood. He wasn't afraid. "Yeah, I think I better."

Reggie the Anthropologist

Red Oak, Oklahoma. 1997.

The visitor Chockie sat at the kitchen table talking with the Christie twins, Janie and Lily, and their great-grandmother, Willie Louise Walkingstick Christie. Chockie lived three miles down the road and was the family's best friend.

Chockie stopped by every day to drink coffee and eat biscuits with the girls' father, Caddo, but for the past month Chockie had been in Okmülgee tending to his sick sister. Now he was back and in time for lunch.

"*Chim a chuk ma*," said the girls' father Caddo, holding out his hand to Chockie as he entered through the screen door. Caddo held a string of gutted catfish in his left hand.

Behind him followed Reggie, a young white man, thin and sunburned, his face spotted with acne. He wore khaki pants, a dingy Jefferson Starship T-shirt, and tennis shoes. It had started to sprinkle and both men were wet.

"*Halito*," said Chockie, standing. Chockie, of medium height, was very dark and had full lips and almond eyes slanting slightly upward. He wore his long kinky hair brushed back in a tight ponytail. All the people Reggie had met so far were older than they looked so maybe he was forty-five, the same age as Caddo.

Chockie looked at Reggie. Chockie was handsome and sure of himself. He made Reggie nervous.

The two dark-haired, light-skinned girls were at the sink husking corn into a metal bucket. One was about five feet and slim, her long hair tied back with a red cloth. The other girl was two inches taller, heavier set, with her hair cut short. The sisters were nineteen. They graduated from high school the year before and worked as checkers at the Piggly Wiggly grocery store.

"This is Reggie Whittaker from California," said Janie.

"He's an anthropology student," said Lily.

"What are you doing? Writing a book on your travels?" asked Chockie.

"No, I have a grant to write my dissertation on indigenous peoples of Oklahoma. I wrote Mrs. Christie in May and she agreed to allow me to interview her. I meant to stay in a hotel," Reggie jabbered on, "but she graciously invited me to stay here."

Chockie's right eyebrow lifted.

Reggie thought Chockie was puzzled. "See, at the end of one's course work, he writes a dissertation—a thesis on. . . ."

"I know what a dissertation is. We're not indigenous to Oklahoma. We came from Mississippi. We're *Chahtas. Chahta hapia hoke.*"

"Yes, well, I'm interested in how the Choctaw adapted after moving west."

"Choctaw? Which one?"

"Pardon?" Reggie said as his eyes widened.

"You said 'Choctaw in Oklahoma.' Which one do you mean?"

"I meant the tribe."

"Then say Choctaws," Chockie said.

Reggie stood very still.

"So, Whittaker, what are us Indians like?" Chockie picked up a biscuit. "You gonna tell us about ourselves?"

"Uh, I'm learning a lot." Reggie dug his hands deeper into his jeans pockets.

"Like what?"

"Well, we've talked about ball games, food, religion."

"Religion? That so?" Chockie looked at Caddo and raised his eyebrows.

"He said he wouldn't write it down, Chock," said Caddo.

"You got a promise on that?" He turned his attention back to Reggie. "There's a lot you people did to us, like make us move, take our land, kill us. You gonna write about those things?" Chockie halved the biscuit. "What are you planning on doing with this story? Make some money?" He was crumbling the biscuit.

Thunder boomed and emphasized Chockie's question.

"Uh, no. Anthropologists try to preserve history for the tribes. A lot of

Indians want to know about their past and we help them to find information. We write down stories and tribes can save them." It was a simplistic explanation and one he hoped Chockie would accept.

"Why would you want to do that?"

The smell of catfish was pungent. Reggie became queasy when he heard the lunch menu included catfish. He hated the thought of eating scavengers that consume things like fish poop off the creek bottom. "Well. . . ."

"And you think you'll know all about us after one short visit? Why are you so concerned?"

Reggie didn't want to say what he was thinking: *I'm concerned about finishing my degree. My armpits are wet.*

Chockie put the pieces of biscuit on the table and looked at Reggie with folded hands. "So what makes you think you can understand what we're about? You've only been here two weeks."

"Well, I'm trying to understand." Reggie's voice rose a few octaves like it did when he was a child trying to explain why he used his father's spaghetti colander to sift dirt for doodlebugs.

"What are you going to pay this good family for their time and information?"

"Oh, Chockie," Willie Lou said. "He's not gonna pay anything. He's going to help reroof the barn."

Reggie was relieved Willie Lou spoke. The old woman was spry and mentally quick.

Despite his fondness for Willie Lou, Reggie was surprised at her comment about him reroofing the barn. *I had never thought that I should pay an Indian for information. My adviser would be horrified at the thought. He would never pay.*

"Lunch is ready," said Lily. "You all go wash up."

Reggie headed out the door fast enough for everybody to notice he was upset. The rain increased and he was drenched by the time he got to the guest room. He sat on the bed, breathing fast. He left the door open and Blackie the rooster ran in and jumped on the bed. Reggie wondered for the hundredth time why the bird didn't stay with the hens and leave him alone.

Reggie stared at the floor. *Is Chockie going to convince Willie to stop talking to me? What if they don't want me to use what they've already told me?*

The kitchen conversation was loud and Reggie could hear their argument. Reggie put his left ear to the bedroom wall. He could hear Chockie's clear voice.

"Reggie won't pay you, but after his book's finished *he'll* get paid. Then more just like him'll see they can do the same thing and they'll start pestering all the tribes. How do you know what he'll write? Those white men write whatever they want."

He continued, angry. "What's wrong with all of you anyways? What were you thinking, telling him about our religion? That's not anyone's business and there's plenty of people who'd tan your hides or worse if they knew you'd been talking."

Then Reggie heard Lily. "Maybe we can ask to read it before Reggie turns it in for everyone else to see."

Reggie continued to stand with his ear against the wall, his mouth hanging open. *Oh shit. What if they don't like the end product? What if they say my conclusions are wrong? Chockie will scrutinize every word and tear it to shreds. Then my committee won't like the new version and I'll never graduate. Since when do Indians not want to be researched?*

Reggie contemplated not writing his dissertation, but what would he do then? He could continue to lecture at UCLA but the pay was minimal. He wanted to play baseball, but he wasn't good enough to play professionally. *Maybe I'll just start over and write about Pueblo religions.*

Reggie had planned to graduate and become a part of the circle of enlightened professors he envisioned sat together at lunches and at seminars pontificating intellectualism and theory, setting the methodological standards the less influential scholars followed. *They understand cultures besides our own, don't they? After all, these are the men who author books and articles about Indians and determine which scholars are worthy of fellowships and scholarly awards. Could it be that these people are only formally educated academics with vivid imaginations? Could it be that the Ph.D. merely gives license to speculate and publish?*

Reggie considered how little he knew about Choctaws. Before his trip he had only read Adair's *The History of the American Indians*; Bartram's *Travels*; Benson's *Life among Choctaw Indians*; Bushnell's "Myths of the Louisiana Choctaw"; Cushman's *History of the Choctaw, Chickasaw, and*

Natchez Indians; Galloway's *Choctaw Genesis*; Swanton's "Early Account of the Choctaw Indians"; and a variety of essays by Halbert, many of which discussed Choctaw myths. By the time he was to leave for Oklahoma, Reggie figured he knew enough about the tribe to start his own research.

The information he had only confirmed his belief that Choctaws were as superstitious and unsophisticated as other tribes. So what if they had a little formal education? That probably didn't mean much. He believed that all he needed to do was to keep his patience around the simple people and get the information he needed to graduate. How difficult could that be?

Reggie chewed on his thin lower lip. He was starting to think differently about them.

Two weeks ago, Caddo had picked Reggie up from the train station and drove in silence the three miles to Willie Lou's farm. There were only four farms along the way, each surrounded by thick woods. Were there larger things than bugs that thrived in the lush vegetation, like wolves or bears? Reggie didn't want to ask Caddo and appear stupid.

After a sharp turn, they arrived at Willie Lou's. A creek meandered to the south and large trees shaded the house and barn. Two dark brown horses with long manes stood with their heads over the range fence, ears pricked. The front parts of their long manes were braided with red ribbon and hung to their noses. A large barn faced the house eighty feet away. Hens walked around the yard with their heads moving forward and back.

Four mature pecan trees stood in back and one in front of the well-kept, white house. Birdhouses hung from high branches or were nailed to tree trunks. A thriving, manicured garden bordered by a latticework fence grew to the south. Rain barrels stood at three corners of the house, positioned to catch the rain from downspouts.

The yard was clean and free of clutter. Many farms were unkempt and dirty and smelled of animals and humans. They were places to buy eggs but not to visit. Unlike the owners of this farm, many people grew blind to the trash piles they created.

Sitting on the covered porch in the largest rocking chair he had ever seen was an old woman wearing a cotton dress and white shoes. The back of the chair was six inches above her head and whenever she rocked back her feet came off the porch deck. Lying next to her was a red hound dog with long droopy ears. As soon as Reggie reached the first porch step Willie Lou stood up so fast it appeared that the rocker threw her out.

"Come on in and have a drink." She had a clear, high-pitched voice. Then she entered the house with her dog without waiting for him.

Reggie was surprised at how different the people looked from each other. Willie Lou was five-eight with light brown skin. Her hair was gray and probably long under the thick bun. She stood straight, not hunched over like Reggie's grandmothers. Willie Lou and her grandson had the same eyes: dark brown color, heavy eyelid, and distinct eyebrow arch. Caddo was darker than Willie Lou, and the two great-granddaughters even darker still. Willie Lou could have passed for a white woman.

Willie Lou said her dog was named Tecumseh; one person in each generation of her family owned a Tecumseh. When Reggie laughed and asked why a female dog was named after a man, Willie Lou's face became serious.

"Tecumseh was a great Shawnee leader," Willie Lou lectured. "He came to visit the Choctaws before the war with Britain. They killed him at the Thames. Don't you know your history?"

"Yes, I know about Tecumseh," Reggie replied. He didn't like people to lecture him on topics he already knew about.

"My great-great-grandmother heard him speak," she said.

"She saw him?" Reggie had asked loudly.

"He came to Mississippi around the time of the war trying to get tribes to fight with him. He didn't have much luck, though. My Great-Uncle Ellis wanted to go with him but he was a doctor and needed to stay at home."

Willie Lou sipped her lemonade. "Pushmataha and the other leaders didn't want to go with Tecumseh. They sided with the Americans. My great-great-grandmother Danny McKenney said she wished she had gone to fight with him. So many whites were around us that a lot of Choctaws were ready to do something. It was too late. Some of them were part of our families."

After that conversation Reggie and Willie Lou followed a deeply worn path to the creek so she could wade. A funny little creature that looked like a cross between a lobster and a shrimp scooted past underwater close to the bank.

"What in heck's that?" Reggie asked.

"Crawdaddy. He won't hurt you much, Reggie," Willie Lou laughed.

Willie Lou waded back to the bank, slowly picked up her shoes, and started toward her house, which was, incredibly, almost 160 years old. It had been rebuilt over the years, of course, but the original foundation and the chimney embedded with little crosses of red stones were there, just as her ancestors, William and Danny McKenney, laid it after they arrived in Red Oak in the 1830s. Reggie winced from the small rocks that poked into his bare feet but Willie Lou didn't seem to notice.

Willie Lou sat in her large rocker and Reggie retrieved his notebook from under the chair leg. He saw movement and looked up to see a gray rat walking toward Willie Lou.

She looked down and picked it up. "There you are," she said gently. "I got a new friend last month. He found his way into the laundry basket Janie left in the yard. She was about to throw my clothes on the bed to fold when my dress moved. He was just a baby and small as a mouse. The laundry must have been warm from drying outside and the clothes basket was a fine place to sleep."

"Willie Lou, it's a rat," Reggie said.

She put her head back and laughed. "Reggie, dearie, it's a possum. Don't you know the difference?"

He leaned closer to look. Reggie had never seen an opossum before.

Then they were silent, content to watch the branches move with the warm July breeze. Birds of various colors drank at her birdbath and ignored the brightly colored wooden birdhouses. They would pay attention to the homes again next spring.

Janie stuck her head out the door. "*Im pat min tih.*"

"Dinner's ready," said Willie Lou.

They sat to a meal of beans, cornbread, and biscuits. Caddo put a piece of cornbread in his bowl, then doled out his red beans. Reggie thought that made more sense than eating them separately. Willie Lou doused her beans with pepper sauce. She grew red and green hot peppers and marinated them for herself and for Christmas gifts, just like her great-grandmother Billie did. Several dozen amber jars sat on top of the refrigerator.

"Do you speak Choctaw?" Reggie asked Willie Lou.

"*Paska kallo sa banna*," Willie Lou said to Lily, who passed her the biscuits.

"Some. My daddy spoke Choctaw real well but my mama didn't at all. My son married a Choctaw who speaks it and that's how these two learned." She pointed at Janie and Lily with her fork. "The schools around here have books in English and Indian."

"Do you girls speak Choctaw when you're at home?"

Janie looked at Lily, who answered, "A lot of the time. Daddy makes us."

"You need to know your language. That's part of who you are," Caddo said. "Who's going to teach your children if you don't learn it?"

Neither daughter said anything. They had heard this lecture before.

They finished eating and put their bowls in the sink to soak. All five moved to the porch. Tecumseh ran off to the creek and Janie brought out a pitcher of tea. The sky darkened as branches swayed. Nighthawks joined the bats in their quest for insects.

"Willie, time for bed," said Janie.

"*Cheki*." Willie looked at Reggie. "A little longer."

She sat in her rocker and told stories until late. Every day after meals Willie Lou and Reggie moved to the porch to talk while Tecumseh ran to the creek and Janie brought a pitcher of cold, strong tea. She told him of her great-grandmother Billie. She told him of bonepickers, *shampes*, and Little People. She matter-of-factly discussed the violent deaths of her ancestors at the hands of Indian Territory outlaws, the Crows.

She proudly told him about her relatives who were medicine people, strange men and women who seemed apart from the family, yet at the same time were the glue that held them together. She related stories of her grandmother Tish Walkingstick, coal mines, ball games, and Lighthorsemen and showed him boxes of sketches that her great-grandmother drew. Reggie enjoyed the tales, but the stories seemed embellished and incredible. *Perhaps that's why my professors don't trust Indians' oral histories*, he thought.

He was moved when Willie Lou tearfully recounted the Choctaws' removal to Indian Territory. Willie Lou's great-grandmother lost her brother and beloved aunt on the trail. Her story caused Reggie to wonder how she could trust white people. Chockie didn't.

Whites could never understand the Indian mind-set, even if they could define it, thought Reggie. *Indians' perspectives of the world aren't the same as those who won, and I'm on the winning side.*

After Reggie went to bed, he lay still thinking about Willie Lou's family. Nothing was what he thought it would be. Were all of Willie Lou's family like her? Were other Choctaws like Willie Lou's family? They're educated and like him in a lot of ways, but also different. They've blended blood, cultures, and ideas, something his family didn't have to do. He assumed that all Indians were the same. But were they?

The hot afternoon breezes cooled with the daily storms. Reggie could relax at Willie Lou's, rocking in an oversized chair and thinking about his past and future. His aunt had told him that when your brain is full, the mind doesn't have room to allow wandering thoughts to settle in and take hold.

She was right. For years Reggie had focused on his studies, hardly finding a half hour to read newspapers. The only quiet moments he had were in the library. His head ached a lot and he realized that he was degenerating into a single-minded bore.

Each morning at Willie Lou's farm Reggie awoke to the sound of Blackie's loud crow, then he ate a large breakfast and moved to the porch to hear Willie Lou's stories. They drank pots of hot coffee, although Willie Lou only drank it in the mornings. Any other time of the day, coffee gave her bellyaches.

Each afternoon the rains fell, a light shower that turned into a downpour. Peals of thunder vibrated the room so hard that Tecumseh rose from her spot near the door and moved closer to Willie Lou.

After an hour of cleansing rain the clouds passed and were replaced by blue sky. The air steamed and they had to step around mud puddles and plump earthworms that washed from their underground homes.

Willie Lou's stories confirmed his belief in how dull he was becoming. Reggie wished he had known his family better. His father didn't care for his parents and for his wife's even less. Reggie had several cousins his age, but he rarely saw them. He never visited anybody, but they wrote him anyway in an attempt to communicate. While at Willie Lou's, Reggie started thinking that he should get to know them.

Reggie had wondered what Willie Lou might tell him and how he was to interpret the information. She didn't look or act like any Indian he ever read about and he wasn't sure about his topic anymore. He knew after only a few days that he was either on to something or out of his league.

When he was a child, Reggie read stories of Plains tribes that fought and often defeated the United States Army. The mention of Sitting Bull, Crazy Horse, and Quanah Parker conjured images of warriors with a love of fighting. Oklahoma had once been home to fighting tribes such as Kiowas, Comanches, and Apaches. Their descendants lived here now, of course, but they were sedentary and held little interest for Reggie.

On the train ride to Oklahoma, Reggie imagined painted warriors galloping across the plains on their ponies with their long hair streaming behind them. Then he blinked and realized that he was looking at pastureland dotted with grazing, almost motionless cows and horses.

He didn't know what to do. *I'm almost finished with this project*, he thought. *I have so much information on Choctaw life after removal it'll be a great dissertation. Then I can revise it into a book*. Satisfied with what seemed a good plan, Reggie shooed Blackie out of the room then washed his hands in the rain barrel and dried them on his damp shirttail. Time for lunch.

Janie and Lily fried enough catfish to fill two platters. Mashed potatoes with their skins on filled a large red bowl. Steam rose from the string beans mixed with fried wild onions in a blue one. The white gravy boat held thick brown gravy next to the basket that overflowed with hot biscuits. The green pot filled with tomato and onion relish sat in its usual place at the center of the table. The pot was full at the start of every meal and empty when the plates were cleared.

Nobody had filled their heavy white plates. They were waiting for Reggie. He sat at the opposite end of the table from Chockie.

Chockie ignored Reggie and started a discussion with Caddo about the fishing at Brazil Creek. Reggie felt a little better since he wasn't the center of attention. The food smelled wonderful but Reggie wasn't hungry. Chockie, however, had an enormous appetite. He ate three helpings of everything and drank glass after glass of water.

After they put their plates in the sink to soak and Chockie left, Reggie felt both relief and guilt, like he was about to do something wrong. Willie Lou continued with her stories and Reggie diligently took notes. By the time he was scheduled to leave he was no longer sure about what to do with the information.

On the morning of the fifth day since his confrontation with Chockie, Reggie woke early and packed his clothes for the trip to Los Angeles. He wanted to bathe in the creek, then investigate Willie Lou's cemetery. He planned to wait until his last day because he didn't want to get caught wandering around among the dead so early in his visit. Willie Lou hadn't mentioned the roof, but he would help her if she did.

During his stroll to the creek Reggie wondered how many times Willie Lou and her ancestors had walked to the same bank, stooped to fill their buckets, waded in the shallows, or sat barefoot, thinking about Mississippi. Like the water flowing past, Reggie only visited the bank briefly. Still, he felt at peace on the cool, shaded bank.

Reggie wondered if Willie Lou would be wading. He saw bare footprints in the soft clay coming and going. Dog prints had pushed through the human's. Reggie followed the bank for fifty yards looking for a deep spot. He found a bend in the stream that sloped into the dark water. He looked around to make sure nobody was looking, then stripped off his clothes, hung them on a branch, took up his washcloth, and waded in.

The water was warm to his ankles but turned cooler as he walked in deeper. He turned and floated on his back, looking up at the gray morning sky. It would turn blue shortly. Bats had flown back to their dark places. In less than fifteen minutes Blackie would crow. In an hour Reggie would hear the locusts sing and smell the aroma of Janie and Lily's coffee and biscuits.

He touched the bottom with his toes, estimating it at six feet down. He walked back to where it was waist deep and scrubbed himself with his cloth. He was leisurely rubbing his neck when he had a sudden thought about snakes.

Without checking to see if there actually were any, Reggie ran out of the water to his pile of clothes. He forgot a towel so he jumped up and down a few times and used his dirty shirt to dry. He dressed quickly, all the while glancing to his right and left, but he saw no snakes. It didn't matter. He was spooked.

Reggie hurried back to the house faster than he left it. Eager to see the cemetery, he went to the back of the house and to the stand of oaks he hadn't paid much attention to before. Walking around the trees, he saw the tops of tombstones set in neat rows. He entered through the gate on the west side.

It was a lovely area. Two elms shaded most of the yard. The grass was recently mowed and edged, revealing flat stone markers interspersed among the tombstones. Each grave had a glass jar set in the ground next to it. Five were filled with fresh-cut wildflowers while the rest held flowers in various stages of wilt. The largest marker stood nearest the gate. Most of the writing was worn away, but Reggie could make out the last name: Lamb.

Some of the stones were smooth, forever concealing who lay beneath them. Some were fairly legible, like those of Tish and Biff Walkingstick, Gilmore and Alexandra Lamb, and especially the large headstone in the west corner with an elaborate stone bear carved on top of it. It only said

BILLIE LOUISE WATCHMAN

1822–1926

If this was the Billie Louise that Willie Lou kept talking about, she certainly didn't seem the type who would dictate that such a marker be made for her. The family must have wanted it.

A jay screamed from atop an oak and Reggie realized he better get to the house. As he walked to the gate he glanced over the field to admire the yellow flowers and saw three oil pumps clustered together. One was tall and cone shaped; the two others looked less elaborate, their hammerheads churning up and down. Two more pumps, of a different shape, stood at the far end of the field. He presumed they searched for gas.

When he reached the front porch Willie Lou wasn't there but her chair was rocking like she had just gotten up. She was inside at the table. There were plates of biscuits, ham, and eggs. The coffee and relish pot sat in the center next to a bowl of white butter, a jug of water, and a jar of what looked like strawberry jam. There were enough biscuits for twenty people.

Reggie was not happy to leave. Although this was not his world, it was a comfortable one, and perhaps better than his. His mind and body had fallen into the rhythm of their days.

"I don't have to make any biscuits for lunch," Janie explained. She was in a fresh maroon dress with green squares and her hair was tied back with a matching cloth. The morning was warm and signaled a hot day, but all three women looked comfortable in their thin linen and bare feet.

"Nice swim, Reggie?" asked Willie Lou.

"Uh, yes. Nice and cool."

"Worried about snakes?"

"Snakes? Oh, yes, you told me about them." Reggie wondered if he looked stupid or just felt like it.

Willie Lou smirked. "Did you see that big snake track?"

"Snake track?" Reggie gulped his coffee and burned his throat.

"A big one's been down at the water. His curly trail went along the bank down to where you went."

"Well, I guess I was a little nervous, like something else was around but I couldn't see it."

"He could have been smelling you, or maybe was in a branch above your head."

Reggie's stomach churned. "I'm glad I came back. Reptiles are back luck to Indians." Reggie was certain he was right about that. The three women just looked at him.

"Bad luck?" asked Lily. "Bad luck if you get bit." All three laughed.

Well, they are bad luck to some tribes. So maybe they aren't bad luck to Choctaws, thought Reggie.

The tender, salty ham and sweet jam were a delightful combination. Reggie put an egg, a slice of ham, and jam on a biscuit and after eating it made two more. The women ate just a little of everything, which explained their tiny waists.

Reggie watched Lily put half a biscuit and a slice of ham into her napkin and then fold it over and tuck it under the edge of her plate. "So you set some food aside for your ancestors," Reggie commented. "Some Pueblos do that."

"No, it's for Tecumseh."

Reggie felt foolish again.

"I put flowers on five graves at a time," Willie Lou said.

Reggie wondered how she knew everything he did.

"That's why some are wilted and some are new. We mow once a week in the summer. It's pretty in the fall when the leaves change."

Janie sat down opposite Reggie. "I'm glad our graveyard's here and not out in the woods like some of the others. Last summer some men came around and asked if that was our graveyard and that they'd pay for what they found."

Reggie put down his egg-, ham-, and jelly-filled biscuit. "You mean bodies?"

"Well, I guess so. They said they were looking for artifacts."

"Were they archaeologists?" It hurt Reggie to ask that question.

"No," said Willie Lou. "They were boys, wanting to sell Indian things. Some of the cemeteries towards town have been dug up. Bones thrown everywhere. Now family cemeteries that aren't close to homes are allowed to grow up with weeds so robbers can't find them."

Caddo came in halfway through breakfast and stuffed a biscuit smothered with jam into his mouth. "I wanna show Reggie some places today," he mumbled.

"Where are you going?" asked Lily.

"Over to Survella's place."

"I want to go." And with that she and Janie went to the porch door for their shoes.

After Willie Lou finished eating everyone piled into Caddo's brown Bonneville. A mile down the road from Willie Lou's house she pointed to a stand of tall pecan trees, about a quarter mile up a winding dirt road that was well traveled. Reggie could see a house painted white, and a barn and corral. The farm looked like an island in a sea of wildflowers. Horses and cows milled about.

"That's where my Great-Uncle Teague and his wife Dicey lived," said Willie Lou. "It's not the same house but that's the original chimney. Luckily all my family got to keep their lands during the allotment. Now his grandson Charlie lives there. He raises horses and sells real estate. A lot of Choctaws sold their allotments. The land was open to anyone to buy and sell, you know. A lot of whites around here live on land that used to belong to Choctaws."

"You can say that about Indians in the rest of the country," Reggie said.

"Yes. The whole country," Willie Lou repeated in a quiet voice.

Caddo drove another half mile and Willie Lou pointed to another farm. It wasn't far off the road and Willie Lou had Caddo drive into the yard. It was a farm but not one with any life to it. The only things left were gray, rotted two-by-fours and chimney bricks settled into a pile.

"This was Survella's house," Willie Lou said, opening the car door. "None of the grandkids wanted it."

Reggie closed his eyes and wondered what life had been like here. There was no smell of coffee or baking biscuits, nor any sound of children playing. What stories did Survella tell her family at night around the table? What flowers had she placed at its center? Survella's children were born here. Somewhere in the perimeter of the ruined fence that once enclosed her garden, Survella and her son Skarloey had died.

Reggie opened his eyes. Willie Lou had been watching him. "Lookie over there by the oaks," she whispered.

Reggie squinted but saw nothing but leaves. "What is it?"

"It's a ki-ote," said Willie Lou. "He's a pretty one. Nice and fluffy. Lots of ki-otes around here. They sing in the mornings."

The next stop was Ollie McKenney Glenn's old property. "This is where the house stood," Caddo said, walking through the knee-high grass. "You can see the old wood through the weeds."

Sure enough, Reggie found the outline of the house and the garden fence and corral, just like at Survella's.

"Ollie and her husband Watson were found lying over there where that Virginia creeper's growing."

Reggie didn't move, wondering what they had looked like, all burned up. And what Ollie's mother Billie had thought when she found her daughter and son-in-law.

The five stood quietly for a moment, hair blowing in the growing breeze. Dark clouds ran over their heads. "Better go before we get wet," said Caddo.

As they rounded the corner to Billie's farm, Reggie wondered about Survella's house. Would Willie Lou's house look like that in a few years? After she died, who would live there? How long would it take for the flowers to wither and for the roof to collapse?

When they arrived back in front of the small white-painted house with a long-eared hound dog waiting patiently by the large rocker, Reggie hurried to get his bags from the guest room. They would eat lunch together, then Caddo would take him to the train station.

Lunch was catfish dipped in cornmeal and fried. He tasted salt, black pepper, garlic, and onions. There was a plate of sweet tomato slices, a big bowl of corn scraped off the cob, and a slimy green vegetable Willie Lou called okree. Dessert was peach cobbler. Reggie was as full as he'd ever been. After dessert they took turns pouring coffee from a blue-speckled pot.

Reggie looked at the photographs on the wall. He saw Willie Lou in her youth, her long dark hair pulled back with a bow. Her great-aunt Ollie McKenney Glenn looked a lot like her, except she wasn't smiling.

"Who's this?" Reggie asked, pointing to a middle-aged man dressed in a suit.

"That's my uncle Hammy Hallmark. He served in the 36th Division in the First World War. He was a code talker, one of the men who spoke Choctaw over the radio to confuse Germans during the Meuse-Argonne campaign. Then he went to Yale for a few years."

"Yale?" Reggie sounded surprised.

Willie knew he had a hard time with that. "Studied literature. Then he came back and taught at the University of Oklahoma."

Caddo walked over to where Reggie stood. "He also built a pecan sheller. Folks came from everywhere with their bags of hard-shelled. He made enough to buy a Hereford bull. Named him Hercules. That bull must've been the daddy of a thousand calves." Caddo chuckled. "Hammy made a small fortune."

Caddo pointed to the pictures in turn. "That was one of Billie Lou's husbands, Peter. Pretty for a man. That's why we kept his picture. There's Teague, Billie Lou's brother. This here's their sister, Survella."

Survella was about forty-five, her hair piled high. Her arched eyebrows gave her an exotic look. She was a stunning presence, a school teacher and farm woman who took care of her family and friends until the Crow gang cut her throat one sunny afternoon.

Reggie looked across the wall at the old photographs and sketches of family members, and newer, lighter pictures, such as the one of the old man in the running shorts and a German shorthaired pointer hunting dog at his side. "Who's this?" he asked.

"Colbert McKenney, Teague's son," said Caddo. "Ran his whole life. He was a funny man in that he won almost every race he entered but never kept any of the medals or ribbons. His daughter has them. He's a lot like my sister Ariana, who won all the cross-country races in high school then had a scholarship to any university in the country. She even qualified for the Olympics, but had a bone spur that year and couldn't go. That's her." He pointed to a color photo on the opposite wall.

Reggie saw that Ariana Christie was tall and thin and had a face that would always stay young.

"Sometimes she drinks too much," said Caddo. "I think for a while when she was married she had a real alcohol problem, but she's back to normal. She's a lawyer in Washington."

Reggie looked at her again. This was the kind of woman that scared him. Smart, successful in something, and good-looking. He wondered why she wasn't married anymore.

Next to Ariana's picture was a color photo of young Richard Hallmark with a rifle crooked in his arm. The old black-and-white picture next to it was of Ralph Glenn, a smiling boy standing on his horse.

The next row featured Tosh Wilson holding a newspaper over his head, obviously proud of the headline; a lovely but serious Tish Walkingstick sitting on her horse that had a shaved mane and tail; Gilmore and Alli Lamb, a tall, stately couple in front of a building that said Lamb Law Office. The last was a fuzzy portrait of two Indian men standing side by side and wearing oversized cowboy hats, one man terribly bowlegged and with a large gap between his front teeth. The other boy smiled so big his eyes were forced shut.

"That crippled boy was Teague's idiot son Romy," Willie Lou explained. "He killed his best friend standing there next to him after that was taken. I keep the picture 'cause it's odd."

"No kidding," said Reggie. *What a family*, he thought.

Reggie never had ventured into Willie Lou's bedroom, so he didn't know what hung on the south wall.

"Look here," motioned Caddo. The wall was covered with old drawings, some framed, others covered in plastic and tacked up.

"Those are my great-grandmother's," Willie Lou said, walking over. "Look closely."

Reggie leaned forward and inspected what at first looked like a sketch of oak trees. Then he realized that interspersed among the trunks and branches were tiny human faces. The next was a waterfall featuring a faintly drawn wild man standing at the top of the falls. The colored picture below that was of a bear standing in the shadow of a much larger animal, bearlike but more of a furry monster.

"Wow. These are what she saw?"

"Oh yes. Those are just some of her drawings." Willie Lou watched Reggie gape. From the ceiling to floor hung portraits of old people, animals, gardens, and houses. "Got a hunnerd more in a box under the bed. Medicine people, bonepickers, people dead in the snow. Billie Watchman was better at drawing her life than writing it down. Ariana has Survella's journals. Keeps them in a bank lock box."

"Here's your dinner, Reggie." Lily handed him a heavy sack. She had cooked ham and beef that morning and there was probably a sandwich of each in the bag.

"Are you ready?" asked Caddo.

Reggie turned from the wall to say good-bye to Willie Lou but she started talking first.

"Enjoyed your visit, Reggie. I got to hear my stories out loud all at once. Never done that before. Gives me more to think about now."

Janie and Lily gave him a big hug and even Tecumseh came over, wagging her tail. He patted her, then went to Willie Lou, who was rocking in her chair. He reached down to hug her and was surprised by the strength in the squeeze she gave him back.

Reggie walked to the car and waved once at the woman sitting on the porch with Tecumseh at her feet. It struck him that he was leaving Willie Lou in the same position as he'd found her.

The car window was still down and he breathed deeply of the damp heavy air. Locusts hummed and blue jays screeched from the oaks that lined Willie Lou's road. Not for the first time he wondered how such beautiful birds could sound so grating.

The sky was bright blue in the south without trace of a single cloud puff, but to the north, where the clouds had headed, it was dark.

This is surely a land of contrasts, Reggie thought.

A year later.

Reggie tentatively titled his dissertation "Civilization Reformed: Choctaw Indians of Oklahoma." He sent the first draft to Willie Lou asking her if Chockie would also read it. To his surprise, everyone liked it. It was not liked much, however, by Reggie's dissertation committee. All agreed that it was "too revisionist" and that time spent among his subjects resulted in "unobjective analysis."

The committee tolerated his discussion of the Choctaws' historical background, their creation stories, and other cultural aspects, as well as his description of the identity confusion that many mixed-heritage Choctaws felt. But they were not happy with the thesis Reggie put forth. In regard to his claims that Indians do not stay the same, that Indians do not always adhere to cultural traditions, and that Indians do not always look like Indians, his committee's position was that Indians are not Indians unless they are all three. Nor did they favor Reggie's opinions that (1) Indians have been sorely abused by the government and the non-Indian public; (2) Indians are sensitive to what is written about them; and (3) Indians can retain a strong sense of Indian identity despite their acculturation to white society.

As far as Reggie and a large number of scholars in the field of cultural anthropology were concerned, these ideas are quite obvious. Just as clear was the reality that his committee had a vested interest in Indians staying "traditional." His adviser was also incensed that Reggie had sent his manuscript to Willie Lou for approval.

Reggie could not satisfy his committee for he would not make the changes the men with archaic ideas demanded. He therefore abandoned the project. It does not bother him anymore.

He secured a job with a large California newspaper as a movie critic and makes an exorbitant amount of money. In his spare time he writes adventure stories for young boys. He married his longtime girlfriend Robyn and she gave birth to their son four months later.

Reggie corresponded with Willie Lou for two years after his visit. He wrote her twice as much as she wrote him. He told her his thoughts and concerns and hoped that he didn't bore her.

One August day, when the thunderheads grew in the south and a cool breeze scurried through the neighborhood, Reggie received a box post-marked from Red Oak. The address was printed in a man's hand. He did not have to read the enclosed letter to know what it said.

Reggie took the letter and the box out to his west fence post where he could sit without his family seeing him. He cried until he could not see. He cried for he knew his dear Willie Lou was gone. He composed himself long enough to open the envelope.

Reggie,

Willie Lou passed last night in her sleep. She watered her plants yesterday morning, waded in the creek afterwards, and helped Janie cook catfish. She sat on the front porch rocking last night until very late. Janie asked her when she was coming to bed and she said she was thinking. I believe she knew her time was near. She kissed us all good-night. Tecumseh's whining let the girls know she had gone.

Willie Lou liked you a lot Reggie.

We wish you well.

Caddo.

Reggie removed the red napkin that covered the object in the box. It was a small framed sketch of a coyote, signed Billie McKenney. It was a part of Willie Lou, Reggie reasoned, and he held it to his chest and cried.

In the evenings Reggie sits in his large rocking chair and talks with Robyn while they watch their children Billie and Janie play. In the after-noons he putters about in his garden with his Pomeranian bitch, Tecumseh, paying particular attention to his tomatoes and that odd vegetable Willie Lou called okree.

He wrote to his father last week—the first time in eight years—telling him he wanted to come visit. He received his reply five days later and his family is leaving for San Francisco next week.

Romy and George

Jefferson's inaugural speech. 1801.

"Good talk, huh?" asked Romy McKenney.

"I guess," answered his companion, George. "I couldn't hardly hear him. Got it on the handout, though. I can read it later."

"No. Cain't take it with you. Leave it on the chair."

"Yur right," said George. "Well, I always thought Jefferson was interestin'. Glad I got ta see him."

"Presidents always sound good but they never do what they say they will," Romy said, putting on his hat.

"I hate talking politics with you," said George.

"How 'bout some religion, then?" asked Romy.

"Let's go."

Nanih Waiya, Mississippi. Prehistory.

"Okay, where are we?" asked George.

"This here's where Choctaws and Chickasaws'll come out of the ground," answered Romy. A loud roar sounded not too far away. "It's too early. No people yet, but it'll be a holy place."

"What d'ya mean, outta the ground? It's just a hill like every other hill I ever saw," said George. He looked around, squinting in the afternoon sun.

Romy turned to George. "Didn't anyone ever tell you? What kinda Indian are you, not knowin' where you come from?"

George looked down and kicked at a rock. "Nobody ever told me nothin'."

"See, Choctaws and Chickasaws used ta be all one people when they came outta the ground. 'Cept they weren't people, they was locusts. Now I don't know if they were like the ones we hear buzzin' or if they was grasshoppers. Anyways, after dryin' their wings they started marchin' and musta turned into people."

"Yur kiddin'." George put his hands on his hips.

"Nope. Eventually they split up and became either Choctaws who followed Chocta, or Chicasaws who followed Chickasa. They were brothers who wanted ta go different directions."

George thought a moment. "What d'ya think about that?"

"I been here a lot but never at the time when anyone's come out. I'm not sayin' I do or don't believe. It's supposed to happen." Romy sat on the ground and looked at the mound like it was an egg about to hatch.

"And you keep comin' here thinkin' you'll see it." George took a few steps forward.

"Hope so. I cain't picture in my head locusts comin' outta the ground. And I cain't picture Adam and Eve in the Garden or Moses partin' the sea neither."

"Ya left out loaves and fishes." George was quiet, then smiled. "Hey, if ya really need ta know what happened, there's one way ta find out. I always wanted ta see Moses and Jesus."

"No. There's a few things I don't wanna see," said Romy.

"Maybe yur right," said George. "Why do ya suppose Christians believe in Jesus and the loaves and burning bushes and all that?"

"How do you know they do?" asked Romy.

"They say they do."

Romy shrugged. "Maybe they're afraid ta say they don't."

"I don't like talkin' religion. I git confused."

"One day there'll be bones buried here," said Romy. "And medicine people'll draw their power from this hill."

"How do you know they'll git power from here? Maybe they'll just say they do?"

"I don't like talkin' religion, either." Romy stood and dusted off his rear with his hat. "Let's go."

The roar was closer and very loud. "What in heck's that?" asked George.

"I ain't never heard nothin' like it," said Romy. "The ground's vibratin'."

"So where to?" George asked. "There's horse races over in Oklahoma City," he said as he adjusted his hat. "State fair."

"Better go," Romy said nervously.

Oklahoma City. 1920.

"That was some noise. I'd like ta see what it was," said Romy.

"You can go tomorrow by yurself," answered George. "There's more people here than at the stickball games. Look at that doofus."

He gestured to an old man in tattered black clothes standing on an apple crate preaching about God. He pointed at George and Romy, who, this time, were dressed in suits and had short hair. "You, you there," he yelled at them. "You Indian savages. You're on your way to the Devil. You. . . ."

Before he got any further George ran into him full force and pummeled his face until Romy pulled him off.

Romy handed George his hat that got flattened when the old man rolled on it. "Thanks, Romy. I woulda hurt him. Hey, Derby Day's tomorrow. Wanna stay?"

"Don't like horse racin' much," answered Romy.

"Why not?"

"I 'member a race once over in Tulsa. A pretty white mare fell and broke her leg. They shot her right there on the track. Liked ta make me sick. But I do want ta see Man O' War run. He'll win the Kentucky Derby, ya know."

"Yeah, I was there," George reminded him.

"I ain't got ta see him yet." Romy fanned himself with his program while they watched the first two races. "Man, it's hot already. By one o'clock there's not gonna be a place to see anymore. I'm ready ta go."

George gave up trying to straighten his ruined hat and pulled it on, the ripped brim bouncing with each step. "Let's."

Maui. 1750.

"Prettiest horses I ever saw," said Romy, drinking his rum and watching the surf roll to shore. The blue-green water looked inviting, but neither man knew how to swim.

"Notice how white people keep multiplyin'?"

"Yeah. These Hawaiians are gonna git run out, just like what happened at home." Romy poured more golden brown liquid into his cup.

"Yeah. I knew that'd happen when Columbus barged in," said George. "Then everyone else came."

"Shouldn't have let him stay."

"Easier said than done, buddy boy," George said as he moved his toes around under the cool sand. "What difference did it make if Columbus or someone else was here first? More foreigners woulda come anyways."

"Probably. Hey, I never understood how white ladies could have so many babies," said Romy. "There were two who lived next to Aunt Survella and Uncle Jincy who had ten children each. One had more than that, I know. Seemed the white folks I saw were like rabbits. They was poor and thin and didn't have enough food but kept having babies anyway."

"Some Choctaws had a bunch of kids, too."

"Well, I know it, George. But there were a lot more white babies than Indian babies. That's why they're everywheres."

"I'm done," said George. He stood and brushed the sand off his pants. "Now where?"

"Wanna go ta Krebs?" asked Romy.

"Only if there's fights," said George, pouring out his unfinished cup.

"Deal," said Romy. "Let's go."

Krebs, Oklahoma. 1922.

"Darn it, Sadie," Romy said to his small brown mare. "We're almost to Krebs. Couldn't ya throw your shoe there?"

"Just a mile or so," said George.

"What's this?" Romy kicked Sadie over to a fence post to read a poster. "Says there's fights today in town. Told ya so."

They walked the horses past the ballpark where a fight arena was set up with double ropes around it. They dismounted and hurried to the ring, Romy's short bowlegs scurrying to keep up with George Coyote's long striders. By the time they reached the arena, a man dressed in white pants, white shirt, and a black bow tie was announcing the fighters.

"Saw fights here a while back," said Romy. "It was between 'Gentleman'

Tom Abbott of McAlester and 'Mysterious' Billy Ross from Seattle. Went fifteen rounds and Tommy had Ross every round but three. Tommy hit that boy's kidneys so hard he couldn't keep the pace. That year a group of churchgoers came to protest. Even a blind man walked around with a protest sign. They wanted the fights canceled but the militia wouldn't let nobody in. It wasn't that good a fight since the fighters had to promise not to knock out each other. Can you imagine that?"

"That referee looks like he can whip everybody here," said George.

"Carl Morris," said Romy. "A lot of fighters train with him."

"How'd you know that?"

"Thought everybody did." Romy looked at the program. "First fight's George Ward and 'Fireman' Wade. Wade's got a good right." At that moment Wade threw a right to Ward's jaw and knocked Ward cold. "Told ya."

"Didn't take long. Who's next?" asked George.

"Carl Fleming and Leslie Jennings. Leslie sounds like a girl's name. Hey," he nudged George and whispered, "it ends in a draw."

An old man with no teeth turned around and looked up at Romy and George. "A woman put herself up as the prize. This oughta be a good one."

"Wanna bet?" asked George.

The old man's eyebrows danced up and down. "I put five on Fleming."

"I bet it's a draw," said George, then he shook the old man's hand.

After thirty minutes Romy was fidgeting. "Long fight," he said with a yawn. Finally, after fifteen rounds, it ended in a draw.

"Well, drat," said the old man. "Both men shoulda got her."

"Don't know about that," said George. "What she look like?"

As they discussed the fight the section of bleachers next to Romy and George moaned and splintered, then collapsed. It wasn't a far way to fall but some people lay on the ground screaming in pain. Those who were unhurt ran over the injured to other seats or to spots where they could see the next fight.

"You sure picked the good seats," said George as he leaned to his right and looked straight down at the ground where the bleachers had fallen. Several injured people were being tended by spectators not as interested in the fights.

"Nobody dies here, you know. I'm tired," said Romy. "Ready? Wait. Oh, no. It's my Aunt Billie. Over there, the lady who looks like she wants to get in the ring."

"Spry old thing, ain't she? I'd like to talk to her," said George.

Romy bit his bottom lip. "She dies in a few years. I cain't ever talk to family no more. Let's go."

"Guess we ain't got a choice," George said under his breath.

After lemonades and ham sandwiches courtesy of the old man's lost wager, Romy and George visited the farrier, who replaced Sadie's lost shoe.

"Good fights," Romy said an hour later. He sat on Sadie with his fists in front of his face.

"Wanna go see Wart?" asked George. Wart was a half Muscogee, half Chickasaw who died thirty years before.

"Sure. Always like ta see Wart." Romy got off Sadie while George dismounted from his stallion, Nocona. The men unfastened the horses' cinches and bridles and pulled them off. Then they slapped the animals on their rumps and watched them run off into a field of dry, yellowed grass, just like they had done a thousand times before.

Okmulgee, Oklahoma. 1892.

"These drops are cold," Romy whined. "Look at the hail. It's not little any more. Geez. Some a these are bigger'n melons. We got ourselves in a fix, George."

"Mama told me when I was little that rain meant God was tinkling. Man, he's got a full-scale piss goin' here."

A piece of hail hit a branch and fell on George's leg. "Shit," he yelled. Another hailstone hit one of the horses, Shivers, on the head. The gelding fell as if the ground had moved under him.

"Git under the tree," Romy yelled.

The other horse, Marco, pulled the wagon and the unconscious Shivers to a tree and put his head next to the trunk. Romy and George wiggled along underneath. The wagon had chunks broken off the sides and driver's seat.

"I don't usually like wagons. Glad ya brought one this time," said Romy.

After a few minutes the hail stopped and a light sprinkle fell.

"It's safe," George said as he walked over to Shivers, who had his head up, blinking his eyes.

Romy looked around. "For now."

"Let's git on ta Wart's."

"Look at them houses," said Romy as they trotted Marco and a wobbly Shivers down the road. "That one's got no roof. We ain't never gonna git there with these branches and trees layin' on the road. Look at that wall of rain, George. It's comin' towards us. What were you thinkin'? Comin' here durin' all this weather?"

"We need ta," George said, looking straight ahead. "Almost there."

Romy and George finally came to a small white farmhouse that was surrounded by trees and dozens of chickens, ducks, and baby turkeys that ran to the wagon when they stopped. "Watch yur step," said Romy.

"You two," said a deep voice behind the wagon. It was Wart, wearing a broad-brimmed hat and carrying a pick. "Daisy made pies this mornin'."

Romy took in Wart's face. His friend was blessed with two warts the size of baby green tomatoes, one on his left eyebrow and another on his chin. Romy always wondered if Wart could have cut them off.

"Come on in," said Wart.

"This house reminds me of Mama's," said George as he and Romy climbed the stairs to the porch.

"Cain't see your mama's house again, George, or any of your family, so you better enjoy this. Howdy, Barf." Romy reached down to scratch the old hound's head.

Romy looked around the kitchen and sighed. It was clean and full of plants and old furniture. A half tin of Towle's log cabin maple syrup that served as a planter for dill and parsley sat on the windowsill. An ivy plant held by tacks grew up the wall and around the perimeter of the ceiling.

Daisy boomed into the kitchen. "Well, there ya'll are."

Daisy was the daughter of a freedwoman and a full-blood Choctaw. She stood an inch taller than Wart and had almost-black skin and hair as long and textured as a horse's tail. She wore a light gray dress with a white apron. The dress was hemmed below her knees and her hair fell two inches longer. She shook Romy and George's hands very hard.

"Sit down, boys. Where ya been? How long since I seen you? A year?"

"Yeah, we been out travelin'." Actually, Romy and George had been gone enough days to add up to thirty-five years, but it was only twelve months to Daisy and Wart.

"Want some pie? Got some rhubarb this mornin'. Or I got cake. Made it with duck eggs. Tastes better that way."

"Well, okay. Both?" Romy asked innocently. He felt something brush his ankle and looked down to see a gray kitten using his leg as a scratching post. This would be Bunky. The first time Romy saw Bunky she was an old, slobbering, grumpy cat, but now she was a new kitten, playful and alert. He was afraid he'd cry but that wasn't allowed.

"What you gonna name her?" asked Romy.

"Oh, still thinkin' on it," answered Daisy.

"How 'bout 'Bunky'?" asked George.

Romy shot him an angry look.

"Well, that's a good one," said Daisy. "*Bunky*. I like that."

Thunder crashed so loud the kitten hooked her claws into Romy's hand and jumped to the floor. She ran to the bed and disappeared under the spread. Wind blew raindrops under the porch and through the screen door into the kitchen. It smelled good, but meant trouble.

"Look how dark it is, ya'll," said Daisy. "Think we oughta git to the shelter?"

Angry winds sprinted through the yard causing chickens and other birds to bounce across the dirt.

"Grab your stuff, Daisy. Tell us what ta carry," said George, standing.

After ten frantic minutes of hauling clothes, tools, birds, and Bunky to the underground cyclone shelter, Wart shut the heavy overhead door. "Hope them pigs and cows git outta the way."

"Most will," said George. Romy kicked his leg hard.

It was cramped and smelly in the damp cellar and the tornado that swept over them sounded like a freight train. "Did you forget about the tornado or what?" George quietly asked Romy.

"Hush. Not now," rasped Romy. Within moments it was quiet.

Wart opened the door and shooed out the birds. Daisy, Romy, and George followed, looking at the property. Branches and leaves and hailstones lay everywhere. Most of the barn was gone, but the house still stood, minus most of the roof. "Could have been worse," said George.

Daisy walked to the creek. "Here's the cows and your mules down here," she yelled. "The tornado went right over them."

"This ain't so good," said Romy. "Look up there."

"That's my pig in the tree," said Wart. "Pieces of him, I mean. Cain't reach them hindquarters. It'll just have ta fall out, I guess."

"Look at them chickens," said George. "They ain't got no feathers." A dozen chickens and two roosters scratched the ground but looked as if they'd been almost cleanly plucked. "Never saw that before. Well, let's git busy."

For the next two days George and Romy helped Wart and Daisy repair their roof and trim branches, and Romy noticed that George talked to Wart constantly. They decided to spend the night and leave the next day after finishing the porch roof. Before the two men entered the barn for the night they looked up and saw stars streaking across the cloudless sky. "Witches're out," said George.

"They're always out," said Romy, very quietly.

The next morning, two miles south of Wart and Daisy's farm, Romy stopped his horse.

"What's wrong?" asked George.

"Someone's . . ."—Romy turned his head to look into the trees—". . . here. See him? Right there on his horse. Jackson Crow."

"Crow? We better git," said George nervously.

"Cain't hurt ya," Romy said, smiling.

Jackson rode into the sunlight on his muddy-legged black mare, her mane adorned with scalps and ears. Four other Crows emerged from the shadows and stood behind Jackson, waiting. "Look at their faces," said Romy. "Uglier than mud fences. They're thinkin' they can take our hair. Let's have fun."

Romy and George got off their horses. Jackson walked his horse until she was five feet away, then dismounted. Jackson stepped up to Romy and stopped two inches from his face. He lifted his nose slightly and sniffed. "You smell dead, boy."

George walked over next to Romy. "Know what, ugly man?" he said. "I got news for you. You *are* . . ." and Romy hit George's arm hard enough to make him stagger. "Hey! Romy!"

"Cain't tell him," Romy said to George, still looking at Jackson.

Jackson stopped grinning and looked back and forth between Romy and George, puzzled at what George was about to say. As he backed up, he pointed at the two men with a long-nailed finger and whispered, "I'll be seeing you later."

"Three more times," smiled Romy. "Yup."

Jackson walked to his horse, said something to his gang, mounted, and all five spurred their horses hard to get away from two men who were even stranger than they were.

"They're gonna kill your family, Romy."

"Already did, George."

Four nights later Romy and George fished the Columbia River north of the Saddle Mountains.

"Why'd ya talk so much ta Wart?" asked Romy. "Ya never did that before."

"Been thinkin' 'bout him getting shot an' all and I wanted ta get my questions to him before he went. We can only visit him one more time." George reeled in his line and replaced the lost worm.

"Right," said Romy. "After ya see him three times, the fourth time has to be soon after."

George threw his line back out into the fast-moving water. "Hey, how 'bout some oysters ta go with this? Wanna go to the Norwalk Oyster Festival?" he asked.

"We got enough." Romy set his pole against a tree and emptied his fish basket onto the ground. Two large salmon flopped on the green grass. "Hey, no sittin'. I caught 'em so you clean 'em."

George tossed his pole into the water and pulled out his knife. He settled down next to the fish and spoke as he filleted. "Daisy acted like she knew somethin'."

Romy shook his head. "Nah. She cain't know. I tell you one thing, though, buddy. Ya cain't put ideas in their heads. Like namin' that cat. They were gonna name it Bunky anyways."

George was quiet for a moment. "Couldn't help it."

Romy took a deep breath. "I know."

Both men were quiet while the fish cooked.

"Good salmon," said Romy, wiping his mouth. "Where ya wanna go now?"

"Let's just rest."

"Cain't," Romy said with a full mouth. "Not allowed. We gotta go somewheres else. Now."

"Okay. There's a fair at Muskogee," said George.

Romy set his unfinished plate of fish on a flat rock and stood. "Let's go, then."

Muskogee, Oklahoma. 1966.

People came from the towns around Muskogee with their canned foods and handiworks to show. There were horse races, lemonade, and all kinds of food. A man in front of a tent said there were human oddities inside and they could be seen for just five cents.

"Oh, man, I just gotta take a look," said George. "I'll pay."

The two men walked side by side through the entrance into the shaded tent.

"Well, I never," said Romy. There were two fat people, a man and woman as big as milk cows, sitting together on a large bench. "Are they just gonna sit there and look at us lookin' at them?"

"Hey, Romy, what d'ya think a this?" In the next area, Siamese twins, two boys, were joined together at the waist facing each other. "They look to be 'bout twenty so they've spent some time like that," said George. "I wonder how they get around."

"Do they get tired of each other?"

"Not much they could do about it, I expect."

In the next room was an alligator with a monkey's head that came from Africa alongside a skeleton of what was supposed to be the world's smallest person. "Looks like baby bones to me," said George.

"What in heck's this guy doin'?" asked Romy. The last exhibit was a man in a cage, squatting in a corner eating a raw snake. He was dirty and hairy and the sign said he had been captured in South America. "You think he stays in here all the time?"

"Nah. Probably his job to act crazy," said George.

"Now, I don't know about that," said Romy. "Who'd eat a raw snake and let blood run all over himself if he weren't crazy?"

"You have a point."

"Probably a hoot to talk to," said Romy.

"Why would you want to? I'm tired of this."

"Well," Romy said as he thought. "There's a powwow in Tuba City."

"I'd rather go ta the Crow Fair, but this should be interestin'."

Tuba City, Arizona. 1997.

"Since when did these tribes out here start doin' Northern Plains fancy dancin'?" asked Romy.

"Beats me. Looks kinda weird, don't it?"

Romy strained to see the middle of the arena. "My Lordy. There's a woman drummin'."

"That guy there's dressed like a Comanche 'cept he's got the roach backwards."

"Check out the Indian Barbie," said Romy. "Everything she's got on's from a different tribe."

"This what ya call pan-Indianism?" asked George.

"No, that's what lost Indians call it. I call it copycattin'."

"As long as we're close, wanna see that Miss Indian Powwow Pageant I told ya about?"

Romy picked a small salmon bone from between his teeth. "Let's go."

Anadarko, Oklahoma. 1990.

"Strange," mused George out loud. He and Romy sat in the darkened seating area of the local junior high school auditorium.

"Sure is," said Romy. A Kiowa girl, about sixteen and dressed in her white powwow buckskin dress, was earnestly mixing cake batter under a spotlight. "Never saw a contestant bake a cake for the talent portion before."

"Wonder how they score that. Do all the judges get a piece?"

The girl melding the cake fixings moved out of the light to make room for the next girl's talent presentation.

"Beats me. Geez, what's this girl doin'?"

"Looks like she's gonna do black face," said George. "I cain't hardly believe it."

"Curious thing for a Seminole to do. Half the audience looks like they'd be insulted. This is all bullshit, you know. The winner's the one who raises the most money for the powwow organization and that cake-mixin' girl got her family to donate more than anybody else. Hey, I'm in the mood for some real dancin'."

"No," answered George.

"Oh, come on." Romy elbowed him.

"No."

Romy knew he'd have a hard time convincing George to visit Wounded Knee in that particular year. "Just for a little?"

"I don't like goin' there," said George. "We cain't tell nobody what'll happen and I don't like it."

"But we cain't tell anybody anywheres," Romy said matter-of-factly.

George was getting agitated. "I really don't wanta go *there*."

"We always learn somethin' from him."

"And I get sick afterwards. I get sick when I see that picture of ol' Big Foot frozen in the snow." George crossed his arms. "No."

Romy thought a few seconds, then smiled. "Well, then, how 'bout sayin' hello ta Geronimo?"

"Where?"

"Fort Sill?"

"I like him better in Mexico." George watched the girl put her cake in the oven.

"Hot in Mexico."

"Hot at Fort Sill, too. Forget it, then."

"I'm goin' back to Muskogee to see if I can find that snake-eatin' guy," said Romy.

"What the hell for, Romy? He's crazy."

"I know. I wanna talk to someone who I don't care how he dies later on."

"You mean like Cortés and Custer? You talked to them."

"Well, yeah," Romy shrugged. "Who wouldn't want to?"

"Me."

Romy turned to his partner. "You don't even wanna see what they look like? See for yourself what they're about?"

"No, I'd kill them."

"Cain't," said Romy. "Ya cain't kill nobody. I wanted ta kill Custer but I cain't. Cain't kill Hitler, cain't kill Jackson. I've wanted to scream to them Cheyennes what was gonna happen. I wanted ta kill Chivington. I wanted to tell Geronimo to stay south and Chief Joseph to get north. I almost punched out Buddy Holly's pilot in the hangar and shot a hole in the tanks so the plane couldn't take off. I wanted to throw Dillon Myer over a cliff. I was standin' next ta Tecumseh at the Thames when he got shot. Twice. Don't ya think I wanted ta. . . ."

"But I'd do it," said George.

"You ain't been at this long enough. I've learned ta just enjoy lookin' at 'em. I like to see if I can understand their thinkin'."

"I could do that," said George.

"Bet ya cain't. Not if it's someone you care about."

"I'll show you." George stood and tucked in his shirttail, which had come out seven years before.

Wounded Knee. 1973.

". . . and what I say goes," yelled the tall, mixed-blood Lakota to his underlings. He was tall and paler than the other Indians, but he hadn't been in the sun much lately. His braids were still short, their length camouflaged by leather wrappings.

"The making of a star," said George. "Hey, I don't care about him."

"Yeah, I know," said Romy. He looked around the church. "There's Anna Mae."

George stared. "Oh, hell," he said and started for her.

Romy grabbed his arm. "Cain't say nothin'."

"Romy, I gotta tell her."

"Cain't. Not allowed. Cain't even tell ol' hot shot he'll be in the movies one day."

"I don't like this, Romy," said George. "Someone's gonna kill her."

"Let's go," said Romy.

"What's the harm if I tell her?" asked George, knowing full well the harm. "Look, there's Buddy Lamont." George looked panicked.

"Let's go, George. Ya know what happens if you tell. Ya gotta stay here forever."

"No, I. . . ."

"Let's go," Romy said quietly.

Santa Monica Downs. 1922.

"There he is, the greatest horse of all. Man O' War. Quit poutin', George. You gotta get it together, buddy."

"But we *know*."

"Yeah, we do," said Romy. "And we cain't tell. This is what I get for hitting my buddy in the head with a pick. And what you get for killin' that kid." Then he drank his lemonade, the good kind with pulp floating at the top. "There's a lot we can do without tellin', ya know. There's places ta go, things ta see. Any time, any place."

"I know, but it ain't easy," said George. "Ain't easy at all. It's like, like, hell."

"I think that's the idea," said Romy.

Eternal Owls

ARIANA

The Braden place, McAlester. 2000.

Reg! In here!" yelled rookie officer Walter Agee. "In here," he repeated, more quietly. Walt felt dizzy and leaned against the bedroom door frame.

Agee and his partner, the more experienced Reginald Blackwood, had been eating a late dinner at McDonald's when they received the dispatcher's call. A frantic neighbor heard the Bradens screaming and called 911. The two officers were the closest to the small, wood-sided home of the fortyish couple.

The white-blond Blackwood stepped through the house carefully to avoid corrupting the bloody tracks that led from the bedroom, down the hall, and out the back door. *Size 11, Nike basketball shoe tread*, he thought.

From the bedroom door Blackwood could see that the Bradens' throats were deeply cut, and their ears, hair, and scalp were gone right down to the eyebrows. He didn't have to walk into the room. Burgess and Meg Braden were dead, all right.

"Someone's been on the warpath," Blackwood said seriously. He chewed his gum faster. "Get out of there, Walt. You got blood all over your back. Walt?" He lightly hit his stunned partner's arm. "Come on, let's report. More here than we can handle." Blackwood didn't tell Walt that he'd get used to this, because this kind of thing usually didn't happen.

Washington, D.C.

"Stay up, stay up," I pleaded with my curtain rod. After I screwed the heavy rod into the white wall, I stood back and decided it was uneven. Then I took the whole thing down and started over. I looked at it again from across the room and realized it looked better the first time. Now I had to put the screws back in the same spot they'd already been in and the fit wasn't tight.

"Mom, I'm hungry." My nine-year-old, Kim, had said that four times already.

"Just a minute," I said. "I'm busy."

After threading the Pier 1 sheer ivory curtains onto the brass rod, I discovered they were a foot too long. Apparently, they were made for those elegant *Architectural Digest* windows that were designed for draperies that fell to the ground then spread out on the floor in front of them.

"Should have measured them. F—," I started. Curbing my cursing after Kim was born was harder than losing the forty pounds I'd gained.

I had no intention of folding the curtains up, cramming them back into the plastic case they came in, then taking them back. So I turned the ends under back toward the wall.

After heating up leftover California vegetable pizza from the Pizza Palace we didn't finish the night before, Kim settled into his math homework and I started unloading the dishwasher. Halfway through, the phone rang.

"Ariana?" asked a voice, hoarse from a lifetime of smoking. It was my ex-father-in-law, Junior LeFlore. Junior was his given name.

"Yes, Junior. What is it?"

"Well, well, I. . . ." His voice cracked.

"Junior, what is it?"

"It's Butter."

My ex-husband. His real name was Len, but he was nicknamed Butter in high school. I thought that a vile name, but it stuck through his adulthood. His parents called him Butter and I called him Len in the same conversation. Len was the father of our son Kim, and Len was a no-good son of a bitch. The latter being my dead ex-mother-in-law.

"He's in jail."

No big surprise there. Junior better not ask for money.

"They say he killed some people."

That stopped me. Usually Len just got drunk, picked fights, or drove drunk.

"Who? Why?"

"Burgess and Meg Braden. It was bad. They had their hair and ears cut off. Len wouldn't never do nothing like that. You know that, doncha, Ar?"

"No, no he wouldn't." My mind reeled. Len was an angry, passionate man, who used words instead of fists to abuse, but he could hurt nevertheless. He learned that behavior from his daddy. Junior picked at his wife, Ivey, until the day she died. Len verbally abused me for six years until the shit bucket finally tipped over and I lost all desire to clean it up.

I knew what he was about to ask and I closed my eyes. Junior cleared his throat. "Can you come?"

"No. I'm sorry, Junior, but I can't. I won't." I said that because I was on vacation. Also because I didn't want to.

"Ar." His tone turned angry. "You used to be married to him. You owe him."

"I don't owe him a thing."

Junior played out his hand. "He's the father of your son."

"I'll think about it. Got to go. I'm checking Kim's homework." I hung up.

"What, Mom?" Kim asked. He stood in the kitchen doorway, his left hand in a box of vanilla wafers. He heard me talk and figured something was up with his dad.

What a handsome kid, I thought. Dark brown hair, almost-black eyes, and dimples. No one in my family has dimples and neither does anyone on his dad's side and I haven't figured out where they came from. Smart and polite, too. Clever when he wants to hide something from me.

"Honey, your dad's in trouble. He's blamed for something he couldn't have done."

"What?"

"Well, they say he stole something," I lied.

Kim had an exalted view of his daddy. "Dad wouldn't do that."

And on we went for a while, discussing what Dad may or may not have done. I planned to keep my opinions to myself until Kim was old enough to handle the truth about his father.

Two days later the doorbell rang while I was finishing my crunches and watching a rerun of *Xena: Warrior Princess.* Standing on my porch was Junior and the one individual who could convince me of anything: the old medicine man Winchell Sill.

"Had to come, Ar," Junior said. He dropped his cigarette onto my clean, flowerpot-covered porch and crushed it out with his foot.

I had just finished a long run and still wore my sweaty, stained, Cabo San Lucas T-shirt. It had holes in the armpits and was revolting, but it was my favorite. "Hello, Winchell. Come in."

When the old man walked through the door I turned to Junior. "Geez. You could have called," I said.

"I did call," Junior said as he walked past me into the den. I caught a whiff of beer. "Where's Kim?"

"At a friend's. He's spending the night." *Thank goodness.*

I got us Diet Cokes and sat in my rocker opposite the sofa where Junior and Winchell sat. The old man hadn't changed much since I'd seen him three years before at the family reunion at Willie Lou's in Red Oak. Winchell was married to one of Aunt Ange's best friends, a full-blood lady named Roxie who made wedding cakes. Since I was a child, Winchell and Roxie attended our family events.

I figured Winchell was about seventy. He was shorter than me, about five-seven, and had thick gray hair cut so short it stood up. Unlike many of the old fulls, Winchell spoke Choctaw fluently and was as culturally Indian as one could be in the year 2000. He was one of the few medicine people left and many of us looked at him with awe. Whether he could really perform magic didn't matter. He was a walking, talking encyclopedia of the old ways and the tribal stories, which was impressive enough.

I looked at Junior. "And, so?"

"We need you to come see Butter. He didn't do it."

"You told me. Junior," I said slowly, "I don't practice law in Oklahoma."

"Don't matter," he said. "You need to come see. Then you can recommend someone." He looked to Winchell.

"Ariana," he said in that voice that sounded like honey mixed with gravel, "maybe you can tell us what to do after you talk to Butter." He leaned forward with his fingers laced together. "I think you need to come home. They'd do it."

Winchell pointed to the pictures that hung on the living room wall of my grandmother Willie Lou; her grandmother Tish Walkingstick; Tish's mother, Billie Watchman; and aunt Survella Wilson. Daddy inherited the pencil sketches of Tish, Survella, and Billie from Willie Lou when she died, and I had to copy the one of my grandmother because cousin Sam Hallmark wanted the original. Apparently, Billie drew all of them, including the one of herself while standing in front of a mirror. "Them women, they'd come. All of them."

"It's not my home anymore." I didn't actually mean that. Oklahoma really was my home and it always will be. I just didn't care to be in the same state as Len, so I accepted a position at a Washington law firm even though I didn't like the city. It was too big, rushed, and violent and I didn't trust many people here. Nobody waves at you like they do back home. Worse, I didn't know any Indians here. I can pass for a white person with a mysterious lineage mixed in, but as soon as the office found out I was Choctaw I quickly became the token "Indian princess." Since most other people said that they, too, were "part Indian," nobody took my attachment to my heritage seriously because they had no connection to theirs.

Winchell leaned back into the soft sofa that I liked to sleep on. "Len didn't do it," he continued. "His tracks were in the Bradens' house, but someone else did the killings."

I knew they meant business. It cost some money and time to drive out here from Oklahoma and Junior would do anything to protect his son, even if he was guilty as sin. After another hour of talking in a circle, of Junior and Winchell trying to convince me to go and me resisting, they decided it was time to leave.

"Think about it, Ariana," Winchell said. "You need to come." He reached to touch my forehead with his hand, the index finger growing as it came closer to my face. It touched me, then shrank back to its normal size. I flinched and felt like I had missed a few seconds.

"Yeah, I'll think about it." It didn't matter what they said. I'd already made up my mind. It had taken me long enough to get away from there and I wasn't going back. Still, I was being pulled to the west.

I took a very hot shower, ordered Chinese, and spent the evening watching *X-Files* videos. I tried not to think about Len, but like every other time I tried to ignore him, he intruded into my thoughts.

Three days later, as I was driving to Dulles Airport to board a plane that would take me to Oklahoma City, I cursed myself for giving in. Winchell and Junior had come over again the next morning for another round of arguments as I was on my way to the grocery store. Junior knew I couldn't say no to Winchell and that's why he brought him to see me.

I left Kim with my neighbors Pat and June Marks, a retired couple who always offered to watch my son if I needed a hand. They were kind, energetic people who thoroughly enjoyed catering to a nine-year-old.

I adjusted the lumbar support in my Mercury Marquis. When I was twenty-eight, I slipped off the roof while cleaning the chimney flue. I grabbed the gutter, pulled it loose, and my body hit the maidenhair fern bed like a 135-pound rock, fracturing a vertebra and pulling a ligament that refused to heal. I still run every day even though my physical therapist tells me it does me more harm than good. After almost thirty years of running, I'd fade to nothing if I couldn't do it. It's my nature to run, regardless of the back pain it causes.

I landed in Oklahoma City at four in the afternoon, picked up my Ford Taurus at one of the easiest airport car rental pickups in the country, and took off to McAlester. I decided to go the old way, through Shawnee and Seminole. I like the small towns and the possibility of finding a treasure in one of the highway antique shops or junkyards, but I especially love the open fields cut by creeks and thick stands of trees. When my brother, Caddo, and I were little, we occupied ourselves on trips with our parents by seeing who could spot the most hawks on telephone poles and tall treetops. That game kept our eyes off the crushed turtles, opossums, and armadillos on the road.

I crossed the South Canadian River and recalled the time I went hunting outside the small town of Calvin with Daddy and his friends. I never wanted to be a hunter, but Daddy wished me to hunt. So did Len and my cousin Sam. Hunting was not something I understood and I gritted my teeth while tolerating their conversations about racks and spikes, the Sunday mornings filled with *Ducks Unlimited* television shows featuring guys with accents thicker than any Okie I ever heard, and endless the-big-one-that-got-away stories.

To appease my father, I tried hunting white-tailed deer one fall when I was twenty-four. Daddy and I left camp at 5:00 A.M. and for two hours sat in the tree stands we had put up the week before while scouting. At seven we climbed down and walked east. I found tracks and scat so Daddy and I followed.

After half an hour, I sighted the 110-pound buck at 170 feet. Daddy's arm was going up to point him out to me, but I said, "I see him." I aimed precisely at the base of the white-tail's neck.

"Easy, girl," Daddy whispered behind me, thinking I might get excited and yank the trigger instead of squeezing.

"Hush," I said.

I aimed again, exhaled, and said, "Got him." Then I lowered the rifle without having pulled the trigger.

Satisfied that I could procure venison in the unlikely event that I was ever starving, I turned and left the buck to worry about more serious predators.

As we walked back to the truck, I jingled the 30-30 shells in my coat pocket, where they'd been all morning. Daddy heard.

"You don't have to hunt with me just to make me happy, you know," he said.

"Well, I'm glad you finally said so."

And I never went hunting again.

McAlester.

When I arrived in McAlester that evening, I filled the Taurus with gas then called my cousin Annette Strong. She was a descendant of Teague McKenney, the brother of our family matriarch legend, Billie McKenney Watchman. Annette and I were the same age, forty, and we had been runners since childhood. I missed her when I went to college, then to law school, but we managed to stay in touch and to see each other several times a year. When I was married to Len, she had been my confidant. She knew all my secrets.

"Hey, Annette," I said, "I'm here."

"Come on over. I got vegetable stew in the Crock-Pot."

Annette was single, mainly because she was too picky. She said repeatedly since high school that "no frigging guy is going to tell me what to do." Annette thought that because they were generally insecure, Indian men were the best at being domineering, so she never dated any. She taught high school biology and lived in a small three-room house by a creek. She loved animals and had entirely too many dogs, cats, and miniature pigs, one of whom stayed in the house and used a litter box. That first night the cats kept jumping on and off my bed and woke me up.

"So, when you gonna see Len?" she asked over breakfast of bananas, Total cereal, decaf coffee, and a vitamin the size of a horse pill. Annette was still the health food fanatic, watching everything she put into her mouth. At least she started eating chicken and fish; for eighteen years she abstained from all meat and didn't look particularly healthy.

"I'll get it over with this morning," I said. "Want to run this afternoon?"

"Of course. The last class ends at three. Come on over and we'll run." Then I watched her pack a lunch of tofu franks, mandarin oranges and raisins, peanut butter crackers, lemonade Snapple, and a box of animal cookies. She brushed her teeth and left.

I cleaned the dishes and went to the county jail. I stopped at the 7-Eleven to get a Diet Coke and saw an old high school friend, Ned Swanson, filling his truck.

After high school, Ned became a bull rider. He was around five-ten, the same as me, and had uncommonly good coordination. He won the Mesquite Bull Riding Championship twice and traveled the circuit for six years, winning or close to it. His career came to an end when he entered the Guthrie rodeo with an inner ear infection that caused him to be tossed off a big ugly bull with no horns, an unforgiving nature, and enormous testicles. Freddy Krueger stomped Ned's legs until the bones snapped.

The surgeons managed to pin Ned's shattered bones together, but they mended in the same way a favorite coffee mug gets glued back together after a fall to the kitchen floor—less reliable and not as attractive as before. Ned was at least more fortunate than his buddy, Lonnie Don Barber, a freckled white boy who lost his life when his ride, Marilyn Manson, threw him into the rails then butted him so hard his ribs broke and punctured both lungs.

I always thought Ned a fool for participating in a sport with a 100 percent injury rate, but at the same time, I was jealous that he could ride something so powerful. He said that bull riding was the same as hunting buffalo. Not that any of our Choctaw ancestors hunted buffalo to great extent. To many Indian men with no culture except their tribes' history, however, buffalo hunting is a pan-Indian symbol of manhood. And Ned had been good at bull riding. Now he looked small and broken, uninspired to do anything except remember the crazy days of twirly-birding on a wild, thousand-pound animal.

"How ya doin', Ned?" I asked while standing in line to pay for my drink.

"Uh, okay." His eyes were red from drinking and he didn't know who I was. I walked out, sad that a successful guy could become such a mess.

At the jail I identified myself and a uniformed woman with a power-lifter's physique led me to a questioning room with two chairs and a table. A few minutes later a guard led in a handcuffed and shackled Len LeFlore. "I'll be outside the door, ma'am," the middle-aged, pockmarked jailer said.

Len sat. My ex, even though he was tall and physically attractive, at least when I felt good about him, looked scared, and I don't recall him ever looking frightened. He had dark smudges under his brown eyes and his hands shook. Len had always been on the thin-but-muscular side and he lost weight easily. Now he just looked thin.

"Hello, Ar. Nice of you to come." Before I could say anything, he continued. "I mean that. I didn't do it."

"All right, Len. Incidentally, Kim is fine. Thanks for asking."

"Don't start that." He got angry, then slowed. His energy was gone. "You know I care about him. And you."

"Don't *you* start *that*."

"Okay, okay. Let's start over. Ar, I didn't kill those people. Someone else did."

"So I hear. Tell me. What were you doing in the house?"

I was a defense attorney and could usually tell when a person was lying. This would be easy, I thought.

"Well, I knew that Burgess got a new 357 Dan Wesson 'cause he showed me the week before. I got drunk and decided I wanted it. Simple as that."

Thieves give me the creeps, especially those who are supposedly friends with their victims. Here sat a thief and I used to be married to him. I wonder what that says about me. "How did you know where he kept the gun?"

"He showed me on Saturday after we came back from fishing at the lake. He kept it in a gun safe in his hall closet, but he lost the keys to it."

"How lucky for you." I blinked twice and he ignored it.

"Around two I went in the back door."

"Wasn't it locked?"

"Yeah. Burgess keeps a key in the barbecue grill out back."

"God, Len. He was your friend."

He shrugged. "Not a real good friend." He got my look. "Well, anyway, I went in and their bedroom light came on. I thought maybe they heard me, but then I heard voices—three or four men talking all at once. Quiet, sort of whispery, but normal. Their sound hurt my ears. I can't explain it."

Len pulled a Lucky Strike from the pack in front of him and his shaking hands made the cigarette difficult to light. When we were married, I made Len go outside to smoke. Sometimes he would, and whenever he wouldn't, I'd take Kim outside instead.

"I decided to leave when Meg and Burgess started screaming. Those other voices laughed and then something flew past me, like a big bird. I ducked into the pantry until everything was quiet. A few minutes later I ran to the bedroom to see what happened and got blood all over my shoes. Then I hightailed it back down the hall." He pushed his brown ponytail back over his shoulder. Len had poker-straight, shiny hair that never got split ends.

"There weren't any other tracks, Len."

"I didn't do it!" he yelled.

The jailer came back in, his chest puffed out like a pissed-off bullfrog. He was ready to beat the liver out of Len.

"We're fine," I said. "Just a bit excited."

The jailer looked at me, then back at Len, and nodded. He stepped reluctantly back and closed the door.

"I didn't do it," Len said again. "That Gary Busey cop saw me in the kitchen as I was going out."

"Who?"

"The cop that looks like that actor."

"Okay. It took the cops ten minutes to get there. Why were you still there? Why didn't you leave?" Len bit his lower lip. "Len?"

Len studied his cigarette butt. His nails were gnawed to the quick of his long brown fingers. I had never seen him bite his nails.

"Tell me."

"Ariana." He put his hands over his face and slowly pulled them down his cheeks, his mouth, his chin. "You know I've done some bad things. Not awful things, but, well . . . I . . . I swear it happened. I'm not making it up and I wasn't drunk enough to see things. I never see weird things when I'm high." He drummed his fingers on the table.

What is going on? I thought. Not speaking his mind isn't one of Len's problems. Usually Len blurts out his feelings without editing them, which was one of the major issues in our marriage. He said what he thought when just thinking would have been best.

"I ran out to the backyard and stopped," he began. "After another bird—or whatever it was—went past me, I looked after it. When I looked back towards the house, there was this . . . this face. This face," he repeated with no sound. He looked at me with watery eyes. That made three things I had never seen him do.

"It was round, with brown teeth, and huge yellow eyes. It was an *opa*-man. I couldn't move. I stood still thinking about him. Then he just . . . disappeared, and I was frozen there until the cop pushed me down and put the cuffs on me. Those *opas* killed Meg and Burgess, and they made it look like I did."

I sat ramrod straight, my mouth open. Daddy and Grandma Willie told me many times of the Crows, the owl-men who almost destroyed our family. It couldn't be, I reasoned. I was sensitive to the tribal stories and even more so to the family ones. Non-Indians and white Indians called our stories myths and legends. But I knew the Crows were real. Len knew better than to use my fear of them to get me to help him.

"You better not be lying to me." I knew he wasn't.

"Not about this I wouldn't."

"I find this difficult to believe." I stood. "We've heard Crow stories a hundred times. Maybe you were drunk and imagined owls at the Bradens'."

Len shook his head no. "Ar. Talk to Winchell."

"I will." Then I knocked on the door and the jailer let me out.

I had a hard time swallowing and drank at the cold water fountain almost a minute. I walked out the door into the warm sunlight and took off my light blazer. My pits were wet and sweat ran down my back. *What had the Bradens thought when they saw the Crows?* I wondered. Willie'd had Survella's old journals, and when we were young, Caddo and I spent the summers with her. One evening she read a passage to us:

> Mama had the runs, so she took off her clothes to wash in the warm river. A gray and brown mother duck and her yellow babies swam across the slow water. Aunt Adele looked at them like they were her family. "What a happy family," Adele said. "See how they keep up with her? Maybe they're going back to their nest." I was almost undressed when I felt a chill. "Adele?" I said. She looked up. "I hear them, child," she answered. "Start back to the wagon." I didn't even know what scared me. Then I saw the owls walking towards us through the shallow water. They were dressed like men and wore hats, except one, who had running sores all over his round head. His ears were too small. . . .

The memory made me want to run. Or to eat, but then I'd feel guilty, so running was better. I looked to the sky and considered who might encounter the Crows next. Then I heard a cough.

Winchell was leaning against my car drinking a Diet Pepsi. "Len told you."

I fished for my keys, which had fallen to the bottom of my purse. "Winchell, there's no way that the Crows are here again. They died a hundred years ago."

Winchell was always patient and soft-spoken. "No, they didn't. They're here. I went to the grave. They got out."

I stared at him. I had seen the grave only once, when I was a teenager. Caddo and I heard the story once again from Grandma Willie and we pressed Daddy to show us the rocks. He had seen them when he was young and didn't care to see them again, but he relented. Many Indians—and descendants of the white townspeople who saw the cremation—knew of the burial site, but they weren't eager to tell people about it.

We arrived late in the evening. The rocks had spread out over a thirty-foot area; there was no longer a tall pile, and each rock was covered with large gray slugs that shone in the setting sun. Nothing grew among the stones except thistles and poison ivy. Afterwards, my brother and I felt sick and unclean, like we had walked close to evil. No wonder Daddy stayed in the car. Mom didn't even come with us.

"Satisfied?" he said once we got in.

"I guess," said Caddo.

My neck had tingled. That was the Crows' grave, all right. I didn't require a lot of explanation for many strange things I believed in. I am what anthros call "superstitious."

In high school, Annette and I had competed against some Pueblo runners at a race in Albuquerque where some of the Acomas were convinced that a Jemez medicine person threw dirt at their top runners during the last quarter mile of the race. Both girls got cramps in their legs and had to stop fifty feet before the finish. I remember running past them, perplexed that both were down and couldn't even crawl to the end. A month later at another race, one of those girls told Annette that they had to have a ceremony at home, and that their medicine person pulled snakes out of their legs.

I found that bizarre, but I didn't not believe it. I thought that owls were beautiful and graceful animals, an important part of the food chain and all that, but I also was scared silly of them. When in doubt, better to be safe.

Winchell believed that the Crows were loose, just as surely as he knew the sun was shining. "You need to be careful, Ariana. They're at work. They've been at work. They killed Teague, Ollie, and Watson, and tried to kill Gilmore."

"Willie told me. I'm always careful. Well, should I just go home or what?"

"No," he said abruptly. "Go on with your run. We'll talk tonight."

How did he know I was going to run?

I got back to Annette's, changed into my shorts and Brooks shoes, and drove to the school. She was already dressed and stretching, using the chain-link fence as a support.

"Ready?" Annette asked, tying her bandanna around her forehead. Her new short hairdo looked funny to me because she was a long-hair person.

"I need it. You wouldn't believe what's going on. Winchell thinks the Crows are out and about."

She acted like she didn't hear me.

"Hello?"

"I heard you. I know. They are."

"Why didn't you say?"

"Winchell needed to talk to you first, Ari." Then she leaned against the fence. Annette called me Ari. Junior and Len called me Ar. Winchell called me Ariana. My brother Caddo still called me Banana because when he was little he couldn't say Ariana; he said "Aribanana." "What did you hear?"

I told her a bit about what Len told me.

She leaned on the fence. "These're the bogeymen of our childhood. When I did something bad, Dad always used to say, 'The Crows'll get you if you don't straighten up.' Mom would get furious because she knew how much they scared me."

"Maybe the Crows aren't real," I said. "I mean, they did exist once, but they can't live forever. It has to be someone imitating them." That wasn't right, but I was hopeful.

"Yeah, someone as nasty as them." She wiped her nose on her T-shirt, then smiled. "Well, we can't stand around worrying. Ready? We're losing time."

"Yep."

"I got tired of this trail years ago so I found other places," Annette said, "but since the murders I haven't wanted to get too far away from people so I came back to this one. They're some dirt roads behind the neighborhood that circle around just a quarter mile from the alleys."

We went through the opening in the fence behind the school. A worn trail led upwards into the trees. This was the trail Annette and I trained on for four years as part of the McAlester High School Buffaloes cross-country team. It was perfect for cross-country training: Ascents came when we were tired and descents when we weren't, and there were enough twists and turns at the beginning of the six-mile trail for us to learn how to maneuver among the mass of runners who were fresh at the start of a race.

"The oak's still here," I said, meaning an old gnarled tree with a branch the circumference of a plate sticking out across the trail at nose level. More than a few inattentive runners had collided with it over the years. It was smooth where thousands of hands had rubbed it while ducking under as they passed.

We seemed to be running as fast as we did twenty years ago. The trees I was so familiar with flew past in the opposite direction with the same speed they used to. We reached the two-mile mark and I was feeling good, the same way I felt in high school.

A few minutes later I caught a strong burning odor. Not just wood smoke, but also plastic and metal.

"Smell that?" I asked.

"Sure do."

We came out of the trees and could see smoke about half a mile to the east, the direction we were headed.

"McCulloughs' place," said Annette. The McCullough family had lived here for almost a hundred years, growing corn and potatoes. I had been to their place once with Daddy when I was in elementary school, and had run past it five days a week for years. They raised goats and I enjoyed watching the kids grow.

We ran on the road through the McCulloughs' potato field and around a gentle curve that would eventually take us past their house and back to the high school. The McCulloughs' old house stood around the bend, but on that day it was burned to the ground. Firemen were to the point of making certain the embers didn't spread to the surrounding woods. Several police cars and an ambulance were parked on the dirt driveway. The lights and sirens were off, so either no one was hurt or, more likely, there was no hurry to take bodies to the morgue.

We ran to the yard. Annette walked up to the officer who looked like that goofy actor Gary Busey and asked, "What's all this? I was here yesterday and waved to them. Are they all right?" She asked the last question in a high pitch because she knew they weren't.

"Fire killed everyone inside. You saw them yesterday? Would you come with me, please?" and we followed the blond policeman to his car.

Annette leaned against the patrol car with her arms crossed while Blackwood asked her routine questions: What time did you see them? Did you talk to them? Did you see anyone else? Did you see any cars on the road?

She answered that it was merely another day of running for her, which included waving to the people she had known for twenty-five years.

"Oh, geez," she said suddenly. "What about the goats? There were some babies."

"In the pen in the garage. I need to call Animal Control."

"I'll take them. I can get my truck and come back."

"Well . . . I need to check on that. I got your number so I'll call and let you know. I don't see what's wrong with it, unless there's next of kin that want the animals."

"Let me go check on them, okay?"

It was just like Annette to be worried about the animals. She went to give them hay and water and closed the barn door securely so they couldn't get out. Then we hung around for another hour watching the firemen. The spring day wasn't all that hot, but my body hadn't shut down yet and I kept sweating. Annette, however, was shivering.

We watched the firemen and paramedics finally pull the bodies out from the rubble of the second floor that had fallen on them. Both Mr. and Mrs. McCullough were blackened, their arms bent stiffly in a fighter's stance, characteristic of most burned victims. I heard the ambulance driver say rather loudly that even though they were charred, it was obvious that both had their throats cut and their ears were missing.

Annette and I ran back to the school as fast as we could go. My lungs burned like they do on very cold winter runs and I was afraid I'd trip and fall. Annette was sobbing the entire three miles back and I feared that she'd hit a tree. When we reached the car, she fell to the ground and cried. I leaned against the trunk until my legs stopped shaking.

Annette wiped her eyes. Black mascara started to run. For all her concern about "natural living," it was odd that she piled on the eye makeup. Her lashes were jet-black and I didn't understand why she bothered with it.

As soon as we were calm, I drove us back to Annette's house, turned on the shower and made her get in first. After we dried off and sat on the sofa in our T-shirts and shorts, I made yogurt and orange juice smoothies.

"Got any whiskey?" I asked.

"No." She started to hiccup. "But there's Amaretto in the cabinet by the dishwasher."

Thank God, I thought. I used to drink too much when I was married to Len. We moved to Oklahoma City so I could attend law school and the stress of school, combined with an inconsistently happy marriage to a man who was excessive in his use of drugs and alcohol, caused me to drink beer, wine, or sweet whiskey concoctions in the evenings. The next day I'd run and lift weights until I thought I was punished enough for imbibing. I figured my self-abuse and healthful exercise all evened out. When I got pregnant and was having difficulty concentrating, I quit drinking cold turkey and didn't miss it.

"I'll call Winchell," I said, picking up the phone. "He'll get us back on track." Annette sat with one arm wrapped around her drawn-up knees and the other rubbing her potbellied pig Peggy Sue. She leaned her head back to look up at the wall filled with the same family portraits I had in my home. Her frames were antique and looked better than mine.

After briefing Winchell on what happened, the old man said he'd be right over. Meantime, I found a cheese pizza in the freezer, which I enhanced with fresh mushrooms, onions, canned green chilies, and spaghetti sauce. Luckily, Annette also kept Red Devil hot sauce and Parmesan cheese on hand. I'm picky about my food and almost everything on my menu calls for heavy spices. Billie Watchman grew hot peppers that were legendary, and Aunt Ange in Tuskahoma swore that the red and green serrano pepper plants in her garden came from Billie's seeds. I doubted that, but got some seeds from her anyway and planted several dozen for myself.

Half an hour later Winchell knocked. Annette jumped up and ran to the door, the agile Peggy Sue behind her. She threw the door open and hugged him hard. He steered her in and closed the door.

I hugged him too. "Winchell." I shook my head. "You're right."

"Yes I am, Ariana. I guess you're wondering how to help Butter. It looks for all the world like he killed the Bradens."

"I know. Pizza's ready. Come sit." Annette and Winchell sat at her old table that once belonged to Arie and Opal's son, Charlie. It was old as Moses and she rubbed oil on it every week to keep it from drying out. I put the hot pizza on the wicker charger and cut it into eight triangles. Neither she nor Winchell was interested. I, on the other hand, can eat no matter what crisis surrounds me. If I ever stop running I'll have to be buried in a piano crate.

"What can we do?" Annette asked him.

He didn't answer the question. "The Crows are spirits that keep getting loose. They always find a way. They got shot, hung, and burned, but they came back."

"So you're saying that nothing can kill them? They just keep living? How can anything do that?"

"There are several things that can, Ariana," Winchell said calmly.

The idea assaulted my sensibilities. I believed that God could be angry and vindictive, but I never thought He would create something as vile as the Crows and allow them to live forever. Evil might stick around, but it seems to me that it circulates through a variety of people who eventually die.

"I'm not saying they can't be killed." Winchell stood and walked to the window. He peeked through the shade. I wondered if he thought the Crows might be lurking on Annette's front lawn. "What I mean is, none of us can kill them. The only way they can die is by the hand of someone they tried to kill, but didn't. And, that someone has to be marked."

"But there's no one like that," I said. "Anyone they tried to kill is dead now. Is there someone else that you know of?"

Winchell sat down, took a piece of pizza, and crossed one leg over the other. "No. There isn't anyone alive like that. Sit, Ariana. Now, you and Annette tell me again everything you were told about the Crows."

The next morning I awoke at seven, rather early considering that Annette and I talked to Winchell for almost three hours about the most upsetting entities we had ever heard of. We were so worked up we thought we'd never fall asleep, but ended up sleeping very soundly.

I had not realized how much I actually knew about the Crows. Annette knew the same stories, but also a few more that I had not heard, like when Mac and Jeke Crow were shot here in 1895 by Tish and Arie, both were smiling when they were dead and wrapped in burlap to be burned to ash. Before he escaped from prison with Dixon, Wirt told Arie that morning that he'd see him again someday.

Winchell asked us twice about Annette's great-great-grandfather Arie catching the Crows outside McAlester, and about the Crows killing Survella and Skarloey. He was especially interested in Tish. After the last go-round of stories, he stood and smiled. "Could be."

"Could be what?" I asked.

"I have to go now. I can't talk to you for a few days." He took his car keys from his pocket. "If I'm right, help'll be here when you need it." Then he kissed our foreheads. "There's nothing you can do right now, Ariana. If something happens to me, then you'll know I was on the right track. You'll also know what to do."

"Wait. Someone who was almost killed by them? You're going to Arie's old place, aren't you? Winchell, everyone's buried in Red Oak. What are you thinking?"

He smiled. "No, not everyone's buried in Red Oak." Then he stepped out the door and walked quickly to his car.

I didn't watch him drive off because when I was little Mom said that if we watched visitors leave they would have bad luck.

"So, what do you want to do?" Annette asked the next morning. She had slept hard and her hair stuck out in all directions.

"Right now, I have no idea. Winchell said I'd know what to do if we don't hear from him. What I want to do and what I need to do are different things."

"What do you mean?"

"Are you kidding? I want to go home, but I need to stay here and help Winchell. And Len."

Then I used her phone to call Pat and June Marks. I told them where my will was, and that if anything happened to me, Kim was to stay with them until his Uncle Caddo came to get him.

For the next two days, Annette and I stayed close to home. Neither one of us wanted to go outside running and, fortunately, she had a few of the *Firm* videos. They were the best I'd seen, but exercise videos bore me to tears and knowing that they lasted fifty minutes, I kept watching the clock.

We went to the jail once so I could talk to Len. Annette didn't want to stay by herself, so she came along and sat in the waiting area with her back issues of *Runner's World*.

The same jailer led him in. Len looked even thinner and the circles under his bloodshot eyes were darker. He looked like a terrified child.

"Can't sleep?" I asked.

"Not a bit. I keep seeing their faces."

Len asked me if I knew anything and I said I didn't.

"I'll see if Winchell can get you something to relax," I said. "Not sure if anything's allowed in here, though."

"What's gonna happen to me? Can you see if Winchell can keep the Crows outta here? I'm afraid they're gonna come in and get me."

I thought that unlikely. The Crows set it up to look like Len killed the Bradens, so why would they hurt him? That would defeat their purpose.

"Yes, I'll ask. You need to eat, Len. Are you eating anything?"

"Not hungry. I eat the bread. That's the only thing that doesn't make me sick."

"Don't worry." I couldn't think of anything else to say. "We're working on it."

"What's gonna happen to me?" he asked again.

"You'll be okay," I said and left.

I was irritated because Len didn't ask about his son and he didn't ask how I was. At the same time, I was angry with myself for being upset with a person I didn't care much about anymore. In addition, Len was in a very bad situation and I shouldn't be mad at him. Instead, I should be more sympathetic. Curse you, Junior, for making me come here. Prior to me getting married, I could simply break up with a guy and never see him again. But when you have a child with someone, ignoring the father isn't so easy. It's impossible.

I called Caddo in Red Oak the second day to apprise him of events.

"Banana-girl, you don't need to get involved," he said over his screaming one-year-old son, Frankie. "This is serious, bad business and you could get hurt. Winchell's an old guy and he can only do so much. If Dad were here, he'd kick your butt and Mom would kick it even harder."

"Yeah, well, they aren't here." They died in a one-car wreck by Lake Eufala two years ago. For some reason, Dad drove into the lake and neither he nor Mom could get out of their seat belts. They drowned in twenty feet of water. There were skid marks, but no flat tires, and nothing mechanically wrong with the Dodge Dakota. Dad couldn't have fallen asleep because it was two in the afternoon and he always listened to loud country-and-western music.

"Maybe I should come. Frankie! Cool your jets. Sorry, he's got a tooth coming in. Banana, you stay away from all that."

"I'll be fine. Annette and I are sitting tight and the cops are all over these cases like ducks on June bugs. Later."

"Hey, wait. . . ."

"Bye."

"Well, he was supportive," I said to Annette. "Let's go to the store and get food. I'm starved."

After a dinner of broiled salmon, asparagus, and cheese rolled up in whole-wheat tortillas, we watched *Dateline*. I called Winchell a few times and got no answer. Both of us crashed around nine.

The next day we watched talk shows, then some absurd soap operas. Around four I needed a nap. I went to the guest room, turned the fan on high for white noise, and stared at the framed animal prints until I fell asleep.

I dreamed of a woman, her dark hair piled on her head and her cream-colored blouse and long skirt blowing in the breeze against a purple sky and pink clouds. The short young man at her side held a multicolored basket and they gathered enormous green beans. My great-great-great-aunt Survella and her son Skarloey.

I watched as the Crows rode into the Wilson's garden, their horses covered with ears and scalps and bloody froth. The owl-men had feathers for hair and talons instead of feet. Their faces all looked exactly the same.

Jincy and his son Corn stood on the porch. They looked alike except that Corn had his mother's eyes and eyebrows. The Crows killed Survella and Skarloey, in fast motion. My brain needed to consider what happened, but my inner eyes didn't want to watch. After they were dead, the clouds blew around the sky like a blue norther was pushing them. Interspersed among the pink cumulus clouds were running, yellow stars. Jincy and Corn sat in the flowerbed, crying red tears.

My last dream was of the rockpile. The rocks were breathing and the shiny slugs had grown to the size of potbellied pigs. Winchell and Ellis Battiest stood at the base of the mound, their arms at their sides, but their mouths working hard. Standing behind them were a dozen people. I knew the faces of Ellis, Billie, Teague, Gilmore, Ollie, Tish, Arie, and Matthias from the scores of sketches Billie left behind. My parents stood to the left of Billie, dressed in the same clothes they had on the last time I saw them alive.

The medicine men chanted and chanted, until finally the mound caught fire and sank until the ground closed over it. Then both men looked at me and along with the rest of my family said in unison, "Come here." I awakened, sat up, and expected to see them in my bedroom. My head felt surprisingly clear and I was not scared.

I found Annette in the backyard, tending to her rabbits. She had a garden hose in one hand and a shot glass in the other full of Wild Turkey that we had bought that morning. "Is that booze? Wish I had a picture. We need to go now, Annette. Winchell said so."

"He called?"

"Sort of. I dreamed it."

She squirted my bare feet with the water hose. "Ari. A dream? Get real."

"I don't have dreams like this, Annette. This was a message. He said to come to the mound. So did Ellis, Billie, Survella, Gilmore, and. . . ."

"God, I can't believe this. Okay, then. But I got period cramps bad."

"As much as you run? You shouldn't."

"Always do."

"I need some Midol," Annette said fifteen minutes later. "My period started yesterday and these cramps are killing me."

"You should see about getting on the pill. I'm regular and hardly even know my period's here."

"That's because you have no body fat, Ari."

"Neither do you."

"Well, my period's regular. The pill's not natural. Who knows what it's doing to you? I'll just guts it out until menopause. Stop there at Wal-Mart."

It was 8:30 and wasn't far to Lake McAlester and the grave. I had thrown extra clothes and one of Annette's flashlights into the trunk along with a six-pack of Arrowhead water and a sack of apples.

We drove out of town and it was pleasant enough without the air conditioner. The warm air rushed through the car. I was glad I pulled my hair into a ponytail and braided it. Otherwise it'd be a tangled bird's nest.

"So, what do you plan on doing when we get there?" Annette asked. She was slightly tipsy.

"Good question. No idea."

When I looked back to the road an owl with enormous eyes was headed straight for the windshield.

"Watch out!" Annette screamed. I swerved hard to the right shoulder and corrected.

"Shit!" I yelled.

Then from behind us a truck appeared. It didn't turn on its lights until it was on my bumper. Suddenly it changed lanes and pulled to the side of us.

"Oh my God," said Annette.

I turned to look and in the lighted front seat of the silver Dodge Ram were three men who looked exactly alike. Their yellow eyes and large brown teeth took up their faces. In that second, I also saw two other men in the crew cab; they looked just like the ones in front. The truck sped ahead, then made a U-turn, almost tipping the truck over. It sped back past us, the way we had come.

"There they are," I said. My heart beat so furiously it made my T-shirt move.

"And they know where we are," said Annette. She was panting and checking her seat belt. She was staring at me as I looked at the rearview mirror, watching the truck's taillights vanish.

"What happened there?" Annette pointed to the road ahead of us and the flashing lights of patrol cars and an ambulance. As we got closer, we saw an overturned Bronco and the firemen who were extricating the occupants. Blackwood kneeled at the passenger's door.

"Oh no, oh no," Annette repeated. "The Crows did it."

I slowed the Mercury and stopped, amazed at how calm I was. Or I thought I was. At least I wasn't crying.

"We have to tell Blackwood," Annette said.

"Tell him what? That we saw some owls that are men, or men who really are owls? He doesn't know what's going on."

"We gotta tell Winchell."

"That's where we're going, Annette."

I parked ahead of the accident and waited until Blackwood stood and looked like he had nothing to do. I got out and he saw me then walked over.

"Are they okay?" I asked.

"Yeah. Maybe broken ankles."

"Did a bird hit them?"

He looked at me without expression. "The driver said a couple of owls headed for the window and he swerved, then overcorrected."

"One came at me, too, but I'm a good driver."

"Where you headed? Nothing this way but the lake."

"There you go."

"Hey, Blackwood," yelled a highway patrolman from the Bronco. "Need you here."

"I need to talk to you," Blackwood said to me, turning back to the wreck. "I may call later. Are you still at Annette's?"

"Yeah. Don't know when we'll be back, though."

"Better be careful."

"I got my cell phone." Then I made the peace sign and went back to the car.

"Ariana!" he yelled to me. "You need to be careful."

I waved back. "I know."

"Do you think he's cute?" asked a nervous Annette when I got back in the car.

I adjusted the rearview mirror. "Too white for me."

We turned at the dirt road turnoff that took us to the Crows' grave. The two-mile drive seemed to take only a minute.

"There it is," I said. Under normal circumstances, I'd say it looked like a lot of regular rocks. But it wasn't. The rocks were old and scary with only God-knows-what under and around them. I parked a good seventy feet away, turned off the lights, and got out.

"Coming?" I asked Annette.

"In a minute." She gripped the door handle very hard.

I looked around, hearing cicadas. I knew from Survella's journals and

Willie's stories that if the Crows were here, the other animals would become quiet. I said as much to Annette. She got out slowly.

"Well, let's look around. Maybe Winchell will show up."

We walked into the trees where the underbrush was scarce and wandered around for an hour, then we went back to the car for water. By then it was ten o'clock.

"Dang," said Annette, scratching her legs. "Got chiggers. Ari, there's nothing here. Winchell's not coming. Let's go home."

"No. Let's wait a while. How else would Winchell contact us? If he ran into a problem, then he sure couldn't call."

"But a dream? Come on."

"And I'd say you don't listen enough to the old ones," I said.

"Oh, I hear them. I just don't have to believe them," she said, still scratching.

"I thought you did."

"Sometimes."

"Sometimes, nothing. You just saw the Crows."

"All right, Ari. Get off it."

We sat on the car hood in silence until midnight, then walked back into the woods farther south than before. We came to a clearing, about forty feet around, with an old campfire circle in the center.

"Let's stay here a while," I said. I was determined to wait until Winchell showed.

It was very warm and the cicadas still hummed.

"Nice night," I said, sitting on a campfire rock.

"Yeah, right," said Annette.

"Well, talking about where the Crows might be will only make us scared and want to leave. Besides, Winchell's here someplace."

"Oh geez, did you see that?" Annette asked. "Stars going sideways."

"Yes, I did." Now I was scared. "Well, maybe we should go." We both stood.

Annette looked over my shoulder. "What is that?"

I turned and squinted into the darkness. Two silver-dollar-sized circles about ten inches apart and almost six feet above the ground lightly glowed. "Looks like an elk in headlights. It's not moving. Wait here."

I walked forward until I could see the outline of the animal behind the maroon-colored eyes. It was a horse. "Here, boy." I took another step, clicking my tongue. "Easy, boy." The horse didn't move. Its eyes were lit as if rose-colored flashlights shone outward from inside his head. I put my hand to the horse's nose so he could smell me. He didn't move and I felt no breath. "Annette, come here."

She walked hesitantly to me. "Feel his nose," I said. "He's cold and isn't breathing."

Annette walked to his side and ran her hand along his rib cage. "No, he isn't. Can he be dead standing up?"

I moved in front of his face. Without my flashlight I could see glowing eyes with black pupils following me. Then I saw the large dark circle in his forehead. I shivered because I knew the horse's name.

I shined the light between Archie's eyes and into the gaping hole that Wirt Crow had made in the stallion's forehead 105 years ago. Crow had tried, but did not kill Archie.

"Archie, Archie," I whispered and rubbed his nose. "Winchell brought you back. He did." I shined the light on his mane and saw that a rolled-up paper was tied to his hair. I took it out. The lids blinked twice, then Archie walked past me and turned to face the rising moon. He stood still.

Annette came up behind me and took my hand. "He's waiting, isn't he? What's the paper?"

I unrolled the yellow ledger paper.

It just said *Winchell*. "He wrote this. It had to be him." I felt lightheaded. "Let's wait."

"With that dead horse?" Annette hugged herself. "That can't be Archie. Ari, what's wrong with you?" She put her hand to her mouth. "Ari?" She started to cry. "I want to go home."

"Annette. If it's not Archie, then what other dead horse is it? We have to wait. Come on, let's go to the car."

As we left the clearing, I looked back and Archie was standing in the same place.

I had dozed off and woke with a start. My watch said 5:30. "Let's go back. Winchell should be there."

"Only for a minute, Ari."

We reached the clearing and found Archie still there. "I need to pee." I walked into the trees to find a spot. As I started to stand and zip up my jeans, I heard men's voices laughing.

"Well, and heeeeere she is," said one of the Crows. I looked through the branches. I supposed it was Jackson from his dominant posture. "And all alone."

I looked to where Archie had been standing but he was gone. Five more Crows—presumably Wirt, Dew, Dixon, Jeke, and Sweeney—came out of the bushes and stood next to Jackson. The ancient, evil men were dressed like the Beach Boys in Bermuda shorts and Hawaiian shirts and looked bizarre and obscene. All they needed was a branch under them and they'd look like a row of owl-men going to a picnic.

"And whar's little Ar-ee-ah-na?" asked the youngest one. That had to be Dew. "I need me a new one."

"She's not here, you son of a bitch," hissed Annette.

Oh great, I thought.

"You're not right by half." Dew backhanded her so hard she fell to the ground on her back.

Jeke walked over. "She's mine." Then he ripped open her shirt and grabbed the waist of her jeans, tearing the denim as easily as the cotton T-shirt. Then he looked to his family and said, "Maybe you'll learn sumthin'." And he proceeded to rape her.

Annette slapped him hard at least a dozen times and it didn't faze him. I took the deepest breath of my life and walked out into the open. They all turned and looked at me, apparently aware that I had been there all the time.

"Wondered when you'd come out, Ar," said Dew. He was as revolting as his father and uncles. I could smell his breath ten feet away.

"Why doncha come here?" he said with a grin much too large for a human face. "Ya look just like Survella 'cept skinny."

I thought fast but my brain wheels spun. *How can I get out of this?* I wondered. *If I run, they'll catch me and I can't leave Annette. I could pick up that stick over by that ugly guy with the sores all over him, but it probably wouldn't hurt anyone. Maybe if I. . . .*

And then I saw Archie in the trees behind Sweeney. The still horse watched.

One of the ugly men put his nose into the air and sniffed. He moved his shoulders like he had an itch on his back.

"What's with you, Wirt?" another asked.

Dew stopped grinning and looked into the air. "Sumthin' ain't right here, Jeke," he said.

"Yur dreamin'," said Jeke as he looked down at Annette and drew his long knife from the sheath on his belt.

"Wrong, wrong," said Dew. He looked around nervously and then he began to shrink. He fell to his knees and his head began to deflate like a balloon.

Then Archie ran from the trees. In the daylight, Archie's coat, mane, and tail were blood-red. The brand M^c on his rump was black and stood out like car tracks on a golf course. Archie ran to Jeke first, stuck out his right foreleg, and stiff-legged him in the gut so hard his hoof broke through the Crow's spine and out his back.

After he stomped Jeke's body off his leg, Archie looked to the man who had tried to kill him a century before. I was closest to him and kicked Wirt in the knee. He screeched in pain. It gave the stallion time to turn his rear to Wirt and kick him under the chin. Wirt's neck snapped, his head hyperextended backward. If he had been alive, he would've seen behind himself and upside down.

Sweeney and Jackson had dropped to their knees and were shrinking fast. The horse ran to the clothes that started to billow to the ground and began stomping the short-sleeve shirts and shorts. A head emerged through one of the collars, a weird half-man, half-owl face that made me remember the Thing in John Carpenter's remake of that movie. I glimpsed the almost-formed beak, the tiny disappearing ears, and eyebrows that were gray feathers. It started to fly away and I threw the pants over it. Then Archie stepped on it.

I kicked the bird named Jackson and it got tangled in the shirt. Archie ran over and stomped the small head. I watched the eyes pop out of the crushed skull and I put my hands over my face.

Two shrill cries cut through the morning and when I looked up, the owls

Dew and Dixon emerged from their clothing and flew up and over the trees to the north. A furious Archie screamed a high-pitched reply that horses can't make and ran into the woods after the evil birds, who knew they would have to finally die.

I looked at the broken bodies of Wirt, Jeke, Sweeney, and Jackson. These were very dead bird-men.

"What a show," Annette said. She was still lying on the ground, naked and dazed. I ran to her and sat her up.

"You're okay, you're okay." I was stunned and kept repeating myself.

"And how do you know?" she laughed. Then she looked around and began sobbing. "Hurts."

"Let me look." There was no bleeding between her legs, and no torn flesh, at least not on the outside. "Well, your period stopped."

"Very funny." She tried to stop crying and couldn't.

"Let's get out of here." I got her dressed, went to the car, and called 911 on the cell phone. Within thirty minutes we met officers Blackwood and Agee at the McAlester Regional Hospital. We didn't have long to wait and Annette was hustled into a room where she was examined.

Blackwood left the waiting room and returned with a cup of black coffee, which I loathed. He handed the Styrofoam cup to me and I sipped the foul drink. "Thanks. How come you're still on duty?"

"Supposed to be off half an hour ago. Long shifts. With what's going on, though, it's probably a good idea. The Crows were some kinda men," he said matter-of-factly. "My grandmother lived here her whole life. She heard a lot of stories and then I got to hear them." He played with his hat brim. "I been hearing about the Crows since I was a towhead."

"You're still a towhead," I said.

He ran his fingers through his thick white hair. "Yeah." Then he was serious. "I know Len didn't do these killings."

"You've got bodies of the Crows along with their finger- and footprints. What about hair samples? DNA?"

My speculations were interrupted by another officer who walked through the entrance and quickly over to Blackwood.

"We got a problem." The patrolman was sweating and breathing hard, the way overweight and unhealthy cops do. His badge said Riggs.

"Problem?" Blackwood laughed. "No kidding."

"No, a real one." He looked at me.

"She's okay," Blackwood said. "What?"

"Well, the bodies aren't there."

"What?" Blackwood was still calm. "They were deader'n doorknobs."

"The bodies are birds. No men. Ma'am? Are you certain of what happened?"

I started to answer, but Blackwood interrupted. "Yeah," he said. "She is."

Less than an hour later, the doctor came to the waiting room to tell me that Annette was fine, a little bit in shock, and was she aware that she was pregnant?

Where is Winchell? I screamed to myself.

Annette was still asleep in her bed when Winchell, Junior, and my young cousin Richard Hallmark came by. I was surprised to see Richard, but even more astounded at how much older Winchell looked. His wrinkles were cut deeper and he stooped like he carried a heavy weight.

"Winchell. Come in." I took him by the arm and led him to the sofa. He sat down hard. Junior stood by the door. "Richard, what're you doing here?"

"Helping," he said with his hands in his pockets.

"Helping?" A light was trying to click on in my head. *Richard helping Winchell? What for?* "What happened, Winchell? Are you all right?" I asked. His eyes were very tired.

He put his hand on my forearm and squeezed. "Yes."

After I poured them bland herbal tea that tasted like grass, Winchell told me what happened.

"Richard and I drove over to Arie's old place," he said, trying hard to talk and breathe at the same time.

"Why's Richard here?" I loved my cousin and was worried about him. We knew he had an interest in medicine, and a few years before had disappeared for several days after scouting for deer on Uncle Ralph and Aunt Ange's home place. Ange insisted that he was fine and would be home soon, but Richard's mother and father went ballistic, launching a huge search that stopped when Richard arrived at Ange's door four days later clean and well fed. He never said what happened, but he had changed. More quiet, thoughtful, and a lot older. Despite his parents' objections, Richard spent time with Winchell. I suspected he wanted to become a medicine man, but I thought it more likely that he'd win the Publishers Clearinghouse sweepstakes. But there he was, my cousin Richard, apprentice to a medicine man.

"Nobody lives there anymore," Winchell went on. "Colbert's grandson Larry lives down the road, you know."

"What was in there?"

"I didn't need to go in. We were trying to find the horse yard."

He was referring to the horse pits where Arie buried his dead animals. Most ranchers burned their livestock, but Arie wanted his underground.

Winchell continued. "We went through two burials before I got a sense of Archie. He was by himself, under an old cherry tree. We had to pull it out with the winch."

"We?" I looked to Junior. "*He* went with you?"

"I needed help. Archie was four feet below the main roots."

"So, you made him live again. How did you do that?"

"He's not alive. Not really, Ariana. I have to use the bathroom." Then Winchell got up and headed down the hall. His posture stooped more as he walked.

"What did he do?" I asked Junior.

"Can't say, Ar."

"Don't act like you're privileged, Junior."

"No, he really can't say," said Richard. "Winchell made him sit in the truck."

"Yeah," Junior nodded. "After a while Winchell got back in looking like he does now. Then we took him home. I never saw Archie. You tell me what happened."

"Sorry." Then I revealed what happened to me and Annette. All the while we listened to the sink water run in the bathroom. "Go check on him." Richard went.

They emerged a few minutes later. Winchell looked even older, dehydrated. His hair and shirt were completely wet. "I got hot," he said. Clearly, he was rapidly aging.

"The doctor says Annette's pregnant," I told him. "That's not possible because she's in the middle of her period."

"It's very possible," Winchell said.

"There have to be more children out there. Winchell?"

He ignored me. "I need to take care of it before it grows. Junior, go get that gym bag from the truck. Ariana, wake Annette. I can't rest until this is dealt with."

Winchell mixed something truly bad-smelling with hot tap water and made Annette drink it. Within minutes it started working because my cousin sat up screaming in pain. Whatever was inside her, it surely didn't want to let go.

Winchell told me and Junior to leave the room. Soon, Annette was quiet. Richard and Winchell came out with something bundled in Annette's blue sheet.

"Junior, we need to go. Ariana, Annette's body will let her run in a few days. I think she may not completely remember what happened. Come here." He touched my forehead. His finger made me jerk backwards against the wall. Then I watched the visions he had put in my head.

The visions began with me looking at Billie, Teague, Jincy, and Gilmore, but I was seeing them through someone else's eyes. I saw their faces clearly, the blemishes, the worried looks. Their voices! I now knew what they sounded like. Then I saw a black man with no nose picking onions and corn in a healthy garden and he said good-bye to my family when they left. Through those eyes, I watched the person's life rush past, a torrent of color, people, blossoming flowers, and aging faces. I saw the cemetery at Willie's house, except letters on the headstones were visible, not smooth and faded. Model T's faded to Subarus, kites to airplanes, clear skies to polluted haze. Lucy, Lassie, and Tonto on television morphed into *All in the Family* then *NYPD Blue*. Then I saw my face; I was leaning against the hall wall at Annette's house. I blinked and looked back at the withered face of Ruel Battiest.

"Winchell? Ruel?" I whispered.

"You know who I am," he smiled.

"But, Ruel? How?"

"I just can. But no more. I've done what I needed to." He was dying, his fluids drying up, his bones turning to ash. "Junior. Come now. Don't worry about your family, Ariana. They're fine." I watched him shuffle to the door.

"Bye," Richard said with a smile.

"You better explain this to me, Rich."

"Someday."

Then they left me to clean up my cousin.

Afterwards, I turned on the news for company. I sat on the sofa, stunned. Ruel, alive? All this time Winchell was Ruel? My family is "fine"? What did Ruel mean by that? They're dead.

A soft knock at the door interrupted my thoughts. It was Blackwood. He was dressed in jeans and a long-sleeved button-down with the sleeves rolled up. "Can I come in? I got some news. And some McNuggets."

Yuk, I thought. "Thanks," I said.

Blackwood came in and looked at the wall of portraits. "Nice faces," he said before sitting.

"Who's here?" Annette came out of the bedroom in a sundress. Her hair was slicked back and she had on makeup.

Good heavens.

"Feeling better?" he asked.

"Great. Wow, McNuggets. Thank *you*." Then she dove into what I thought she believed to be poisonous junk food.

He watched intently while she ate. "You can come get the goats. I talked to the McCulloughs' son and he doesn't want them."

"Cool," Annette said between bites.

"Uh, look," Blackwood said to me. "There was a knife under all the birds and clothes. Funny thing, it's from the Revolutionary War period. Perfect condition. Should be in the Smithsonian. Len couldn't have had something like that. Somebody else used it to kill the Bradens and the McCulloughs."

"But Len was in the Braden house," I said.

Blackwood shrugged. "So what?"

"Not that you want him to stay in jail or anything," giggled Annette as she slapped my back. "I just feel great!"

What's got into her?

"There was another item in one of the pockets as well. Car keys to a

Dodge Dakota with your maiden name on them, Ariana. 'Christie,' isn't it? I understand your parents died at Lake Eufala a couple years back and the keys were never recovered."

My stomach lurched. So, we had come almost full circle. The Crows killed my ancient family and then, a hundred years later, killed them again. At the urging of that same family in my dream, I got to see the Crows, but I also got to help kill them.

"You feeling okay, Annette?" asked Blackwood. "There's an Orson Welles film festival starting next week. Want to go see *Citizen Kane* on the big screen?"

Things seemed fine here. I wasn't so sure about myself. "Excuse me," I said as I stood. "I'm going to the bathroom."

The next day, I discussed Len's case with a McAlester attorney who had gone to law school with one of my partners. As we left it, he was going to have the knife tested for fingerprints within the day. If Len's prints weren't on it, then he'd be freed.

Then I went home. I was desperately homesick for my boy and almost got a ticket speeding home from the airport.

I ran up the sidewalk to the Markses' home and Kim answered the door. He jumped up and hugged me so hard we almost fell. He smelled of pizza and chocolate.

"You were right, honey," I whispered in his ear. "Daddy didn't do it."

Later.

As the years passed, the runner grew older and slower, but she still ran. She took her dog with her, but he pulled her along too fast, so then she left the yellow lab at home when she ran and took him to play Frisbee at the park instead.

Ariana wanted to run fast like she did when she was young, but her body would not allow it. Still, every morning she tied her shoes and shut the door behind her. First, she ran east to watch the sun rise. In the evenings she started in the opposite direction. If her neighbor's pear trees held ripe fruit she picked one for breakfast. She knew all the dogs she passed and spoke to them as she ran past their yards. She picked up newspapers and threw them to her neighbors' front doors.

Ariana finally had to walk. Seventy years of running had caused her knees and feet to ache. She did not have arthritis, but her joints were worn. So she walked.

One morning, ten years after she began walking, she felt very light and her breath did not come easily. She slowly made her way to the Canadian River and stood there watching it; the river was swollen with rainwater, and she was jealous that it ran so fast. Then everything was black.

Ariana opened her eyes and saw the clouds. She could not remember hitting the ground. She watched fast birds fly below the clouds and she wanted to join them. *At least they're not owls*, she thought. Then she closed her eyes and was still as she watched the events of her life rush by. "Your family is fine, Ariana," she heard Ruel say. "And so are you."

Then the runner flew.

Afterword

Stories in *The Roads of My Relations* evolved from my family stories, many of them odd and fascinating, others interesting but in need of embellishment to be of interest to anyone outside my family. I do, therefore, consider this a work of fiction.

"The Death of Matthias Lamb" was originally the nucleus of this book and is based on the death of my great-great-grandfather Charles Wilson, a Choctaw merchant who was shot and hatcheted in 1884 by a violent Indian Territory gang. Jackson Crow led the group of Indian men, and their murder of Wilson and subsequent hangings are chronicled in S. W. Harmon's *Hell on the Border* (Fort Smith, Arkansas: Phoenix Publishing Co., 1898).

My grandmother, Eula, was an original Choctaw enrollee born and raised in Red Oak. Her family sold their allotted land but retained the mineral rights and my widowed mother receives a small royalty check every now and then. Eula married the boxer Thomas James Abbott—featured in "Romy and George"—who was the middleweight boxing champion of the Southwest in 1914 and later served as police chief of McAlester. His father, physician William Elliott Abbott, had drawn blueprints for the town of North McAlester and served as its first mayor. (I chronicle the life of my grandfather in "'Gentleman' Tom Abbott: Middleweight Champion of the Southwest," *Chronicles of Oklahoma* 68 [Spring 1990]:24–37.)

"Big Tom" and Eula's wonderful garden, described as Billie's in numerous stories, was behind their home in Muskogee, Oklahoma, in the shadow of Alice Robertson Jr. High School, where my father, Thomas James Abbott, Jr., ran track.

"The Tamfuller Man" is based on the newspaper story written about my husband's grandfather Joshaway, a Comanche. The reporter's portrayal of the educated Joshaway as an ignorant "Injun" angered me, and I feel certain other Indians have experienced the indignity of being stereotyped as backward, Tarzan-speaking dullards.

Mama, Teague, Survella, and Beula are based on people I know who have issues with their identity, appearance, multi-heritages, and separation from their tribes. Chockie's anger at "Reggie the Anthropologist" is typical of many modern Indians who have been victimized by academics who view Indians as "objects of study." The anthropologists that I know, however, are quite sensitive to the beliefs and concerns of Indian people.

"My Horse" is based on a story relayed to me by my father-in-law, Henry, who wept when he read my interpretation of his remembrances of his horse Skeeter. The photograph of him standing on Skeeter's back hangs on his bedroom wall, which is also adorned with family pictures.

A reader of a very early version of this collection wanted to know more about the bonepickers, medicine people, and Choctaw religion in general. While the bonepickers and the Little People are fascinating entities and are enticing topics for lengthy fiction stories, I do not feel comfortable creating superfluous tales about them. Native religion and spirituality are serious topics indeed, and my feeling is that extreme care must be taken when using these figures as characters in a work of fiction. What I present here are stories based on Choctaw myths and differences of opinion among tribal members over who these entities really were—and are. The true roles of Little People, *shampes*, and medicine men and women are for them to tell.

The majority of the names in this book are in my family. Ariana in "Eternal Owls" is my daughter's name, but the character is much like me. Annette was my best friend in high school and is now a triathlete. I have been a runner for thirty years and I encountered Billie's spider two decades ago on a run and still think of her. The trail Annette and Ariana run on is a fond description of the trail my cross-country team ran, and I encounter the tree with the wayward limb every day on my run in the mountains of Flagstaff. My sweet, dumb, pet opossum, Gerald, wandered off one evening many years ago and never came home; I always hoped he found other opossums to live out the rest of his days with. Archie the horse is patterned after a horse belonging to a friend of mine; for no apparent reason, one day he ran into a stack of fence posts piled in the bed of a truck and was impaled in the forehead. He lived for several years with a bandanna over his wound before he finally succumbed to pneumonia. Bunky the cat belonged to my grandparents and she drooled every day of her twenty-one years.

The sugar bowl that survived the removal stays at my cousin's, Jo Ellen Gilmore Gamble, in Norman, Oklahoma. My aunt who cared for it prior to her death was as possessive of it as was Billie's mother and I was never allowed to touch it. Billie is patterned after my aunt, Billie Mills. Known as B to us, she is exceedingly close to our dead ancestors, makes pepper shakers, and is as smart as her namesake in the book. Her mother, Survella, had knee-length hair that I brushed at night before bed. She fell off a horse when she was a teenager, broke her back, and wore a corset the rest of her long life. Around the same time that she suffered her back injury, Survella's father was killed by a train and his remains were returned to her in several boxes, just as Teague was brought home to his family.

I want to thank Ronald Redsteer and Daniel Boone for helping to design the chart on pages viii–ix that shows the book's complicated family relationships.

About the Author

Devon A. Mihesuah is a professor of history at Northern Arizona University in Flagstaff. An enrolled member of the Choctaw Nation of Oklahoma, she is the editor of the *American Indian Quarterly* and the author of numerous nonfiction books and articles, including the award-winning *Cultivating the Rosebuds: The Education of Women at the Cherokee Female Seminary, 1851–1909* (Urbana: University of Illinois Press, 1993, 1996); *American Indians: Stereotypes and Realities* (Atlanta and Regina, Canada: Clarity International, 1996, 1997); *Natives and Academics: Researching and Writing about American Indians* (Lincoln: University of Nebraska Press, 1998, now in its second printing); and the forthcoming *Repatriation: Social and Political Dialogues* (Lincoln: University of Nebraska Press, 2000).

Her first work of fiction, the story "The Tamfuller Man," won first prize over 200 entries in the 1997 *Flagstaff Live!* short story contest (a publication that reaches 20,000 readers), and her second story, "Medicine Woman," appeared in *Red Ink* 5 (1998).

She is currently working on the nonfiction counterpart to *Roads of My Relations*, tentatively titled *American Indian Women: Issues of Identity*. An excerpt from this manuscript-in-progress has appeared in the *American Indian Culture and Research Journal* 22 (1998), and two more excerpts appear in the journal *SIGNS* (Summer 2000) and in the anthology *Native Women's Lives* (New York: Oxford University Press, 2000).